LOVE & CONSEQUENCES

A LOVE & RUIN STANDALONE NOVEL

J.A. OWENBY

CHAPTER 1

*I*f I were into girls, I'd totally want to do my best friend, Gemma.

I leaned against the door frame of my stepdad Franklin's kitchen and watched while Gemma rummaged through the bowl of fresh fruit on the counter. Her long wavy hair flowed down her back, and she swayed slightly as she hummed under her breath.

"You think you can just waltz into someone's house and take their oranges?" I asked, my tone teasingly accusatory.

Gemma's head rose quickly, her brows arched in surprise as she snatched her hand away from a Honeycrisp apple. This girl was absolutely clueless about how gorgeous she was. Not only did she have the red hair and blue eyes that melted all the guys into a hormonal puddle, but she was one of the most genuine people I'd ever met.

We were in stark contrast to each other in the looks department. My dark brown hair was either in pigtails or hung straight down my back. Unlike Gemma's, my chocolate brown eyes didn't change with my mood or the clothes I wore.

Her entire expression lit up at the sight of the grin spreading across my face.

"Mac! I've missed you so much," Gemma said, darting across the kitchen, applying my signature move and crushing me in a bear hug. "Even though the tour has been awesome, my heart ached to be home with you and Franklin," Gemma said softly against my ear.

"Yeah, me too, bestie. I can't tell you how happy I am to see you."

She pulled away from our embrace, studying me. We hadn't seen each other since the horrific night that changed our lives, almost a month ago.

"How have you been?" Gemma asked, resting her hands softly on my shoulders. "And no bullshit," she added, punctuating her words with a quick squeeze.

I mentally willed my lip not to quiver as the memories suddenly rushed over me, and my stomach twisted into knots. There was no way I could fall apart in front of her. I didn't want anyone's pity or to think of me as weak. Especially her. She'd saved me from my kidnapper, Brandon Montgomery. Gemma had unselfishly traded herself in exchange for my life, and I had no fucking clue how I'd ever repay her for that.

"Hey," Hendrix said, waltzing into the kitchen and breaking me away from my inner turmoil. He'd just provided the distraction I needed to avoid lying to my best friend. I wasn't okay.

"Hey," I said, grinning like an idiot at my rock star stepbrother who was also Gemma's boyfriend. Hendrix's band, August Clover, had just returned from the first leg of their US tour, and when they left again tomorrow, I'd go with them. He flipped his shoulder-length brown hair out of his face and went straight for the food.

"Sorry we got in so late last night." Hendrix opened the fridge door and grabbed the pitcher of fresh squeezed orange juice Ruby, our chef, had made earlier.

Franklin was a prominent attorney in Spokane, Washington with all the right connections. When I was in grade school, he built a ten bedroom Colonial mansion complete with an indoor pool and guest house that sat on fifteen lush rolling acres. Hendrix and Gemma had their own house ten minutes away, but they also had a room and stayed over often. Even though I understood their need for privacy, I wished they were here all the time.

"I was hoping to get in soon enough to spend a few days with Franklin, but we need to leave tomorrow morning," he said, grabbing a glass and filling it.

"Yeah, Franklin was really disappointed," I said sadly. "I was a little bummed too, but this time I'm coming on the road with you!" I did a little happy dance.

"We can all have dinner together," Gemma suggested.

"I'm soooo glad you're here," I said, giving her another hug.

"Me too, Mac. I've really missed you. Are you excited to join us on the tour?" Gemma asked.

I couldn't be prouder of my best bestie. She'd shown up at our dorm room a broken girl, terrified of almost everyone. But in just a year, she'd grown into a confident woman who stared the world straight in the eyes, singing on stage alongside my brother in his band.

"The bus is everything you could hope for ... cramped spaces, no real privacy, sharing one bathroom with four guys, and an overabundance of testosterone." Gemma rolled her eyes and shot a sideways glance at Hendrix.

Hendrix responded with a crooked smile.

"Omigosh. I can't believe I'm going with you. The first few weeks you were gone flat out sucked monkey toes. I mean, don't get me wrong, I love spending time with Dad, but it's not the same without you and Hendrix." Franklin was technically my stepdad, but he was the only father I'd ever known since my sperm donor skipped right out the front door when I was a baby. "And I haven't seen Mom since she took off for Europe." Excited,

I tugged on her hand and dragged her behind me to the tan marble breakfast bar. We slid our butts onto the bar stools and faced each other with silly smiles plastered on our faces. "Plus, since I'm single, I doubt you'll hear me complain about too much testosterone. It would be a welcome change. Well, I mean Dad has testosterone, but ... Like, dudes that are my age, and I'm not related to or sort of related to or ... You know what I'm trying to say. Anyway, the one thing I'm not looking forward to are the beds on the bus. I've gotten spoiled by the California King in my room. Knowing my luck, I'll roll right out of the bed, land on the floor, and wake up John and Cade."

"It won't be bad," Gemma replied, taking a bite of the crispy red apple she'd finally selected from the overflowing fruit bowl. "They can actually hold two people, it would just be snug."

"Girl, snug only works if I'm getting some action, but thanks for the encouragement," I said, giggling.

"Rule number one," Hendrix said firmly, "no hookups on the bus. The guys aren't allowed to do it and neither are you, Mac."

I scrunched my nose at my brother.

"Someone needs to loosen up," I jokingly chided.

"I don't think you want the bus smelling like a sex fest, and I seriously doubt you want to hear John and Cade getting busy. If they had a consistent significant other it would be different."

"Eww. Okay, I get it," I said and raised my hands in surrender. "Bestie, I need a favor tonight." I bit my lip while she and Hendrix both arched an eyebrow at me. I placed my elbows on the marble countertop and leaned on it, inhaling sharply.

"I need to ditch Hercules, my bodyguard, for the evening."

"Hercules?" Gemma barked out a laugh.

"Yeah, it's my nickname for Calvin."

"What? Why? Mac, you can't leave without your bodyguard. I mean, I know Brandon is in custody, but his dad is still running loose. And we have no idea if or when he might retaliate. You know none of us are allowed to go anywhere without security."

4

Gemma placed her half-eaten apple down, concern flickering across her features.

"I don't like it," Hendrix said, frowning.

"You two need to knock it off already. You've not even bothered to hear me out," I huffed.

Gemma sighed and glanced at Hendrix. "Sorry." Her voice softened. "Don't get me wrong, I know you're strong, Mac. I just worry you're bottling up all your emotions and it's going to backfire. After—after everything with Brandon and his dad, I just need to know you're working through it and taking the security detail seriously."

"Dillon Montgomery can rot in hell along with his son. I'm fine. I realize the FBI is only just now closing in on the Dark Circle Society, but I'll be glad when they blow it all to pieces." My stomach had tightened the moment Brandon's name left Gemma's lips. "I mean, any sick fuck that orchestrates rape and trafficking of underaged girls ..." Not to mention what they'd done to Gemma when she was a teenager. I shook my head, unable to articulate what horror I'd like to personally inflict on them if I had the chance.

"I wish it were that easy," Hendrix said. "The FBI has been onto the Society for years, but the organization is large and widespread, which complicates matters. And those sleazy bastards are always one step ahead of the feds. They can't just go for the little guys one by one or it'll tip off the ringleaders and blow the entire op. And now, with Dillon having slipped through their fingers ... It sucks, but we have to stay quiet about it. It also means we're constantly aware of our surroundings. We have no idea if Dillon might show up or send one of his buffoons."

"I get it, but here's the deal. It's not that I want to go anywhere alone, but I can't let Franklin find out."

"Find out what?" Hendrix asked, curiosity flashing across his expression.

"Who I'm meeting tonight. In order to get away with it, I need

Gemma and Pierce with me instead of my bodyguard who blabs everything to Dad. You'd think for such a hunky badass he'd not be such a fucking pussy and report every single thing I do to Dad. But it's my luck."

Gemma frowned. "He does? Like you have no privacy, Mac? That's so not cool." Her nose wrinkled in disdain.

"Can't disagree with you there." Hendrix strolled over and slipped his arm around Gemma's waist. These two had met at the university library over a year ago and were now joined at the hip. It was love at first sight for my brother, but Gemma had a shit ton of demons to overcome and their road to a happily-ever-after was rocky. I was happy for them, but sometimes seeing them together made my heart ache. So far, my luck with guys hadn't turned out too well.

"Where are we going?" Gemma asked, her eyes sparkling.

I leaned in closer to them, bridging most of the gap between us. "I'm meeting Asher," I whispered.

"What? Are you two working things out? I've not even had a chance to talk to you about him or Jeremiah yet. I'm sorry. I'm a bad friend." Gemma wrapped her arm around me for another hug.

Asher Weston and I dated our junior and senior years in high school. We were so into each other, no one and nothing else existed. He was my first everything, and I thought he was my forever.

But I'd been young and naïve. And while I was well aware that life could turn upside down in the blink of an eye, I never thought anything would come between Asher and me. Until I found out I was pregnant.

Asher's father suddenly decided I wasn't good enough for his son, and without even consulting us, used his money and power to silence the situation. I may not have been ready to be a teenage mom, but it still gutted me when Asher remained silent and did nothing while Mr. Weston arranged and paid for my abortion.

Hendrix, not Asher, had been the one who stayed with me during it all.

Shortly after my abortion, I lost Asher too. He didn't have a big enough pair of balls to stand up to his father. Money or not, I refused to be controlled or manipulated by anyone.

Regardless, when I learned Asher was engaged to a more suitable girl, i.e. a rich one, I was devastated. And that was when I'd tried to move on with a great guy I met during my stay with Gemma in her hometown in Louisiana. Unfortunately, I failed miserably with Jeremiah by not realizing he was merely my rebound fling and not my new forever.

My attention returned to the present moment with Gemma and Hendrix. They had no idea how happy I was to have them here. Fighting through the darkness on my own had been daunting, to say the least.

"No, we've not been talking, but he mentioned he'd learned the deets the press hadn't released concerning my kidnapping and Brandon. Apparently he overheard his father talking on the phone about it even though the judge has a gag order in place. Anyway, he wants to meet me. He basically begged, and well, what can I say? I caved, but if you're with me I won't jump him and be tempted to have crazy sex in the park, and if Pierce drives us, then Calvin can't blab to Dad where I was."

My attention bounced between Gemma and Hendrix to see if they'd support my plan or not. If I were honest with myself, I wanted to talk to Asher before we left tomorrow. A part of me needed to hear him out. Maybe I was still seeking closure, so I could truly move on. My heart seemed stuck on him.

"I'm in," Gemma said, grinning mischievously.

"I'll keep Franklin busy when you two are gone," Hendrix replied.

"Omigosh! Thank you. You have no idea what it's been like with a constant tattletale protecting me. Thank God he's not going on tour with us."

"Yeah, Franklin felt like Pierce was enough since Cade and John will also be with us most of the time," Hendrix added.

"It's not like we won't be moving around, anyway. I mean, if Brandon's dad is coming after us ..." My words trailed off while a ginormous knot fisted in my stomach.

"Yeah, I know. Mac, I realize Gemma tried to prepare you, but privacy is a rare commodity these days on the bus," Hendrix said.

I grinned. I'd seen the bus when Hendrix had first bought it, and I figured it would be a hunk of junk metal, but not even close. It sported leather couches and recliners along with dark wood floors. The kitchen even had stainless steel appliances. And although Hendrix and Gemma had a bedroom, the walls were thin, and the space was smaller than a jail cell.

"How's the self-defense training going with Pierce, Gemma?" I asked, redirecting the conversation. Pierce was Hendrix and Gemma's bodyguard who accompanied them on tour.

"She can kick my ass, now." Hendrix beamed proudly at Gemma and placed a kiss on her cheek.

"I wouldn't go that far, but I have come a long way. My confidence is up after working with Pierce. There's a comfort in knowing I can protect myself."

"And me," I blurted. "I mean, you took Brandon down with a single stiletto."

"Mac," Gemma said softly. "I'd do it again, too. You're not just my bestie. We're family. The only one I have." Her eyes misted slightly, and I clenched my jaw in order to fend off my own tears.

Gemma grew up in a small Louisiana town and was an only child. She'd lost her entire family within the last six months. I never got the chance to meet her mom, but I knew they were super close.

I did get the chance to know Ada Lynn, Gemma's substitute grandma. She was a major badass! In fact, she helped Hendrix beat down Gemma's piece of crap dad and send him to jail.

Gemma's dad was involved with the Dark Circle Society that

started this entire mess we were currently dealing with. What he subjected his own daughter to was nothing short of despicable. That bastard was now rotting in hell. I spent a few months with Gemma and Ada Lynn in Louisiana, and when we returned to Spokane, we brought Ada Lynn to come live with us in Franklin's house. Sadly, she passed away six weeks ago from a heart attack. But she'd be the first to say we shouldn't be sad because she'd had a good life. I loved her like crazy and we all missed her so much.

Gemma had a lot of Ada Lynn in her personality, too. She was the strongest person I knew. I had no doubt she was haunted by nightmares and depression, but you'd never know it. She stayed focused on all the good things in her life. Maybe someday I'd get there.

"Do you want me to go, too?" Hendrix asked. "Asher really hurt you, Mac. After all of these months, what could he possibly need to say to you?"

My chest ached with Hendrix's protective words.

"I think I need some girl time, honestly," I said. "If it's okay with you? Gemma's been gone for almost four weeks, and we have a lot to catch up on before we're surrounded by a bunch of dudes and no privacy."

Hendrix grinned. "Yeah, I'd take advantage of the time, too. The guys are great, but as Gemma will tell you, we can get a bit rowdy. Even Pierce joined in a few times."

"Seriously? You all finally cracked his shell to find a human inside of the cyborg?" I laughed.

"Right?" Gemma chimed in. "He's still serious and, as always, damned good at his job, but he's so ... What's the word I'm looking for?" She tapped her chin with her finger.

"Stoic? Stuffy? Stodgy?" I offered, giggling.

Our laughter filled the kitchen, and for the first time since that shitty night with Brandon, I experienced a small thread of happiness.

But it wasn't quite strong enough.

"I need to get ready for tonight, so I'll see you in a little while."

"Do you want company?" Gemma asked.

"Nah, it's okay. I need a few minutes to clear my head before I see Asher." I didn't miss the quirk of her eyebrow. I gave her and Hendrix a smile and walked out of the kitchen.

I closed my bedroom door behind me and turned the lock as a familiar longing for a Xanax crept over me. Ever since my therapist had prescribed them along with some Adderall, it had been easy to pop whatever I needed and add some alcohol on top of it for good measure. With Gemma around, I'd have to go light on the booze tonight until I returned home. I didn't want her nosing around in my business. At least about this.

Rummaging through my nightstand, I grabbed the prescription bottle along with the pint of vodka. I twisted off the lid, popped an orange tablet in my mouth, and washed it down with some liquid courage.

I sank onto the side of my unmade bed and a combination of guilt and anger washed over me as I closed my eyes, waiting anxiously for the much-needed relief. Chewing on a hangnail, I inhaled sharply and willed the flashbacks of Brandon Montgomery away. Fuck Brandon for living rent free inside my head. Fuck my therapist for giving me the prescriptions in the first place. Fuck the guilt. I took another pull on the bottle of vodka, then neatly tucked everything away.

CHAPTER 2

"*N*ow that we're practically alone, how are you really doing, Mac?" Gemma asked, pinning me with her intense gaze. She knew me well, but she'd also lived through her own hell and understood the process of putting up a front for everyone.

I stared out the back-passenger window of the Mercedes and into the darkness. Pierce agreed to drive us, and we explained to Dad we didn't need two bodyguards for the evening. He'd reluctantly given in to our request.

"Right now? I'm nervous about seeing Asher. Even when I was with Jeremiah in Louisiana, there wasn't a day that went by I didn't think about him. But Gemma, I have no idea what he wants. As far as I know, he and Rochelle are still together. I've been super firm with him after they announced their engagement and he still wanted to see me. I'm not interested in being the other woman on the side. That crap won't work for me."

"Nor should it. You deserve better, Mac. I have no doubt in my mind there's someone out there that will love you for all of you. And yes, before you say it, even your ADHD. You have ADHD, ADHD is *not* who you are."

My focus traveled to my new tan Tory Burch sandals and back to her.

"Hendrix is my role model. In the back of my mind, I compare every guy to him. Is that weird? I mean he's super smart, generous, and thoughtful. I always know he has my best interest in mind. I've never admitted it out loud until now, but I do. He's incredibly patient with me, and I never doubt he'll be there when I need him."

"Yeah, we both lucked out there." Gemma flashed a shy smile.

"Right?" I asked, agreeing with her. When I first met Gemma at college, she had insisted on wearing a hat and dark sunglasses to hide her appearance. Her past had left her broken, but she hadn't stopped trying to move forward. With my help, she finally came out of her shell, met Hendrix, and they fell in love. Hard. She'd come so far in a short amount of time. Maybe no matter how fucked up someone was, there was a chance that love could really heal.

I shifted in my seat, turning toward her. "I want what you two have. In fact, I think most women want what you two have. It's like a once in a lifetime thing. And from what I've experienced personally—unobtainable."

"It'll happen, Mac. When it's the right one, we'll all know it." She paused. "I'm going to loop back around to my question you didn't answer while we were in the kitchen, though. How are you doing?"

I scrunched down in my seat. Gemma and I had been college roomies off and on over the last year, and in that short time, we had gained a keen ability to see through each other's facades.

"Fine," I muttered, twirling my braided pigtail around a finger.

"Is it bad? The therapy isn't helping?" Gemma asked, worry lines creasing her forehead.

"Like, what the fuck? I'm supposed to talk to someone I don't know and miraculously feel better about being thrown in the trunk of a car and held at gunpoint?" My leg bounced with my words, and anxiety crept up my spine.

"Mac, you can talk to me. I was there, too."

"I can't talk to you when you're not here," I said, my tone sharp.

Gemma blanched.

"Shit. I didn't mean it like that. You know I didn't. And, like, don't get me wrong. I'm a million percent supportive of you touring, it was just after Brandon ... you and Hendrix left a week later, and everything that had happened fucking blew up inside me. Normally, I'd have you and Hendrix here, but it wasn't like I could wake you up in the middle of the night because I couldn't breathe, or I'd puked from the bad dreams, or—"

Tears streamed silently down Gemma's cheeks, and she grabbed my hand.

"I almost didn't go, Mac. Leaving you right after everything— it tore me up. I'd talked to Hendrix about it and Franklin, too."

"You did?" I asked, sitting up straighter in the black leather seat.

"I did. Franklin assured me he'd be there to take care of you. Plus, we'd only be gone for four weeks, but it seemed like a life-time to be away from you. Especially now. I'm so sorry, Mac. I made the wrong choice. I should have stayed." Gemma wiped her cheeks and chewed her bottom lip.

"You did the right thing. Don't feel guilty. I'm talking out my ass like usual."

"No, you're being honest. You need to talk to me, Mac. What you went through ... what I went through after I turned myself over to Brandon ... No one else experienced it like we did. We will share the darkness and the victory of it for the rest of our lives together. Even if I'm on the road, I'm only a Facetime away."

"Even if it's three a.m.?"

"Yeah, even if it's three in the morning. Now that we've gotten this out in the open, promise me you won't hide what's going on with you anymore. Let me help."

"All right, but it goes for you, too. Brandon fucked us both up."

"I know, but I get to beat the hell out of Pierce, and it's super helpful." She gave me a lopsided grin.

"Are you Gemma's punching bag, Pierce?" I asked, leaning forward and raising my voice. I released a giggle at the thought of Gemma kicking Pierce's ass. The dude was not only a total fucking hottie, but broad-shouldered and solid as hell. If five foot six and a hundred- and ten-pound Gemma could do some damage, maybe I should learn, too.

"She's come a long way," he replied without cracking as much as a smile.

I laughed and leaned back. "Same loveable personality I see."

Gemma giggled and nodded. "Told you," she said under her breath.

At exactly eight forty-five, Pierce turned the Mercedes into the nearly empty parking lot of the well-lit family park. I dabbed my forehead with the back of my hand. Thank goodness the late summer evening was warm, but not overly hot. I was already sweating bullets. A female laugh floated through the air, and I glanced out the window at a couple tickling each other underneath a large oak tree.

"There he is," Gemma pointed toward a lone figure perched on a picnic bench.

"Wish me luck," I said while the butterflies in my stomach set off another stream of anxiety.

"I'll give you some space, but I'll be outside of the car. Don't leave my line of sight," Pierce commanded.

"Yes, sir!" I saluted, rolled my eyes, and opened the car door.

"I'm going to stand outside with him. I'll feel better if I can see you, too," Gemma said.

"Ugh, it's almost like I'm the girl on the other side of the peep show."

"Ew, no, I don't want to watch you dancing around naked." Gemma laughed. "Go, he's waiting, and I'm super curious to know what in the hell is so important he reached out to you."

I nodded and jumped out. The sound of the door closing behind me echoed throughout the empty lot. The sharp scent of the freshly trimmed grass tickled my nose as Asher's head turned in my direction. He stood slowly, watching me meander down the sidewalk while the crickets chirped in the background. My heart thundered in my chest as I neared him, and a part of me longed for the days we were together. No one had compared to him and what we'd had. But I was younger and incredibly naïve then.

"Hey," he said softly, his hands crammed into the front pockets of his dark wash jeans. Knowing Asher, they were most likely Dolce & Gabbana.

I came to an abrupt halt in front of him as I scanned his sandy blond hair, deep brown eyes, and angular jaw. My pulse raced while I fought the urge to fling my arms around him. Regardless of our past, he was safe and comfortable, and I craved that right now.

"Hey," I said. "It sounded important. What's going on?" I glanced over my shoulder and spotted Gemma and Pierce next to the car.

"You have a bodyguard now?" he asked, his voice low and raspy.

"Yeah. Everywhere I go. He's not mine, actually." I said, pointing in Pierce's direction. "Dad has one for each of us."

"I don't blame him. Not after ..." Asher's jaw tensed. "You look good, Mac."

"Thanks. You too." I kicked nervously at the ground with my shoe.

"Can you sit down for a minute?" he asked and motioned to the table.

I stared at him, debating whether to indulge him or not. Finally, I jumped up on the picnic bench and plopped down on the table top.

"How are you after the Brandon ordeal?" he asked cautiously, sitting next to me.

We were so close if I stretched out my pinky, I could touch him. Instead, I turned my body toward him, and for a moment my insides quivered. Then I remembered what had really happened the night Brandon had taken me. The part I'd not told anyone.

"It's taken you a month to ask me?" I looked away, my jaw tensing with a sudden flash of anger.

"Mac, I'm sorry. I—"

"Stop. Is this why you wanted to see me? Because I have a lot of packing to do tonight before I leave with Hendrix and Gemma tomorrow."

"No." His focus dropped to the ground and back up to me. "I know you're mad at me, and I totally get it. But I wanted to tell you I broke things off with Rochelle."

My heart skidded to a stop.

"What?" He had my undivided attention, which was pretty difficult to come by.

"I want you back, Mac. I realize I've blown it. I know I should have stood up to my father sooner. But I did. I am."

I shook my head in disbelief. It had been two years since we broke up. Although communication never really stopped, mostly because Asher kept texting me on and off while I was at college. I did my best to stay strong, ignore him, move on. It was harder than anything I'd ever done because he'd been my safety net for so long. But seven months ago he broke the news of his engagement. In a text! And in the same message, he swore he still loved me. What the hell was I supposed to do with that? It had ripped me into a million little pieces that night. I'd been alone in my dorm room all cozy in my pajamas when my phone had buzzed and his words had sent me reeling.

"She not doing it for you in bed anymore?" I asked, sarcasm dripping from my words. "I loved you, Asher. You were my entire world, and when your father made me keep the pregnancy under wraps and stopped us from seeing each other ... Fuck." Anger coursed through me with the memories. "You didn't do a damned thing. No, wait, I'm sorry. You snuck around behind his back and we saw each other when we could. I became your dirty little secret."

"Babe, it wasn't like that. Please. I asked you here to tell you everything I couldn't before."

Unfortunately, my curiosity piqued, and I softened. My shoulders slumped as I waited for him to continue. An uneasy feeling tugged at me. There was no way I was going to walk away from him tonight with my heart intact.

Glancing at the clock on my phone, I cleared my throat. "You have five minutes, so make it count."

Asher hopped off the table and stood directly in front of me. Memories of us together flooded my thoughts, and I sat on my hands so I wouldn't do something stupid like tug on his expensive T-shirt and press his warm, soft lips against mine.

"Rochelle and I never slept together."

I laughed.

"Mac," he said, leaning into me. I didn't miss the pain etched across his handsome face.

"Don't." I held up my hand, warning him not to move any closer. No way would I be able to stand firm if he did. I peeked at my cell again. "Four minutes."

"The marriage is off. It was a big scam, anyway. You're well aware Dad didn't want anyone to know about you and me, not about us per se, but the pregnancy. He was in the middle of making the biggest financial deal of his life, and he went fucking nuts. He said if I didn't leave you alone I'd never see another penny from him again. He cornered me and honestly, at seventeen, what could I do?" He paused, glancing at his feet and back to me again. "The day I turned twenty-one he told me about the arranged engagement, which was really part of the business deal he'd made when you got pregnant."

I chewed on my bottom lip, mulling over the level of deviousness his father had gone to for money. Anger sparked to life inside me, not just at Asher for not fighting for us, but his asshole dad.

"Maybe you couldn't do anything as a minor, but you didn't even try. You rolled right over with his demands, crushing my heart in the process."

He stepped in between my knees, wrapped his arms around me, and pulled me to him before I could object. The warmth of his muscular chest melted me. Safe. Strong. Comfortable. One thing I could say about Asher, I always knew where I stood with him even if I didn't like it. When Daddy had backed him into a corner, Asher had been upfront the entire time.

"Mac, I love you. I've never stopped loving you," he whispered in my ear while his fingers danced across the back of my neck, sending a tingle down my spine.

I inhaled his musky cologne, and my insides trembled with desire. He was no longer with Rochelle. What if things really were different?

I pulled away from him, sucking in some much-needed air.

"What happened?" I asked, peering up at him.

I shivered as Asher rubbed his hands up and down my arms. His touch still ignited my body like no one else's had.

"Our relationship was strictly a business arrangement, but in the beginning, Rochelle told me—Mac, she's a lesbian. She swore me to secrecy. If her family ever found out, she'd lose everything including her inheritance."

I literally choked on my own spit. What kind of parent would turn their daughter away because she was gay?

"What?" I yelped. "Why in the fuck didn't you tell me, Asher? It could have changed so much between us!" I stood on top of the picnic table and paced back and forth, attempting to digest what he'd admitted.

"I'm sorry. I promised I wouldn't share it with anyone. She was terrified, Mac. I'm not proud of what I did, and I sure as hell didn't handle it well."

"No fucking shit. Like, *her* secret was more important than us?" I put my hands on my hips and glared at him, my toe tapping incessantly on the table.

"Although I wanted to protect her, after a while, I couldn't live a lie anymore."

"Was that the 'something good' you said you wanted to tell me when you asked me to meet you at the movies? Ya know, the night Brandon kidnapped me? Were you going to tell me about Rochelle, Asher?" I stopped pacing, my stomach twisting into knots.

He turned away from me, raking his hands over his short blond hair. A few seconds later he faced me again.

"An hour before I was supposed to meet you, I told Rochelle we were done. I was finished with all the lies, and I told her I couldn't play along anymore even if it cost me everything. I explained I was still in love with you and had stupidly thrown it away because I was a coward."

"You did?" I asked, my voice cracking with emotion.

"Yeah. It terrified her. She'd have to tell her family the truth and risk losing not only them but her inheritance. It fucked me up just thinking about it, but I couldn't live a lie anymore. Mac, I finally did what I should have done a long time ago. Instead of blowing my allowance on stupid spoiled rich kid nonsense the last few years ... I invested it. I finally got something right."

"What?" I gasped. Asher had loved spending Daddy's money.

"During that time, the money grew so even if Dad cuts me off. I'm solid for at least a little bit. I did it for us, babe. When I came crawling back to you, I wanted to be able to tell you'd I'd done something for our future. I mean ... if you'll have me."

Stunned, I remained silent for a moment while I attempted to understand everything he'd said.

"I've never told anyone I was going with you to the movie the night Brandon was waiting for me. Your name never came up, and I wanted to keep you out of it. But why were you late showing up? I waited in the parking lot for ten minutes. Couldn't you have at least texted me you were running behind? If you had, I would have gone on inside instead of waiting outside by my car." My tone showed no hint of the emotion I was really feeling. At this point, getting an answer from him was the only thing that mattered to me. "Why?"

Asher's shoulders slumped in defeat. "I lost track of time. Rochelle started crying, and I caved and stayed with her until she was okay. I figured I'd slip into the movie and find you. I—"

A muffled cry escaped my throat, and I covered my face with my arm and sank down onto the table top. Hot tears stung my cheeks as they fell.

"I'm sorry, Mac. When I heard Brandon had kidnapped you ... It fucking wrecked me," he whispered. "It's all my fault. Please—Please, babe. I'm so fucking sorry."

My body shook with my sobs. If he'd been there like he'd promised, my entire life would have been different. But he hadn't. Once again, I felt Asher hadn't had the guts to show up for me. Maybe in this instance I wasn't being fair, but I couldn't seem to separate logic from my emotions.

I peered up at him through my eyelashes and wiped my cheeks with the palms of my hands.

"I thought about you while I was tied up in the back of his trunk," I said quietly. "I cursed you and pleaded for you to find me all in the same breath."

Asher's eyes grew misty with my revelation. "I'll never forgive myself for not being there for you."

I hiccupped and glanced away from him. Even though it was warm outside, a chill traveled through me as I hopped off the table, my sandals crunching the gravel on the ground. My gaze traveled up to his. Every emotion possible flickered across his expression. A long silence hung in the space between us.

"Mac, please. Can you forgive me? I love you so much, please don't say we're over."

"You were so busy protecting Daddy and your fake fiancée, you failed to protect the one person you swear you love the most. Me. If there's one thing I've realized since the shit with Brandon —I want more, Asher. I want a guy in my life who loves me for all my good and all my bad and continues to show up for me. I'm not interested in a yes man to Daddy, or someone who can't commit to me." I ran my hands over my face, attempting to regain my composure. "Asher, I'll always love you. We have a history, but I don't think there's another chance for us. I'm sorry." And with that revelation, the fog of anger and grief lifted from around me. With determined steps, I walked to stand before him, placed my hands on his shoulders and planted a gentle kiss on his cheek.

"Goodbye," I said softly and walked away. My heart jumped into my throat. Asher had no clue how much I still loved him, but I already struggled with fitting in due to my unfiltered mouth and attention bouncing around faster than the Flash on speed. I wasn't interested in being with someone who wasn't sure where I belonged in his life.

"Mac, don't say that. Give me a chance to prove to you I've changed. All I'm asking for is some time. I know you're going through a lot, and—don't make a final decision. Not tonight."

My feet ground to a stop, and I turned back to him, my pulse rising. Maybe my past wasn't going to let go of me after all.

"I'm going on tour with Hendrix and Gemma for a few weeks. We can talk when I get back," I conceded.

In a few long strides, Asher stepped into me, pulled me against him, and brought his mouth to mine. His warm lips melted all of my resentment, and my pulse sped into overdrive. The tip of his tongue gently brushed mine, and as quick as it had started, the kiss was over.

"I love you. I'll prove to you I've changed. Don't give up on me yet," he said in a hushed tone, his breath hot against my ear.

With that, he walked away and left me standing alone with only the insanity of my racing thoughts.

CHAPTER 3

"*M*ac!" I turned to see Gemma running down the hill. "What happened?"

I sniffled while my emotions ran rampant inside me.

"Are you okay?" she asked, grabbing my hand.

"I don't know," I whispered. I looked around, but Asher was already gone. Only his Beemer tail lights blinked in the darkness as he pulled out of the parking lot.

"Come on," Gemma said, guiding me back to the picnic bench.

Glancing over my shoulder, I spotted Pierce, and a wave of safety washed over me. After the kidnapping, I rarely felt safe unless security was nearby. Gemma situated herself on the table, and I followed.

"I need a minute," I said, attempting to wrap my head around what had happened. Even though my brain could process information at a million miles an hour due to my ADHD, it couldn't do the same with my emotions. Glancing up into the star-lit sky, I gathered some courage to tell Gemma the truth about the events that led to my kidnapping.

"Don't be mad," I said, turning toward her.

"Why would I be mad?" She cocked an eyebrow at me.

"Shit. Because. I never told you ... The night Brandon took me ... Fuck." I groaned and slapped my hands over my face.

"Mac, spit it out," Gemma encouraged.

My hands dropped to my lap, and I huffed loudly.

"Asher had asked me to a movie. He said he had something good to tell me, so I'd agreed to meet him. He was late, and that's when Brandon grabbed me. If Asher had been on time, Brandon wouldn't have had the opportunity to drug me, toss me in his trunk, and take me to the nasty warehouse. There it is. I was supposed to be with Asher when Brandon showed up." My shoulders slumped with the weight of my confession. Asher hadn't been the only one keeping secrets. Once again, he'd made me think with my heart instead of my head. And look where that got me. Lesson learned.

"Mac," Gemma gasped. "I don't know what to say. Had you two been meeting up with each other even though he and Rochelle were together?" Her eyes filled with compassion.

"Nope. Even if we had, it wouldn't have mattered."

"It always matters if someone else is involved. You've never been the type to support cheating."

"And I totally agree, but there wasn't anything really going on with Asher and Rochelle."

"I don't understand. Did they break up?"

"Gemma, you can't tell anyone. I'm not trying to cause problems for Rochelle, she has enough already," I said.

"You have my word." Worry lines creased her forehead while she waited for me to continue.

"Rochelle is a lesbian. She and Asher have never slept together. If she admitted it to her family, she'd lose everything, and she was terrified."

"Poor girl."

I shot Gemma a look. "Really bestie? You're feeling bad for *her* right now?"

"I'm sorry, Mac. You know you're most important to me, but

for a second my heart went out to her. I think it would be agonizing to hide who you really are."

"Not my problem," I muttered, jealousy stirring inside me. It wasn't like I wanted to be her, but she'd ended up with Asher.

"I know, but you just said you weren't sharing the information in order to hurt her."

My eyes squeezed closed as I fought down the ball of emotions that threatened to erupt.

"No, I'm not. It would be an awful way to live," I replied, my throat tightening with the mere thought. Rochelle and I didn't share the same situation, but deep down, we both wanted to be loved for who we were. It was exhausting trying to fit in all the time and hoping someone might love you.

My chin quivered, and Gemma pulled me into a hug while I finally released all the pent-up anger and frustration from the last few months.

I cried against Gemma's shoulder. "Asher chose to protect her secret over standing up to his father and being with me."

"Oh, Mac. I'm so sorry, but he's trying to make things right. He was stuck in a bad place, no money, and no say in the situation as a minor. And maybe this is also good news? I mean, Asher and Rochelle never slept together, right?"

I stared up into the night and chewed my bottom lip, blinking away my tears.

"Yeah. He didn't lie to me about their sex life. He wants another chance ... I ... I don't ... The timing really sucks, ya know?"

"I get it. Take your time Mac, there's no rush. We're heading out in the morning, and we can talk more about it then. Right?"

"Sounds good," I muttered, wiping my nose with the back of my hand.

"Do you want some more time here or are you ready to go home?" Gemma asked.

"I'm not ready to go home, but I know Franklin wanted to spend some time with us before we leave."

"I'd like to see him, too. However, you're my top priority right now."

"Yeah?"

"Yeah," Gemma said, nudging me gently with her elbow.

"Thanks. You're the best bestie ever," I said, flashing her a grin.

"I think the tour will be good for you. It's so hard to wake up every day in the city where someone assaulted you. I know when I came to Spokane ... when I met you and Hendrix, it's when I finally started to heal. Maybe you'll be able to take a deep breath, laugh, spend time with people you love, and get the hell out of here for a while."

"It really helped you when you left Louisiana?" I asked. For some reason, I'd never considered how much it had made a positive impact on her until now.

"It changed everything, and it all started with you." She smiled at me.

I barked out a laugh as I recalled the first time I'd met her. Although she wouldn't admit it, my boisterous personality had scared the living crap of her. Not to mention I talked nonstop. It hadn't taken long before we'd gotten used to each other, and now we were best friends. I'd never had a friend like Gemma, and we'd shared some dark crap. When it came down to it, she and Hendrix were who I trusted with my life.

"Thanks for coming with me tonight and sharing Pierce," I said.

"Anytime. I'd have asked you too if I'd been stuck with Calvin."

"You got the cool one." I hopped off the table and brushed my backside off.

"Pierce has been very good to me, but it's caused a bit of contention between Hendrix and me while we've been on the road." She tucked a stray red hair behind her ear and stood.

My head tilted as I stared at her. "What do you mean?"

Gemma rolled her eyes. "Hendrix is convinced Pierce is in love with me."

"What?" I exclaimed. "This is the juiciest shit I've heard in like, ever! Why are you just mentioning this now?"

Gemma cringed. "It's not been the right time. Besides, we just got home, and I figured we'd full on catch up while on the road."

"Wait. What? Pierce is in love with you?" I whisper-yelled. I loved Gemma, but she could be so naïve when it came to guys. She'd only ever been with Hendrix, and she still had some learning to do.

"Ugh. No, I can't right now, Mac. Hendrix and I discussed this way more than I wanted to. I wish he would get it through his noggin' that Pierce and I are good friends."

"Pierce has friends?" I gasped, clutching my hand to my heart dramatically.

Gemma snickered. "I know, right? It's the charming personality."

I glanced at the Mercedes to find Pierce standing there, his intense focus trained on us.

"Gemma, best bestie of mine, if Hendrix says Pierce is into you ... I gotta side with my bro. He's smart, and there's this thing."

Gemma folded her arms across her chest and glared at me.

"Give me a second to explain. Think about this for a minute. Let's say you and Hendrix were at dinner, and the waitress winked at him and giggled. What would it tell you?"

"That it was time for me to slap her?"

My laugh split me wide open. She'd gotten a bit feistier since she and Hendrix had started their tour.

"But you'd know she wanted in Hendrix's pants." I muffled another laugh as Gemma's nostrils flared. "We know when the skanks are hitting on our men, right?"

"Yes," she replied, her foot tapping against the ground.

If I hadn't been trying to make a serious point, I would have laughed. I'd not seen Gemma jealous before. I assumed the groupie sluts would push anyone's buttons, though.

"It's the same. Dudes just show it differently most of the time. If Hendrix has talked to you about it, something about the way Pierce looks at you or his body language is giving his feelings away. And honestly, you're seriously gorgeous. What guy wouldn't be into you?"

"Mac," Gemma dropped her arms and sighed. "Think about it, though. Who protected me in Louisiana when Hendrix was hurt?"

"Pierce," I replied.

"Who taught me to defend myself against assholes when they put their hands on me?"

"Pierce."

"Who was the one that prepared me to take down Brandon when I exchanged myself for you?"

"Pierce," I mumbled, clearly seeing where she was going with this.

"And who has continued to make sure I'm safe on tour?"

"Pierce," I groaned.

"We share some of the darkest parts of my life together. We've bonded as friends during some intense and fucked up shit. I trust him with my life, and he's proven to me on several occasions he's worthy of it. And how many people in my life have I been able to really trust other than Ada Lynn, Franklin, Hendrix, and you?"

Dammit, she got me. "No one."

"Can you see what I'm seeing? Pierce cares about me, I know that, but he's not in love with me."

I sighed. "I do understand your side, but I'm not going to dismiss Hendrix's concerns, either."

"Whatever," Gemma said, chewing on her bottom lip.

"Are you mad at me?" I asked.

"No, I'm just tired of defending my friendship with him."

"I'm sorry," I said, flinging my arms around her. "We can talk more about it later. I'll keep an eye on Pierce and let you know what I think about it another time. Alright?"

Gemma hugged me in return. "Me telling you not to worry about it is futile. I suspect you won't be able to resist."

I stepped back, nodded, and smiled. "Well, you know once I get something stuck in my head, I'm like a dog with a bone. But for now, let's go home."

"Sounds good," Gemma said, returning my smile.

IF NOT FOR Ada Lynn's empty chair at the table, it'd be a normal family dinner. My heart grew heavy at the thought of not seeing her sweet face or hearing her jokes and pearls of wisdom. She had been the one to get Gemma out of Louisiana and to college in Washington, where we met. Seeing the love between them was something special, and I'd quickly grown to love Ada Lynn, too. If my heart ached for her, I was certain Gemma's was broken. Even Dad had grown close to her.

"Are you excited?" Dad asked me, pulling me from my thoughts.

"Yeah, I definitely need a change of scenery."

Hendrix's chin tilted slightly in the air. He was sizing me up, assessing me to see if I was okay. I wasn't, but he had his career and Gemma to juggle now. He didn't need a clingy sister, too.

"It's an adjustment, but a lot of fun," Gemma said.

"Yeah, but you didn't really know John and Cade. I went to high school with them before they formed the band. I already knew they were loud and obnoxious." I grinned at Hendrix.

"Cade shaved his God-awful beard," Hendrix said, chuckling.

"He probably wasn't getting laid," I said, rolling my eyes. "I mean good grief, you can't walk around looking like you're from Duck Dynasty and expect to get your wick dipped every night."

Hendrix chuckled while Dad tried to hide his grin.

"John and I might have had something to do with it, too," Hendrix said, a mischievous sparkle in his eye.

I leaned forward, my elbows on the table. "What did they do, Gemma?"

"They're like a bunch of fifth graders, Mac. They have contests to see who can burp the alphabet, how much they can drink before they pass out, and other things I won't mention." She looked at Franklin and smiled sheepishly. "Anyway, there was shaving cream, Ben Gay, and other items involved in their practical jokes."

"Oh," I said, my lips forming a big 'O'. "Did anyone mess with you?"

"Hell no," Hendrix said immediately. "She's off limits and all mine." He reached for her hand and winked. A crimson blush traveled up her neck and cheeks. The poor girl was probably thinking about getting naked with Hendrix, and now everyone in the room knew from her reaction.

"Back to the beard," I said, grinning.

"You were right, he was complaining he wasn't getting any action," Hendrix said, laughing. "So one night when he was passed out cold from drinking, John and I got the scissors and whacked it off. It was a mess when he got up the next morning. But we were tired of him moaning and whining all the time."

"I tried to tell him if he wanted to meet someone, he needed to dial down the beard," Gemma chimed in, "but for whatever reason, he didn't. Guess Hendrix and John thought they'd help him out."

I laughed. "That's mean Hendrix, but it's funny."

"Yeah, he finally stopped whining and is back to his playboy ways."

"Hope he wraps his shit up. I bet there's some real skanks showing up backstage."

"You have no idea," Gemma said, her eyes cutting sharply in Hendrix's direction.

He squeezed her hand, and my heart melted. Hendrix had always had women fall at his feet, but it hadn't phased him. He'd never been a player like Cade, he wasn't wired that way. I just hoped there were more guys like him out there.

"To be honest, Cade's dialed things down a lot. I think all the women were fun, at first, but he's chilled out about it."

"Maybe he's growing up finally." Even in high school, he'd had a bit of a bad boy reputation, but at the same time, he was a decent person. John had been more mild-mannered where Cade liked to be the center of the party. Once they all started playing music together, they had something else to think about other than getting laid. It seemed to help. Honestly, I never cared what they did. They both had always been good to me when they hung out with Hendrix at Mom's house. I was with Asher anyway.

"I'll miss you all," Dad said. "I've gotten used to everyone being around. It's been really nice, actually."

"It's not forever," I assured him. Although Franklin was Hendrix's biological dad, I'd grown to think of him as mine as well. Even though he and my mom had only been married for eight years, he was more of a dad to me than my real father who had walked out on us when I was one. Franklin was an alcoholic, though. He'd been sober now for a few years, but it had cost him everything; his marriage, son, and the closest thing he had to a daughter. I was thrilled to see he'd stayed off the booze and had worked hard to rebuild his relationships with his kids.

"I know, but the house will be empty again."

A feeling of dread spiraled through my chest. I knew what loneliness was like. We all did, and no one wanted to revisit it even for a little while.

"You can fly down to any of the shows," Hendrix suggested. "We've added a few new songs since you've seen the last concert."

"We've written a few more, too," Gemma added.

"I can't wait to hear everything!" I squealed, bouncing in my seat. "You two are amazing." I sighed dreamily and flashed them a big grin.

"I'd love to see you guys again on stage, too. As much as I don't want to, I need to make my way to bed. Wake me up before you all leave in the morning," Dad said, scooting his chair away from the table. "I've got court first thing, so I'll need to get up anyway."

"Okay." I stood and gave him a hug goodnight. He walked over to Gemma and placed a parental kiss on the top of her head. Hendrix stood and hugged him. Sadness flickered across Dad's face.

"I sure am proud of you all." He smiled before he turned and walked out of the room.

"Dammit," I muttered. "Maybe it's too soon, and I should stay with him. The last several months have been intense for all of us. You don't think he'll start drinking again do you?" I asked Hendrix.

"Unfortunately, there's always a possibility, Mac. Even if we stayed in Spokane, there's a chance. You can't not live your life because you're afraid he'll pick up the bottle again. He's an adult and has a good system and support group in place. You're coming with us tomorrow. I need my sister with me, and Gemma needs her best friend."

A smile pulled at the corners of my mouth while my focus bounced between them.

"Agreed," Gemma said.

"If you think it's alright, I will. I need to get the fuck out of here anyway."

"Excellent, be ready to go by seven tomorrow morning."

"Ha! I'm already packed. I'm rolling my ass out of bed and straight to the shower."

"Oh," Hendrix said, leaning back in his chair, his gaze traveling over Gemma. "You have the nice big shower in your room. Man, have I missed it."

"Hey now, don't discuss your sexcapades in front of me. Just keep it down for fuck's sake. And yes, pun intended. The last time you two lived here, the walls were shaking with all the booty bumpin'."

Gemma's neck and cheeks flamed red. "I'm sorry. We had lost time to make up for," she stammered.

"I was there, you don't have to explain," I said sarcastically. "But keep it down tonight and every night. It's almost one a.m., which leaves only five hours to sleep, so I'm outta here. See you two tomorrow."

"Night," they both replied.

I stood, pushed my chair under the table, and headed toward the staircase. Heaviness clung to me with every step up the stairs. Maybe it would be better when I wasn't alone. It sounded like the band had grown a lot closer, but I assumed it had something to do with the tight quarters and their career finally taking off.

My skin hummed with anxiety, and I rubbed my arms as I turned on my bedroom light and closed the door behind me. Leaning against it, I stared at my nightstand. Maybe tonight I could sleep without another Xanax and vodka. Shutting my eyes for a moment, Brandon's sneer filled my mind, his hate filled threats ringing in my ears.

I balled my hands into tight fists then made my way to my nightstand and stash.

CHAPTER 4

*T*he last thing I expected to see when we arrived at Hendrix's tour bus was a guy's naked ass mooning us from the doorway.

"Welcome back motherfuckers," Cade laughed and pulled his pants up.

"Dude, in front of my girlfriend and my sister?" Hendrix asked bewildered. Gemma turned away quickly, attempting to maintain her innocence.

Cade spun around, his amber eyes wide and his smile faltering as he spotted us behind Hendrix. His chest and arm muscles flexed beneath his dark grey T-shirt while he ran his hands over his short jet-black hair. My attention traveled over his jawline, noting his beard was completely gone and now revealing a tanned face. In my opinion, Cade had always been gorgeous, but he was more like a brother than dating material. Not only that, I didn't get involved with the players. Talk about inviting disaster.

"Shit, sorry man. I forgot about the ladies." He hopped down the front steps and embraced me. "Good to see ya, Mac."

I stood on my tip toes and hugged him back. At least his ass was a nice one and not all hairy. "You, too. Thanks for being cool about letting me tag along."

"It's good for Gemma. She really missed you," he replied and tugged on one of my braids.

"Dude, seriously?" I glared at him as I flipped my hair behind my shoulder. His ornery grin was his only answer.

"Yes, I did miss Mac, and everyone can see why," Gemma said dryly.

Cade and Hendrix chuckled as we all lugged our duffel bags up the metal stairs and onto the bus, which was currently parked in a high-security RV storage facility. Buses like this, all tricked out with every possible convenience, cost a mint, so when not in use Hendrix took no chances. He also wanted to make sure Brandon's family had no access to it.

We may not have verbalized it, but we all worried about the same thing—when would Brandon's father show up seeking revenge, and what were his evil plans? It was a horrible way to live, always looking over our shoulders. I reminded myself I was surrounded by people who would protect me. I was safe.

The faint scent of leather tickled my nose while I waited for everyone to move forward. The beige leather recliners had been cleaned, and all the surfaces including the kitchen had been polished. The rich brown hardwood floors gleamed in the natural sunlight that streamed through the windows. It was beautiful.

I noted the sizeable 4K TV mounted on the wall and thanked God I could watch YouTube and Netflix on my iPad. Who knew what the guys watched, but naked girls and football weren't my ideas of good times.

Pierce remained quiet as he stood outside and guarded the bus entrance. It hadn't occurred to me he would sleep on the bus with us. I was surrounded by three hot dudes while Gemma shared the bedroom with Hendrix. I couldn't hide my grin. Most girls would kill to be in my position.

"Hey, hey!" John yelled, bounding up the stairs behind me. "Welcome, Mac!" he said, smacking a sloppy kiss on my cheek.

"Dude!" I wrinkled my nose and wiped the moisture off my cheeks. "Was that necessary?"

John's green eyes sparkled as he flashed me a cheesy grin and wrapped an arm around my waist. Before I knew it, he licked my cheek, his tongue flicking over my skin. He laughed hysterically.

"Shit, I'm with a bunch of fucking five-year-olds. Gemma was actually nice when she referred to you as fifth graders!" I shot John a nasty look and wiped my face off with the collar of my shirt.

He ruffled my hair with one large hand. "Glad you're here. It will give me someone else to mess with other than Cade's ass."

"Oh, lucky me," I muttered.

Everyone laughed as we reached the sleeping quarters and the guys flung their backpacks on their respective beds. It wasn't lost on me that John was across from me and Cade directly above me.

John flashed his perfectly straight pearly whites at me, then his shoulders slumped forward, and his expression grew serious.

"Hey, I'm sorry about what you went through with Brandon. If you need anything just let me know." Compassion filled his face.

"Thanks. It means a lot to me."

"My mom said to tell you the same thing. Anything we can do, ya know." He scrubbed his hand over his lightly stubbled jaw and nodded.

I'd known John as long as I had Cade. He had a really sweet side to him when he wasn't being a pesky ass wipe. He'd filled out nicely after high school, but it was the combination of green eyes and blonde hair that had the girls drooling over him.

I scanned the sleeping quarters while Hendrix and Gemma continued toward their room. Although I'd seen the bus and beds before, I'd forgotten that only a curtain separated the bunks from the rest of the area. I mentally scanned my sleepwear selection and groaned inwardly. After Brandon had held me hostage, I'd found pajamas restrictive and had started sleeping in the nude. *Shit*.

"You alright?" Pierce asked, eyeing me.

"Yeah. I need to chat with Gemma." I gulped and full on panicked as everything began to close in on me. I shouldn't have been surprised the close quarters would ramp up my anxiety, but apparently being tossed in the back of a trunk at gunpoint would do that to someone.

Even if I slept in a shirt and undies, the best I had were thongs. One cheek peek out of the sheets, and a sleep induced kick at the curtain would open it. I'd be flashing everyone. Although I considered John, Pierce, and Cade friends, it was a new level I wasn't interested in. Besides, they would never let me live it down. They were already going to be a handful to manage.

"Gemma!" I hauled ass to the back and pounded on their door.

"Mac? What's wrong?" she asked, flinging the door open wide.

"Can we chat outside for a minute?" I squeaked.

"Babe, I'll be right back," she called to Hendrix. "Are you okay? You're pale." She grabbed my arm and led me past the guys who were all staring at me like I had the plague. "Ignore them," she said under her breath. I followed her as we moved through the common area and out the door. I inhaled the fresh morning air the moment we were off the bus again.

"What's wrong? Do you not want to go? We have time for Pierce to take you home if you need to."

"No, it's ... I want to stay. It's just tight quarters with three big dudes, and I panicked. Which is new, ya know? Like, small spaces never bothered me before—Brandon," I choked out. "Plus, I totally spaced and didn't pack any appropriate pajamas. Well, that's an understatement. I started sleeping naked after the kidnapping. I don't know why it made me feel better to not have anything on. It sort of felt constricting, which probably sounds weird, and when I saw the beds—I freaked the fuck out. I'm probably not making any damned sense right now, but I need to borrow something to sleep in."

"Oh Mac, it's okay. I do get it. I have plenty of pajama shorts with cute tops. They might be a little tight across your chest since you're bustier than I am, but you're welcome to anything I have. All you need to do is ask."

I nodded. "Yeah, cool, thanks." I rubbed my forehead and peered at her. "Tight quarters with three dudes," I muttered. "No privacy."

"I understand, and I also know it's not really about the guys, it's about what happened. Listen, I have nightmares every night. It's not going to go away any time soon. I'm fortunate enough I have Hendrix next to me to calm me down, but I'm assuming you're dealing with the same. Insomnia, bad dreams, thinking you see Dillon or Brandon everywhere you look."

Speechless for a change, I merely nodded. I'd not realized she was dealing with the same mental whiplash.

"Gemma, I know you disclosed to the police and FBI what Brandon did to you while he held you captive, but you and I haven't ever fully dived into it. All I know is he tried to rape you, and you had enough self-defense training you were able to take him down ... with your stiletto. Which is impressive as hell might I add."

Gemma glanced at the black asphalt of the newly paved RV parking lot for a minute, her gaze slowly traveling back up to mine.

"I don't know if we need to go into details, Mac. We both know what a monster Brandon is. I can take a good guess at how he tormented you, and I'm not sure I really want to know. All it will remind me of is that I should have been there sooner for you. I was late showing up to help you, and I struggle with it on a daily basis."

"You can't." I shook my head. "No, don't even go there." I

grasped her hand and squeezed. "The important thing is we're both out of the mess, and we're all alive."

Gemma's eyes grew misty and she nodded.

Maybe having her close by again would help both of us. If I could, I'd take on Gemma's nightmares. She'd lived through enough, and until recently I'd been fortunate to not have to deal with a tragedy on this level. Silence filled the space between us.

"Well concerning the tight quarters, think of it like this if it helps," she said, changing the subject. "It's like—camping, sort of. Ya know, like if we were all in a cabin together. You'll get used to it in no time. You'll probably feel safer. You've got three body-guards, and they obviously think the world of you. I mean, I was never greeted with a bare ass or sloppy kiss."

I laughed. "Fucking hams."

"You okay?" she asked me, rubbing my arm.

"I'm good. Thanks. No way in hell would I do this without you, though. I'm not sure how you made it the last month with them."

"Right? It was a huge adjustment, and you know how private I am."

"True. True. If you can do it, then I can too."

"Ya know, we can always rent a car when we're in a city we want to see and have Pierce drive us around. We'll have some girl time, I promise. We'll both need it desperately by then anyway. Just remember Hendrix and I are here with you."

"I'm better. Thanks." I took a deep breath and flung my arms around her.

"You're welcome."

"Ladies," a middle-aged, light-haired, plump man said, approaching us.

My entire body went rigid. I didn't know this guy. What did he want? Where was Pierce?

"Hey Mike," Gemma said. "This is Mac, Hendrix's sister. She's joining us over the next few weeks. Mac, this is Mike, he's the driver."

Oh, thank God. I immediately relaxed. "Hi, nice to meet you. And thanks in advance for not crashing the bus and killing all of us."

Mike's eyebrows shot up. "You're welcome," he stammered.

Once again, my mouth had gotten the better of me, and I'd put someone in an awkward position.

"You'll get used to her," Gemma assured him, grinning.

"The instruments and luggage are all loaded, so let's hit the road," Mike said, boarding the bus.

"Let's roll like a tootsie," I said, finding my inner courage to get back on the bus and winking at Gemma.

We followed Mike up the steps, and the doors closed behind us. Cade had settled into a recliner and had his headphones on. Pierce sat in the seat closest to the door, obviously alert. It hadn't dawned on me he would be nearby when I had my mini-meltdown with Gemma. I wonder if he heard the pajama predicament. Inwardly, I cringed as his dark eyes landed on me. I'd have to be more careful.

"Why don't you unpack and put your clothes in the drawers beneath your bed, and I'll grab some PJ sets for you," Gemma whispered.

"Thanks." I managed a smile before she left me standing there surrounded by massive amounts of testosterone.

My phone buzzed in the back pocket of my denim shorts. I grabbed it and groaned. Asher.

I know I said I'd give you time to think, but I miss you.

I proceeded to my bed and tossed my it down next to my duffel bag. There were three long drawers beneath it. I hoped it was enough. My cell buzzed again. Sighing, I pulled my bag to me and unzipped it, ignoring the additional text. There was no way I'd be able to sort through the situation with Asher if he was smothering me. But my curiosity won out, and I peeked at his message.

I'll wait for you. I always have, Mac. There's never been anyone else.

My heart stuttered. Dammit. How could he still make me feel this way even after everything he'd done? Not once had he stood up to anyone and fought for our relationship. Until now, I reminded myself. But was it too late? Had the damage been done?

My fingers danced across my keyboard with my response.

I need some time and space ... Please.

A row of heart emojis lit up my screen, but he didn't say anything else.

The bus groaned and moved forward at a crawl. I located one of the windows near the beds, and a soft sigh of relief escaped me while we pulled through the security gates and onto the road.

First stop, Portland, Oregon. My stomach fluttered with excitement at the thought of leaving Washington and Brandon behind. I needed a change, even if it was for a short time. I'd never seen Oregon, so I hoped it was one of the places we had the time to stay for an extra day and sightsee. I'd have to ask Gemma what the schedule looked like.

CHAPTER 5

*T*he cool thing about touring on a bus? We were allowed to park at the venue or a close by area and sleep. No hotel necessary and it also gave us flexibility in our day. Since the band wasn't scheduled to perform until the next evening, Hendrix had arranged a full day for us at the Multnomah Falls in Oregon, and afterward, we could sleep the rest of the way to Portland and through the night.

The rush of the crystal-clear water filled me with awe as we approached the viewing area. I'd never seen trees so green and lush during the summer before either.

"You ready?" Gemma asked Hendrix and me.

"It's pretty high up there," I said, gulping visibly while I pulled on the clear plastic rain poncho and hat, I'd purchased from the gift shop.

"We're going to get soaked that close to the water," Hendrix said, adjusting his own rain gear. "But it will be worth it."

We hiked up the steep, narrow hill and made it to the bridge halfway up the falls. Large droplets of water plopped on my hat and poncho. Since I'd never been this close to a waterfall, I'd not realized everything would get wet including my jeans and braids. Within minutes all three of us looked like drowned rats.

"This is amazing." I glanced around me, my heart splitting open at the sight of the wreckage still visible from the fire a few summers before. It had made national news and burned more than forty-eight thousand acres. It was mind blowing and heart crushing to see the damage. The tree trunks were scorched, and the ground still remained blackened even a few years later. Regardless, it was one of the most beautiful places I'd seen.

"Shit," I muttered glancing down from the bridge as I grabbed Gemma and Hendrix's arms for support. Hopefully they hadn't seen me sway.

Hendrix chuckled and patted my hand.

"Still afraid of heights, huh?"

"Mmhm," I squeaked out a response. "But I didn't want to miss this. I mean, how many times have I ever been to Oregon? None, and we literally live five hours away. How does it even happen? I mean I moved to Louisiana for a while, but couldn't find time to visit Oregon?"

Gemma and Hendrix laughed as I contemplated how weird the situation was. But hell, life had been one ball of fucked up strange for a while now.

"Be glad John and Cade are chatting up the girls below us, or I'm sure they'd be giving you grief right about now," Gemma added, squeezing my fingers for additional support.

We quieted for a moment and took in the beauty around us. Even though we were surrounded by people and the roar of rushing water, the falls were still peaceful. Maybe water soothed my soul. Didn't other people talk about how the ocean or mountains calmed them? All I knew was I needed something to help.

The gummy edibles I'd stashed at home were now in my purse, and if I got caught, I'd be in big shit. Not to mention Hendrix would be super pissed I'd brought them on his bus. I didn't want to cause trouble, but some nights I was desperate to shut my mind off and sleep. I'm pretty sure my counselor would say I was self-medicating my ADHD and the kidnapping trauma. Of course I was. I was well aware of this fact, and as far as I was concerned my counselor could go fuck herself. She wasn't living my life right now.

"I'd love to stay up here all afternoon, but by the time we finish hiking to the top, it will be dark. We'll need to eat, then drive into Portland," Hendrix said to us.

"Thanks for making time for us to stop," I said, beaming at him. "This was awesome."

"Sightseeing is definitely one of the best parts about touring," Gemma said. "It's nice to see new places when we can squeeze in the time."

We made our way down the trail and back to the spot we'd seen John and Cade last. John waved and laughed as we approached.

Frowning, I scanned the elbow to elbow crowd of people for Cade. Where was he?

"You guys want to hike up the other trail with us?" Hendrix asked John. "Where's Cade? Or do I want to know?"

"Well," John started and coughed into his hand.

I glanced at Gemma confused. What was going on? Where was he?

"There he is," John said unable to hide his laughter.

We all turned to see Cade and a gorgeous blonde step out from the woods. She giggled and hung all over him while he smacked her on the ass.

Hendrix ran his hand through his hair, unable to hide his grin.

"Dude's got game." He laughed and the girl took a selfie with Cade, then gave him a quick kiss on the cheek before she ran off to meet up with her friends.

"Her skirt's twisted," Gemma commented dryly as Cade approached us, grinning like a Cheshire cat.

"Oh shit. They just fucked in the woods?" I muttered to Gemma.

"Well, they did something." Gemma rolled her eyes and grabbed Hendrix's hand. "Man whores, both Cade and John."

My eyes widened. I knew Cade was a bit of a slut, but this was the first time I'd ever seen him sneak off in broad daylight with a random chick to get some action. Shit, I almost envied him for a minute. I had no problem with a one nighter, but I wasn't down for a lot of them.

"This happens a lot?" I asked her while the guys moved off to the side. I assumed Cade was sharing about his adventure. They laughed, and John smacked Cade on the back.

"Mac, don't get me wrong, being on tour can be lonely. I can't imagine what it would be like without Hendrix. Plus, we have the bedroom, so we don't have to sneak around. Hendrix told the guys to have as much fun as they wanted, just don't bring it on the bus. I think if they had steady girlfriends who were with us on tour it would be different. I don't know. It's Hendrix's call, but in a way, it's not fair he and I sleep together. On the other hand, don't these two have any sort of moral compass? Maybe that's what Hendrix is more concerned about, ya know, like multiple girls on the bus." Her nose wrinkled.

I laughed. "When it comes to getting laid, I don't know. Cade's always been promiscuous. John too, but he had a steady girlfriend for over a year in high school."

"Did Cade? I mean, has he ever settled down in a real relationship?"

My mouth twisted as I thought back over the years I'd known him. "Not in high school. Maybe over the last few years, but Hendrix never mentioned anything, and I've only seen John and Cade a handful of times in the last twelve months. I saw them more often my freshman year, when I had the awful roomie at school, and I stayed with Hendrix a lot."

"Maybe it's the southern upbringing in me, but I hope he finds someone who's good for him, and he can really see how amazing it is with someone special." Gemma's blue eyes sparkled as she directed a dreamy gaze at Hendrix. The connection between them was amazing and only seemed to grow stronger with time. He gave her a soft smile, mouthed *I love you*, and returned to the conversation with Cade and John.

I wanted what Gemma and Hendrix had, too. Deep down inside me though, I wondered if Gemma had found the last good guy on the planet.

"Are you ladies ready to hike on up?" Hendrix asked as the guys surrounded us.

"Yes! This is beautiful, and I'm already going stir crazy. Let's do it," I said, bouncing from one foot to the other like a little kid.

THANK God the hike had worn me out. Not only was I exhausted, but I was the first one in the group to tumble into bed. I put my headphones on so I could listen to some music and block out everyone else around me. In some ways, this trip reminded me of having a roomie in college. No one was ever on the same schedule, and it was typically me that was up at weird hours of the night.

I checked my little curtain in front of my bed for any cracks someone might be able to see through. If it had been all girls, I wouldn't have given a rat's ass, but I'd suddenly grown shy around my male friends.

Flinging myself back into my pillow, I pushed play on my iPhone and listened to the soft music of the Sleep playlist on my Spotify app. Hopefully between the peaceful sounds and killer hike, I'd be asleep in no time. Even the movement of the bus seemed calming. No edibles would be needed tonight.

"Nooo!" I shot straight up in bed, my chest heaving with short gasps, my pulse hammering, and beads of sweat dotting my forehead. I glanced around in the darkness, desperate to identify where I was. Brandon's sneer remained imprinted in my mind as I attempted to shake the nightmare. But where was I?

"Mac."

I froze. Had Brandon been released and found me? I patted the blankets for my phone as a small whimper escaped me.

"Mac, it's Cade."

Cade? Fuck. Fuck. Fuck. I was on the bus. I wasn't with Brandon. I located my cell, the light splitting open the darkness. I was safe. I slapped my hands over my mouth and swallowed down a cry.

"Can I open your curtain?" he asked quietly.

I nodded, then realized he couldn't see me.

"Yeah," I replied breathlessly, still paralyzed with fear.

The curtain parted a few inches to reveal Cade's upper body hanging over the side of his bed and down into my space.

"What's up?" I asked, hoping I hadn't actually yelled in my sleep.

Even upside down I could tell a deep frown had etched itself into Cade's forehead.

"Are you okay? I think you had a bad dream."

"You heard me?" I grimaced.

"Yeah."

"Did anyone else?" I asked, frantic.

"I can't tell for sure, but I don't think so. John sleeps with noise-canceling headphones on, and I'm pretty sure if your brother or Gemma had heard you, they'd be out here by now."

I nodded. Okay, not an ideal situation by any means, but it could be worse. I could have *all* of them staring at me.

"You're shaking," Cade noted.

"Sorry," I muttered, rubbing my bare arms with my hands.

"Come on." Cade extended his hand toward me.

"Huh?"

"You're terrified, Mac. Come up here with me until you feel better."

"Cade Richardson, are you trying to get me in your bed? Dude, do you not have any fucking limits?"

Cade's face paled.

"No. Promise. I'm trying to take care of my best friend's sister right now. I know he'd do it for me. Come on."

He disappeared, and I stayed where I was.

"I don't have all night. We both need some sleep before the show tomorrow so hurry up."

That sounded more like Cade, so I settled down a little. I slipped out of my bed and made my way up the ladder to his bunk.

"I'm going to sleep on the outside of the bed so you gotta hop over me," he said, grinning impishly.

"Cade!" I whisper yelled. "I thought you were trying to help me, not get into my shorts."

He tossed his hands up in surrender then his amber eyes grew serious.

"I won't try to get in your shorts, Mac. Hendrix would fucking have my head. But your nightmare, whatever it was that terrified you ... John was serious, we're all here for you. You don't have to be afraid to sleep."

I searched him for any sign he was messing with me, and before I realized it, my attention traveled down his neck, chest, and across every breathtaking ab muscle. A dusting of dark hair trailed down his lower abdomen and disappeared beneath his navy-blue basketball shorts.

"Hey now, I'm not a piece of meat," he chuckled.

My cheeks flushed crimson. I'd never outwardly ogled a guy I wasn't in a relationship with. Apparently my manners were still asleep.

"Are you going to stand on the ladder all night or are you going to jump over me so we can get some sleep?"

I huffed, slung one short leg over him, and pushed myself off the ladder. But my foot refused to cooperate and somehow wrapped itself around a rung. I flailed around like a one-legged windsock pole at a car dealership and then managed to land right on top of him. The air rushed out of my lungs while my tank top twisted up beneath me. Cade's brows shot up as he got an eye full of my overly exposed D cups. My nipples were the only thing that hadn't popped out to greet him.

I gasped, untangled my foot, and clumsily made my way to the other side of him.

"Sorry," I muttered and refused to look at him. Awkward didn't even begin to sum up the situation. I'd known Cade for a long time, but sleeping in his bed put a new spin on our friendship.

He cleared his throat and moved his hands behind his head. We both remained quiet for a few minutes. I shuddered as the air began to dry the sweat along my forehead and the back of my neck.

"You can get under the blanket. I'll sleep on top of them," he offered.

"Oh. Okay." I was too chilled to argue.

"Go on to sleep, Mac. I'll set my alarm so we can get you back to your bed before anyone realizes you're up here. No one can know. Your brother will kick me right out of the band if he thinks anything is going on."

"But nothing is going on. I'd tell him you were trying to help, Cade. He won't do anything crazy, but I do think it's a good idea no one knows. I really don't feel like dealing with any drama while on tour with you guys."

I inhaled deeply and sleep suddenly tugged at me again.

"And, Mac?"

"Yeah?"

"You're safe now."

And for the first time since Brandon had taken me, I actually felt protected.

At six o' clock in the morning, Cade gently woke me, and I slipped undetected back into my own bed.

THE NEXT DAY, Cade and I barely saw each other as he prepared with the band for the performance at the Moda Center. Neither of us even mentioned what had happened. It worked for me, and it was nice to see he had kept his word and our secret.

After a few hours of practice on stage, Gemma returned to the bus with me, which I assumed was a rare treat.

"Hey, since you've already rehearsed and the guys don't need you for a little bit, we should check out downtown and do some shopping," I suggested, leaning against the door of her and Hendrix's bedroom.

"I'm one step ahead of you," she said, smiling while she gathered her thick red hair, pulled it into a ponytail, and turned toward me. "As promised, we'll have some girl time. Pierce will drive us in a rental car and keep us company, but unlike Calvin, he won't repeat anything we discuss."

"You're sure?"

"Very. Hendrix and I have actually argued in front of him before, and you'd never even know he'd heard us. His facial expression and body language never change. He's never opened up about his background, but I know he's had some serious training. Like, military or martial arts or some other intense shit. He's tough to read. Only on a rare occasion do I get a glimpse into what he's thinking."

"Well it's good though. I mean, he is here on a job, right? He can't protect you and Hendrix if he's trolling on Facebook and Tinder."

Gemma giggled. "He's all hawk eyes and no phone. But sometimes I want to crack his hard exterior and let him know we're not just a job. We're friends, too."

I paused for a moment, selecting my next words carefully.

"Gemma, he can't have an emotional attachment and also do his job to the best of his ability. Like, emotions complicate situations like this."

"Ugh, you sound like Hendrix," she said, closing the bedroom door behind her and sauntering up the middle of the bus. "I mean, emotions make us connect on a deeper level, Mac. Having empathy doesn't make someone weak, it makes them stronger."

I waited for her to continue, afraid to disagree with her about Pierce. I knew they had a history most people would never share. Maybe … maybe it was possible I simply didn't understand their situation.

"Take you and me for example," she continued. "If you'd not had any compassion for me when I'd first arrived in our dorm room, you wouldn't have hugged me, Mac. You wouldn't have adopted me as your pet project or given me the time of day. You would have turned up your nose at my appearance and moved on with your life. Your sensitive, generous side, which is full of emotion might I add, changed the entire situation. We would not be here together if you'd snubbed me like so many others did."

Fuck. I hated it when she outmaneuvered me with her logic. How in the hell was I supposed to respond to her?

"I know, Gemma. Like, I totally see where you're coming from, but I think this situation with Pierce is different. Hendrix is my brother. If he's convinced Pierce wants to go to pound town with you, then you've got to take a step back and have some empathy for your boyfriend."

Gemma whirled around and stared a hole right into me. Oh damn. I'd crossed a line with her.

"I do not under any circumstances want to sleep with anyone other than Hendrix. Mac, you know that about me. I'm not like

Cade, hopping off into the woods for a quick hookup. Come on now."

My shoulders slumped forward. I did know. She'd never cheat on Hendrix, and I suspected they'd end up married. But my best bestie in the world was also seriously naïve when it came to the opposite sex. I almost felt bad for Hendrix while he attempted to educate her about guys and how to know if they were interested in being more than a buddy.

"I've said it before, and I'll say it again: Pierce and I are friends."

Our time in Louisiana earlier this year culminated with an avalanche of crazy. A tornado destroyed the arena where Hendrix was about to perform, injuring him so badly that he was in a coma for two weeks. Not only that, but Gemma's past had come with a vengeance to haunt her. Pierce was by her side throughout all of it.

There was no way I was going to win this conversation. "I'm still keeping an eye on him. I want to see his interest or lack thereof for myself."

Gemma sighed softly and continued toward the doors where Pierce was waiting for us. She halted and turned toward me again, her eyes wide.

"Ugh, sometimes he's so quiet I forget he's around," she muttered to me.

"He's sort of eerie," I agreed with her. "Like, he can sneak up on anyone. Do you think he heard us?"

"God, I hope not. I don't want to make things difficult for him."

I nodded. A little part of me suspected she'd already made things difficult for him, but I was going to try and keep my mouth shut for a change.

"Well, let's try to be careful," I whispered, eyeing Pierce.

"Yeah." Gemma turned around and walked the rest of the way down the pathway and out the door.

"Ladies," Pierce said.

"Hey," I smiled, attempting to assess the situation. His dark aviators hid his eyes, making it impossible for me to tell if he'd overheard us.

Gemma and I talked to him about our afternoon plans, and within minutes we were shopping in downtown Portland. Neither of us brought up Pierce again.

CHAPTER 6

J'd forgotten about the insane energy that coursed through a crowd during a good concert. Gemma and Hendrix were on fire, and the entire crowd was on their feet. It was amazing how much they'd grown as individuals and as a pair.

I'd had my choice of front row seats or hanging out backstage during the show, so I chose a section of the audience next to a security guard who waited for the crazed fans to step out of line. Cade and John were working the crowd while Gemma and Hendrix sang one of their new songs. John was behind his drum set, using sticks that lit up and changed colors. He tossed them in the air as he played, never missing a beat or dropping them. Overall, the band's performance had definitely kicked up a few notches. I was thrilled to see them so alive. Even Gemma walked the stage, reached out to people, and touched their hands. No way in hell would she have even considered something like that before they'd begun their tour a month ago.

The band moved into one of the songs I knew, and I sang along with them at the top of my lungs. It felt good to let go and just have fun.

"They're so hot!" The girl dancing next to me yelled.

"Which one's the hottest?" I asked. I was a little curious about how everyone else saw my brother and his friends.

"All of them, but I'd totally be all over Cade Richardson. Oh my God. He can strum me just like he does his guitar."

I coughed into my hand and attempted to hide my grin. She had no idea I knew them personally. Like really well.

"Do you want to meet him after the show?" I asked her. She stopped cold, her brown eyes widening.

"You can take us backstage?" She ran a hand down her long platinum blonde hair.

"Yeah," I replied. "Hendrix is my brother, and I've known John and Cade for years. We all went to high school together."

She grabbed my hand and jumped up and down, screaming her head off. She turned to her group and explained the situation. Before I knew it, the other three girls wanted to go, too. Shit, I hadn't thought about how many other people were in the group with my new-found friend. Would Cade be pissed? If he got laid maybe he wouldn't care.

"Is it you four?" I asked.

"Yeah, and I'm Marilyn," the girl next to me said. She introduced the other girls, but it was too loud to hear their names.

"Nice to meet you, Marilyn. Stay with me after they're done, and I'll get you ladies backstage for a bit."

An hour later, I led the group of sweaty girls behind the stage and to the VIP room. They were chattering a mile a minute while we walked. I nodded at the security and showed them the badge Hendrix had given me earlier. Finally we reached Pierce, who stood at the entrance of the band's after party room.

"Hey Pierce," I said.

"Hey, Mac," he replied, eyeing the girls I had with me.

"We want to say hi to everyone."

"Are the ladies with you?"

"Yeah, we were sitting next to each other during the concert, and I mentioned I'd take them to meet Hendrix and the rest of the group. I assume it's okay?" I flashed him a warm smile as the girls fidgeted silently behind me and waited for him to respond.

"I'll see if they're ready." He touched his earpiece and communicated with one of the additional security guys located inside the room with Hendrix and the band.

We waited, Marilyn and her friends growing more excited by the minute.

"Alright," Pierce said. He opened the door and let us through.

"Thanks." The room was loaded with a full bar and multiple couches. An enormous aquarium took up the majority of one wall. I swallowed hard as a baby shark swam to the front. No way was I interested in getting close to it.

"Oh. My. God!" I rushed to Gemma and pulled her into a big hug. "You guys were amazing." I ran over and gave each of them a hug. "You guys just get better and better."

"I'm so happy you liked it," Gemma beamed at me.

"Hey, I brought a few people with me. We were all in the front row together."

I motioned for them to join us.

"Hi, I'm Marilyn. This is Katie, Janna, and Lauren. We all love you guys sooooo much," she said, unable to contain her enthusiasm.

Everyone stepped forward and talked to the group. I stood off to the side, watching the interaction. It was fun to see others going cray cray over the people that were my best friends and family. I leaned against the couch Cade and John had been sitting on a minute ago and grinned. Hendrix wouldn't flirt with the girls, but John and Cade had turned up the smiles and the charm like thousand-watt light bulbs.

Gemma joined me and laughed at Cade and John's full on flirtation mode.

"They're super happy tonight. The performance went really well," she said as she rested against the wall.

"I'm shocked at how much better you've all gotten. It's not like you all sucked or anything, you totally didn't. I mean you were amazing before you left for the tour, but the growth in such a short time is insane."

"Thanks," Gemma said, a soft blush creeping across her cheeks. "It might get a bit crazy back here tonight, so stay close so we can see each other."

My eyebrow arched. "What do you mean?"

"Sometimes, depending on how long the VIP list is, they allow the room to get too crowded, in my opinion. It gets stuffy and loud. We'll have the other musicians from the opening band join us in a few minutes, too. I'm pretty sure some weed and coke will start circulating along with the alcohol. There are other rooms the guys can take girls to for privacy, but the ladies aren't shy, and I've seen some flip up their skirt and straddle a guy right in front of us. When the sex starts, it turns into one long party. Hendrix and I sneak out as soon as we can and head back to the bus. I'm not a hundred percent sure, but I think the majority of the time John and Cade stay."

"Oh," I said. "Well, if they can't take a girl on the bus then this is at least a better choice than in the woods."

The door opened, and I caught a glimpse of Pierce while he ushered another group of people in.

"I'd better go be social," Gemma said, pushing off the wall.

"I'm going to stay put back here and have a few drinks," I said while I surveyed the situation. Even *I* knew shit was about to get crazy.

"If you want something to drink the bar is over there." Gemma pointed to the opposite side of the room.

"Thanks. Go have fun. I'll catch up with you later," I said and made my way straight for the booze.

Before I realized it, the room was overflowing and stifling. Gemma's red hair helped me easily keep up with her, and Cade stood a half foot taller than most everyone else in the room. It wasn't long before a string of girls, John, and Cade stepped through the door and disappeared. I shook my head and laughed. No wonder Hendrix didn't want them to party on the bus. It reeked bad enough in here of sweat, weed, and sex. Not to mention this room was way bigger than where we were sleeping.

Even in a crowd full of people, I felt the familiar pang of loneliness. Once again, I felt like I didn't belong and was left observing everyone else having a good time.

After another screwdriver, I glanced at my phone. It was after two in the morning, and I was exhausted. Standing, I searched the room for my bestie. I was ready to go and simply needed a bodyguard to get me to the bus.

"Hey!" I said, tugging on Gemma's hand from behind her.

She turned toward me and smiled.

"Are you having fun?" she asked.

"I think I'm ready to go back to the bus. Is Pierce or someone else available to take me?"

A small frown creased Gemma's forehead.

"Are you alright?" she asked, her eyes moving over me.

"Yeah, it's a lot of activity I'm not used to. I didn't sleep so great last night, and the drinks are making me even more tired."

She nodded and located Hendrix who was currently surrounded by a group of people. He shot a glance in our direction, smiling when his eyes landed on us.

"He's really good about keeping an eye on me after the concerts," she said. "He knows it's not my natural environment. Plus, I worry someone can slip by security and ..."

"No way," I assured her. "You guys have a shit ton of bodyguards in here."

"Yeah, I know, but I still worry sometimes that someone could get to me. I guess old fears die hard, huh?"

"Gemma, after Brandon snuck backstage and got his nasty paws on you before he was arrested ... hell, he had some stealth skills for sure." Hendrix had finally talked Gemma into performing with the band on stage for the first time. After she'd finished her song, she waited backstage for the concert to end, and Brandon had pounced on her like a ravenous cat. "We need to keep an eye on each other, ya know? I don't think there's anything wrong with being alert during situations like this. I mean, we don't know any of these people in here. They could be anyone, right? Maybe even someone Brandon sent over. Even though he's in custody, I don't doubt he and his father have deep connections." I stopped blabbing and cringed. "Sorry, it was the wrong thing to say."

Gemma's face paled with my words.

"Shit, me and my mouth," I muttered, my shoulders sagging.

"No, it's the truth, and just because I don't say it out loud doesn't mean I don't think it. Sometimes I'm glad you blurt stuff out. At least you have the guts to speak up."

"I don't think it's guts," I muttered, glancing cautiously around the room now that I'd spooked myself.

"Let me talk to Hendrix, and I'll get Pierce to take us to the bus. I've stayed long enough."

"No, you don't have to leave, too. I'm sorry, Gemma. I don't want to pull you away from your fans."

"You're doing me a favor actually. I'm exhausted, and I'd love to have some peace and quiet before the guys all come back drunk anyway. Well, Hendrix definitely drinks more on tour than he used to, but he doesn't get smashed like John and Cade do."

Gemma's last statement concerned me. Hendrix hadn't ever been a big drinker, one or two max. I hoped the drinking wasn't turning into an issue. It would tear me up if he followed in Franklin's alcoholic footsteps.

"If they're going to be loud and obnoxious, I'll put my head-phones on."

"Good idea," Gemma agreed, and we made our way toward Hendrix. He wasn't thrilled about the idea of us going back to crash without him, but he conceded when he remembered Pierce would be with us. Five other security guards would remain with the rest of the band, so we knew everyone was safe.

~

HALF AN HOUR LATER, we boarded the bus with Pierce.

"Oh, I'm so happy to be back. That was a lot of people. It used to never bother me, but I've changed. Or maybe I only feel comfortable around people I really know. I guess it's easy to hide in a bubble after a trauma, huh? I mean, it's what you did in Louisiana." I paused, realizing I was rambling again. "Aren't you tired from all the social activity afterward?" I asked Gemma.

Gemma released a heavy sigh.

"You have no idea. Touring is as exhausting as it is fun."

Pierce sat in the recliner closest to the doors and gave us a weary look. Even he was tired, but I don't think he slept as deeply as we did either. Or maybe he was like a mom with a newborn and always had one ear open. Regardless, I think we were all happy to be able to take a breath and chill out.

"Thanks, Pierce," I said, stifling a yawn. "I'm going to crawl into bed and hopefully get some sleep."

"You're welcome. I'll be here if you need anything." His gaze held mine for a brief moment before it traveled to Gemma. Although he wouldn't admit anything, I suspected he'd heard me yell out during my bad dream last night.

"I'm right behind you," Gemma said.

I waved goodnight to them, turned around, and walked to my bunk where my borrowed pair of pajamas and favorite pillow awaited me.

Soft whispers filled my ears, and I peeked over my shoulder. Gemma had crouched down to Pierce's eye level, and he leaned toward her. Gemma nodded and stood slowly. His attention followed her every movement. Then he glanced down the hall in my direction, his dark eyes flashing.

Embarrassed I'd been caught eavesdropping, I hopped into my bunk and pulled the curtain closed behind me. Even though I wasn't sure what they'd discussed, I was clear on how Pierce felt about Gemma now. Hendrix was right. Pierce was in love with her, and he'd done a shitty job of hiding it when he thought no one was looking.

Gemma either didn't want to see it, or she honestly didn't know what to look for when a guy was interested in her. This had to be torture for Hendrix and Pierce being on tour together. How could you even deal with knowing a guy you had to spend so much time with was in love with your girlfriend?

The crazy thing? I didn't blame Pierce at all. It wasn't his fault Franklin had hired him from the Westbrook's security firm and assigned him to protect Gemma and Hendrix. And even if he wasn't very social, Pierce had gone through a lot with our family over the last year and a half. We were all friends. He and Hendrix were friends. Well, as much as you could be friends with Pierce. He had iron walls up and refused to let anyone in. Except for Gemma. Hendrix obviously knew, but he was caught in a tough spot. He couldn't say anything to Pierce without causing a situation that would most likely end Pierce's job with us, but how was Hendrix able to deal with a dude wanting his girlfriend?

Maneuvering carefully in my small bunk space, I changed into my pajamas, then threw myself back on my pillow. I realized I would have to stay quiet about what I'd seen a few minutes ago. Gemma would hate me for coming between her and Pierce's friendship, and I wouldn't be telling Hendrix anything he didn't already know. It was really up to him what he chose to do about the situation. For now, the smartest thing I could do was stay out of it.

My mind continued with a million thoughts about the concert and what it was like to be included in the after party. It was strange watching girls flip their shit over how hot the guys were, but it wasn't just them. Gemma had a line of guys waiting for her autograph and pictures, too. She might not have enjoyed all the eye candy tonight, but I sure as hell had. Tonight would have been a perfect night to get trashed and have hot and sweaty sex, but I wasn't with anyone. Maybe it was time for a one nighter.

After another thirty minutes of tossing and turning, I located my purse, rifled through it and found my stash. Tonight, I needed something to help me sleep. Maybe it was the large crowd and strange people that had sent my anxiety into overdrive. Regardless, I knew what would help. It wasn't long before my mind quieted, and I drifted off into a fitful sleep.

I woke a few hours later to John's soft snoring. Apparently the guys had made it back at some point. I pulled the covers up and tucked them under my chin. Maybe Gemma was right, and I'd feel safer with them close by.

CHAPTER 7

"No nightmares last night. That's good," Cade said softly to me in between sips of his orange juice at breakfast the next morning.

I nodded subtly and kept my focus trained on Hendrix. There was no way I wanted to tip off the group about our sleeping situation. The best way to do that was to keep our distance, and not raise any eyebrows.

Pierce had found a place to have breakfast, and we all huddled into a booth in the back corner of the crowded restaurant. I'd squeezed in next to Cade as John sat on my other side. Hendrix and Gemma were across from us, and he was reviewing the day's schedule with everyone.

I shoveled some scrambled eggs into my mouth and peered over at Pierce, who stood in the corner closest to us where he could easily survey the room.

"What are the next few stops again?" I asked Hendrix after he'd finished.

"Nevada, Arizona, New Mexico, and Colorado. We'll be working on some music, but you're welcome to hang out with us if you want."

"Really? I won't bother you guys?"

Hendrix shook his head. "Nah, we goof off, too. It's a long time to be cooped up though, so we have to get some work done."

"I get it." I grinned. How cool was it I had a front row seat to practices, too?

John slipped his arm around my shoulders and pulled me into him.

"Glad you're here," he said, ruffling my hair. I made a mental note to keep it in braids if John was going to continue to mess it up.

"Hey! You and Cade are actually worse than my brother. You're constant pester bugs." I huffed and pulled away from him.

"Come on now," Cade said near my ear. "We don't get to pick on our own brothers and sisters while we're away, so we're all too happy borrowing our best friend's sibling."

"Lucky me," I muttered as Cade planted his elbow gently into my side.

I whirled in my seat, my next bite of eggs poised delicately on my fork.

"I'm older than your sister, and I have a lot more practice at fighting back. I suggest you back off."

A look of amusement flashed in his eyes. Cade threw his hands in the air, feigning surrender and laughing. I didn't miss his focus drifting down my dark teal T-shirt, ogling my busty chest, though. This wasn't anything new, and I simply ignored the fact that guys looked at my boobs all the time.

"Eyes," I said, giving him a warning look.

"That's my sister, dude," Hendrix reminded him.

"Just looking, man. No offense meant, but they're kind of out there and hard to miss," Cade said, grinning.

"Hey dumbass, you gotta stop while you're ahead," John said, shaking his head.

"John's right. Stop. Like right now, dude," Hendrix warned and chucked a piece of toast at Cade.

"Oh crap," Gemma said, ducking in her seat as Cade snatched my fork with eggs on it and flung it in Hendrix's direction. Everyone at the table burst out laughing and a mild food fight began. I took Gemma's cue and slid into my seat, but not before I saw her nudge Hendrix. Hard.

"Sorry," he said to Gemma before he bounced a piece of cantaloupe off John's ear. "Alright, we'd better knock it off, or they'll kick us out of the restaurant."

It didn't stop the guys from getting Hendrix back before they all settled down.

I sat up and hid my grin with my hand. Franklin would be appalled at the situation, but for once it was nice having fun without anyone breathing down our necks.

THE NEXT FEW days passed by in a big blur. The band practiced on the bus during the day and performed at night. Even though I was having the time of my life while visiting new places, hanging out with the band after performances, and partying all night, I was exhausted. Dark circles had settled in under Gemma's blue eyes, too. At least I wasn't the only one. Some days I felt older than my twenty-two years, and just because I was hyper didn't mean I wasn't tired.

Brandon also continued to haunt my dreams, and I'd had two more nightmares. Each time, Cade reached his hand down and motioned for me to come up to his bunk. Hell, we were almost in a routine. I'd yelp myself awake, and he'd be there within seconds. The next morning he'd nudge me awake, and I'd slip back into my own bed. We never talked about it, either. Until tonight.

"If I weren't desperate to sleep, this wouldn't be worth it," I whispered.

Once again, Cade lay on his back and waited for me to catapult over him. I threw my leg over his muscled, exposed stomach and settled in next to him, rolling over on my side.

"Why do you make me crawl over you?" I muttered, trying not to be irritated with him since I'd woken him up, too. "Why don't you scoot over?"

He rubbed his face and peered at me. His sleep filled amber gaze held mine for a second.

"A few reasons," he said, his voice deep and husky. "If someone opens the curtain, they'll see me first. Second, I can't protect you as well if you're on the outside of the bed."

"Protect me?" I asked, yawning. "From what?"

"Anything, but if Brandon were released from prison, at least the son of a bitch would have to go through me first. I've done what I could to keep you safe."

My eyes widened. It's not that I hadn't considered Brandon might be released, but I was more concerned about his father and the other society members. But none of that information was public knowledge, and I couldn't share it with Cade.

"Thank you. But Pierce is here."

"I know, but even with him nearby, it isn't enough to stop your bad dreams."

"I'm sorry. I know I keep you up at night."

"Don't worry about it. I'm used to being up at all hours anyway."

Where was this coming from? Why did he even care? I was Hendrix's sister and nothing else. He didn't have to be kind to me. Not to mention the Cade I saw at night was completely different than the one everyone else knew.

"Cade, I don't get you. You're a total player, but when it comes down to it, you've been right next to me when I needed you." Heat traveled across my cheeks at my own directness.

"What can I say? I'm a complex kinda guy." He flashed me a lazy smile.

"Yes you are." I paused, collecting my next words as carefully as possible. "Why all the girls?"

Cade didn't miss a beat. "Why not? No strings attached, no commitments, and I'll probably never see them again."

"That's appealing?" I propped up on my elbow and stared at him. For some odd reason, I suddenly wanted to know what made Cade tick. Maybe he was a good distraction from my own hell.

"Yeah. Things at home suck and being on tour is a lot of work. It's nice to blow off steam and not worry about it."

"What's going on at home?" I frowned. I'd been so absorbed in my own crap, I'd never considered what Cade or John's life outside the band was like. Even when we were younger, they'd always come to our place. I'd never even met their parents.

Cade rolled over on his side and stared at me.

"Hendrix never said anything?"

"About what?" I asked, picking at the hangnail on my thumb.

"That's cool he didn't," Cade said softly.

"It's okay, you don't have to tell me," I offered. I didn't want anything to be awkward between us. We were friends and bunk buddies, and honestly, as long as we were on the road, I needed his support.

"I almost had to leave the band," he started.

"What? Why? From what I can tell, you and John love it as much as Hendrix does."

"We do, but things at home are complicated. Sometimes it makes it difficult for me to leave."

"You still live at home?" I asked.

"Yeah, but not because I want too. My mom ... she's autistic."

"Oh wow, like how bad?" I sat up. He had my full attention. I had no idea he had so much to deal with.

"She's what's considered high functioning, so she can handle some stuff on her own, but not taking care of my little sister in the way she needs to. And like with any other person in the world, Mom has good and bad days. On the rough ones, she rocks a lot or gets hyper-focused on whatever it is at the moment. She's great with Missy's schedule, breakfast, school, and daily routines, but most thirteen-year-old kids get sick of eating the same thing every day. Hell, I don't even want to eat the same food every day."

"So you take care of both of them?" I asked, compassion filling my tone. "What did you do when you were young? Who took care of you? Where was your dad?" I rattled off in rapid succession.

"Dad split when I was little, and my grandma lived with us until she passed away a few months ago. Since Mom wasn't able to work, we grew up on the system, but it kept a roof over our head, food on the table, and Missy and I were safe. Grandma attended parent teacher conferences, shopped for school clothes, and assumed full responsibility for us. I was closer to her than my real mom." His voice trailed off as a flicker of grief flashed in his eyes.

"I'm so sorry you lost your grandma." I resisted the urge to hug his pain away.

Cade nodded and ran his hand over his short dark hair.

"Me too. I miss her every day, but I have to step up as man of the house now. If I don't, Missy can't live with Mom anymore. I can't stand to put her in the foster system when I'm capable of taking care of her. Besides, with the money coming in from playing, I can easily support everyone."

"How are you able to tour then? Don't you worry about Missy and your mom at home alone?"

"I do worry about them, but Franklin actually helped me find a trained nurse and caregiver to be with them while I'm on the road. He also checks on them a few times a week and lets me know how they're doing. I had some real reservations about leaving them with someone I didn't know, but Franklin's help has made a big difference for all of us."

"Wow, I had no idea. I can't imagine how difficult it must be to deal with. I mean, autism can be really unpredictable. But if she's on the spectrum at least she can have some normalcy maybe, but it makes it super tough on you."

Cade's eyes narrowed. "I don't need your pity, Mac. I'm just telling you why I like to play hard," he said, his words clipped with anger.

I shook my head. Dammit, I'd really tried not to stick my foot in my mouth this time.

"It's not pity, Cade. Yeah, I'm sorry you're in the situation, but you could choose to not give a fuck, too. Instead, you stepped up and did the right thing. Your family is together because of you. That's a big deal."

An awkward pause hung in the air.

"Somedays, I don't want to go back at all," he confessed as he lay back on his pillow and stared at the ceiling. "Then the guilt fucks with me. I can't do it to Mom or Missy. The only reason I don't feel like a total fuckwad playing music is because I pay all the bills, which includes Mom's medical treatment."

"Cade," I said, reaching for his hand without thinking. "I'm pretty sure anyone would feel like that. Hell, I would. I can barely keep my own life together, much less a family."

He turned his head and held my gaze as sadness flickered across his expression.

"You're stronger than you think, Mac." He squeezed my hand and smiled gently. "We should get some sleep."

"Okay." I slipped beneath the blankets Cade had set aside for me. We each had our own now, so he didn't have to freeze on top of the covers at night when I was there with him.

I turned on my side and faced away from him, my heart aching with what he'd shared. For the first time since I'd met Cade, I saw him as more than a man whore. Why hadn't I seen this other side of him before?

"Mac?" Cade's voice pulled me from my thoughts.

"Yeah?"

"Can we keep this conversation between us?"

"Yeah. Thanks for trusting me."

And with that, I drifted off to a peaceful sleep.

CADE'S CONFESSION concerning his family cemented itself inside my thoughts the next day. I wanted to talk to Gemma about it, but I couldn't. No one could know we were hanging out together in his bed, either. Besides, it would put Gemma in a terrible position. I'd have to swear her to secrecy, and I'm not sure she could really keep a secret from Hendrix. Honestly, I'd feel bad even asking.

We'd reached Vegas, and as much as there was to do, I was antsy. So far, I'd attended all of the on-stage rehearsals and helped when anyone needed me, but today my mood had taken a downward spiral from all the activity and people constantly around. I needed some space, and a Xanax ... or two. I wasn't dealing well with being under Pierce's constant microscope, either. I had to jet, even if it was for only a few minutes.

Overcome with the need to not be watched every time I scratched my ass, I left all reasoning behind and slipped out of rehearsal, making a beeline for the front door of the auditorium. The bright Vegas sunlight blinded me as I stepped outside. Since it was summer, the sidewalks were packed with tourists, so I hugged the inside of the sidewalk near the grass as I looked for a place to hang out. A minute later, my attention landed on a park that didn't seem overly busy. If I weren't desperate for some alone time, the heat would have sent me right back inside.

I set off down the street on my own. Hendrix would be pissed I'd not told him and taken Pierce with me, but we'd been cramped up together for too damned long. I loved all of them, but I felt as though I was about to suffocate. Besides, the temperature was sweltering and too hot to stay out long. I'd be back before they even missed me.

After a lot of maneuvering through the crowd, I reached my destination. There were people at the park, but not a ton. I could work with it. I scanned the green grass and palm trees as I walked toward a vacant picnic bench. A light breeze kicked up, and I sat down. Alone at last. Well, sort of. I laid my forehead on the cool cement tabletop and took a deep breath.

"I'm behind you," a deep voice broke the silence.

My head snapped up, and I whirled around.

"Dammit, Pierce, you scared me."

"I didn't mean to, but I wanted you to know I was here. I saw you leave."

"Fuck. I just wanted a few minutes without anyone hovering over me." My lip jutted out into a full-on pout.

"I won't bother you," he replied, scanning our surroundings.

"It's fine, you're here now, and at least Hendrix won't jump all over me for leaving by myself."

Pierce turned his attention to me, but I couldn't tell what he was thinking behind his dark sunglasses. He'd opted for a beige polo shirt and jean shorts, fitting in with the rest of the tourists.

"You're not sleeping well," he stated matter of factly.

"Shit." I slapped my hands over my face, and my knee bounced up and down. "You've heard me?"

"Yes, but I know you and Cade don't want anyone to know you're sleeping in his bed. It's not my job to report your behavior unless you're in danger. I just wanted you to know that I've heard you. You're safe Mac. I won't let anything happen to you while I'm around."

I squinted against the sun and peeked at him through one eye.

"Really? You won't say anything to Gemma or Hendrix? I know you and Gemma are close."

I wasn't positive, but I thought Pierce flinched at my mention of his relationship with Gemma.

"No. It's no one's business."

"Thank you," I muttered. "It does help to know you and Cade are there for me. Believe it or not, the dreams are worse at home."

"I'm not surprised. You're dealing with a lot. Have you opened up to your therapist yet?"

My eyebrow shot up. "You know I have a therapist?"

"Yes."

He didn't elaborate, but at this point, I had to suspect Pierce knew a lot about our personal life but had opted to keep his mouth closed. I could only hope Calvin would learn to do the same.

"You can sit down, Pierce. You look a little out of place standing next to me, ready to pounce like a hungry lion."

Without a word, he sat down at the picnic table. A moment of silence passed, then he cleared his throat.

"Franklin is worried about you," Pierce said.

"I realize that, but I don't know what else to do. I get out of bed every day even though I'm exhausted. My moods swing from depression to super anxious, then I think I'm alright. I saw what happened to Gemma and how she lived her life when she first arrived in Spokane. She was terrified of her own shadow. I don't want to live like that, too. But I think I see him all the time. Brandon, I mean. Logically, I know he's behind bars for kidnapping me ..." I released a heavy sigh and tapped my fingers against the concrete table top.

"I can teach you along with Gemma."

"How? I mean, you're on tour with them. I'll be at home when you guys travel most of the time."

"I can work with you when we're on the road and have someone take care of you at home."

I hesitated. "Not Calvin."

"No, I'd send someone I've trained with personally."

I paused for a second and watched a family settle in at another table. A small cry escaped the stroller, and who I assumed was the father, picked up the toddler while the mom rifled through a diaper bag.

Would I ever have that? Love? A family? Vacations together? With my history, I'd never trust someone at this rate.

"Alright. I'll do it. I'll do almost anything at this point to feel better."

"Good. It's more difficult to set a routine when we're on the road, but we have some time coming up in the next few days."

"Let me know."

"Mac?" Pierce asked, removing his sunglasses and making eye contact with me.

Dammit, this was serious. He never took off his sunglasses during the day unless he meant business.

"Yeah?"

"Does anyone else know?"

My stomach sank to my toes. Was he asking what I thought he was? I'd been so careful.

"What are you talking about?" I had to play this off.

"The drugs." He didn't even flinch.

"It's not a big deal, Pierce. It's just some edibles for nights I can't sleep."

"And?"

His focus never left me while I racked my mind for a good lie, but there wasn't one. Somehow, he'd found out I had more than edibles. He knew my stash also contained uppers and downers in my bag. I'd only taken a few on days I was exhausted after not getting any sleep or to counteract the downers. It was the only time I got any relief. Each time I closed my eyes, the constant images of the night with Brandon antagonized me.

"It's not every day. How can you tell, anyway? I don't think anyone else has any idea."

"Unfortunately, I know what to look for. Even someone really good at concealing a habit can't hide it from me."

"It's not a habit," I barked. I stood up, my anxiety hiking up a notch. "How dare you! It's none of your business."

Pierce stood with me. "Mac, calm down. I'm not getting onto you. I'm genuinely concerned. I've seen drug use like this spiral out of control very quickly. You're Franklin's daughter and Gemma's best friend. I've grown to see you all as more than a job. We're friends. Please ... take a seat. Talk to me."

"I can't, Pierce. I can't talk about it. I can't tell anyone what Brandon did to me or about the pills. I'll be fine. I'm exhausted, and when I'm awake, my focus is shit. The Adderall actually helps me. I wouldn't even say it gives me much of a pick me up." I sighed and sank back down onto the bench.

"How long?"

"Would it help you to know it's all prescribed by my therapist?"

"No."

"Why? She gave me a prescription for Xanax and Adderall. In fact, the Adderall is the only thing that helps with my ADHD. I'm not even taking them like she wants me to."

"And there's the problem. You're using them to hide from what you're feeling, not to help you stabilize. Taking them as uppers to stay awake then Xanax to sleep, it's a problem. There's a difference, and I'm more concerned about your intent and dependency than anything else. Then there's the fact you hide it from everyone."

"Why should I tell anyone? Do you discuss any meds you take?" Tension snaked between my shoulder blades at where this conversation might end up. If he said anything to Hendrix or Franklin, it could get ugly. I'd never be left alone again.

"I also know the nights you do sleep, you're mixing the Xanax with alcohol. Mac, it's a bad combination, not to mention dangerous."

My nostrils flared. How in the hell did he know what I had unless he went through my stuff?

I leaned over the picnic table toward him.

"Stay out of my fucking business. I won't tell you again," I hissed. "What I do is not up to you. You don't live with my nightmares. You don't even know what he did to me."

Pierce didn't even flinch. "Tell me, Mac. You can trust me."

"Stay the hell away from me. I don't want to see you or train with you." I stood quickly, spun on my heel, and marched away from him. I stopped the moment a thought occurred to me, and I turned to face him again.

"Hey, Pierce," I said.

CHAPTER 8

"*Y*eah?" he asked.

Slowly, I approached him again.

"If you tell anyone about your suspicions that aren't even accurate, I'll go to Franklin and tell him you're in love with Gemma. You'll never see her again."

Pierce's stoic expression never changed with my threat, but I suspected I'd gotten to him.

"If you're willing to threaten me, Mac, you need to consider the change in yourself already. Obviously you're willing to hurt everyone who loves you in order to keep your secret." He stood slowly, his gaze never leaving mine. "My job is to protect you and your family, no matter what the costs."

Dammit, I could have sworn I'd rattled him even a little bit.

"You'd never see Gemma again," I snapped.

"And for some reason, you think it would be a bad thing?"

"You're impossible," I hissed.

Frustrated and pissed, I whirled around and made a beeline through the crowd back to the safety and air conditioning of the rehearsal.

FOR A CHANGE, I was the one not interested in going out.

"Come on, it will be fun," Gemma coaxed while we walked from the rehearsal back to the bus. "There's a great new club down the street, and we can go dancing after our performance. It will be nice not to have to hang around and meet people tonight, too. Besides, there are four other bands so no one will miss us. I need to have some fun," Gemma pleaded and batted her long eyelashes at me.

My shoulders slouched forward in defeat. She rarely asked to go out, which told me she really needed to blow off some steam. Maybe it's what I needed too, but I'd been in a funk all day, and nothing sounded fun at this point.

"For you, best bestie, I will."

"Thank you! It will be fun, I promise." She threw her arm around me and chatted my ear off for the rest of the way back to the bus.

THE BAND HAD A SHORTER SET since there were other groups lined up to perform for the night. The guys were all excited about taking a break and going out afterward. It had been a long time since I'd gone to a club. And unless Gemma had gone with the guys while on tour, I'm not sure she'd been to one yet. She was still a month away from twenty-one, so I suspected someone had hooked her up with a fake ID.

"How ya doing?" Hendrix asked, tossing his arm around me as we all walked down the strip together a few steps ahead of the rest of our group. I'd never seen a city more alive at night than Vegas with the hotel lights, water show, and clubs. It was nuts.

"Good. You?" I beamed at him, hiding all the darkness I really felt. Pierce's earlier conversation buzzed in the back of my mind, and a jolt of panic shot through me. Would he tell Hendrix or keep my secret to himself? I slammed the door shut on the nagging thought and focused my attention back to Hendrix. "You've got to be super excited about how well the tour is going. You guys have sold out every show!"

A lopsided grin spread across his face. "It's been surreal."

"How's Gemma holding up? This is a huge change for her."

"Ya know, she's handling things really well. She's working the crowd, and she's not as jumpy as she was at the beginning," he said while we dodged a drunk dude weaving in and out of the crowd, yelling for someone named Patricia. Hendrix shook his head and chuckled.

"She's my hero," I said, peering up at him. "Everything she's gone through, and she just keeps going. I swear every time I turn around, she's tried something new and shed more of her old self."

"She's amazing," he said. "You do realize she wouldn't be where she is now without you."

If I looked at Hendrix right now, he'd see through me and know exactly what I was feeling, how much I was struggling with the fallout from what Brandon had done to me. And he would be disappointed because I wasn't as strong as Gemma. She'd never needed to rely on drugs to make it through the day no matter what was thrown at her. Here I was, letting my entire family down. They just didn't know it yet. I gave him a half shrug and stared ahead at the couple in front of me. A tattoo of a scorpion wrapped around the girl's neck, the tail ending in her short hair.

Gemma's giggle broke my attention, and I glanced over my shoulder. She, John, Cade, and Pierce were behind us. The guys were picking on her like a little sister. Well, except Pierce.

"Wedding plans any time soon?" I asked Hendrix. A laugh escaped me as his eyes widened.

"I'll take that as a no," I said, giggling. "I didn't mean to throw you such a curveball, bro."

"Hopefully," he replied softly.

"Wait, what?" I stopped in my tracks. "Why haven't you told me?"

"Because—"

Suddenly, my body lurched forward, and an arm slid around my waist, saving me from face-planting in front of everyone.

"Gotcha," Cade said, grinning.

"Dude, watch where you're going! You ran right into me," I said with more irritation in my voice than necessary.

"Don't stop so fast then," he replied matter of fact.

I heaved a loud sigh and smoothed my hair back into place.

"I didn't mean to," I said. It's not like I could tell him why I'd stopped so abruptly, and since we'd been interrupted, I'd have to wait to find out more from Hendrix.

My mood continued its downward spiral as we kept walking.

I honest to God wondered if traveling had thrown off my period and I had PMS. Everything was pissing me the fuck off. Mentally, I reviewed my birth control pill pack. Nope. I was simply in bitch mode. I had Pierce and our earlier conversation in the park to thank for that.

"We're here," Hendrix announced, pulling Gemma into him and kissing her gently.

The outside of the club looked like a boring red brick building with no windows, but I knew from experience it was the inside that would be decked out.

Hendrix and Gemma stepped in front of us, and we lined up behind them to get into the door of the club.

"Sorry," Cade muttered into my ear. I turned around, my attention landing on him.

"It's fine. I didn't mean to stop so fast." Guilt rushed over me for being so damned cranky. It really wasn't Cade's fault I was in such a shit mood. Even though his teasing was irritating sometimes, overall, he'd been a good friend.

"Are you alright? I mean, you seem a bit ..."

My eyebrows rose, warning him to choose his words carefully.

"Uh, un Mac like," he said.

"Un Mac like? What's that supposed to mean?" I huffed and folded my arms over my chest.

"Nothing bad. You're typically laughing and chatty. You've not been yourself the last few days I guess."

He'd noticed my funk?

My hands dropped to my sides. "Yeah. Thanks for checking. I'm just in a mood."

We moved up in line, and I dabbed off the beaded up sweat on my forehead with the back of my hand.

"If you're hot now, wait until we're dancing."

"We?" I asked, cocking my head at him.

"Well, yeah. Why not?"

"I figured you'd find some hottie and take off for the night."

He laughed. "Nah, not for the night. It will only take half an hour, then I'll be ready to drink and dance the rest of the time."

I almost flipped him crap about it, until I recalled our conversation about his family. He really did need to go wild sometimes. Hell, I couldn't begrudge him some fun. The thought had crossed my own mind the other day. A quickie would probably do my sour attitude some good.

"ID," the massive bouncer at the door demanded. I showed him mine and waited with Gemma and Hendrix for them to allow Cade, John, and Pierce in behind me.

"I'm so excited," Gemma said. "My first club," she whispered to me.

"Ah, I wondered." I turned to Hendrix and smiled. "Guess you're popping all her virgin cherries, huh?"

"Mac!" Gemma said, smacking me lightly on the arm.

Hendrix chuckled and pulled her in for a kiss.

"Get a stall, man!" Cade yelled at them from behind me.

"Bathroom sex? Seriously?" I asked Cade while we all made

our way down through the door and a hallway that led to a two-level dance floor and multiple bars.

"Holy shit!" I yelled to Gemma.

"Wow!" Her mouth hung open as she scanned the gyrating bodies and packed club scene. Pink and green strobe lights slashed through the darkness, illuminating a large crowd of people and half naked girls dancing seductively in cages.

A warm hand gently took hold of my arm.

"Stay close to one of us tonight, and don't leave your drink unattended," John said.

My heart softened with his words. It was almost like I had three brothers on this trip.

"I won't. I can stay with Gemma and Hendrix when you and Cade go off to get laid."

John shook his head. "Not tonight. I think I'd rather hang out with everyone and dance. Sometimes those hookups get old."

"I wondered if they did."

He nodded, took my hand, and waved to everyone while he led me to the bar.

"What do you want to drink? It's on me."

"John, you don't have to. Really, I can buy my own."

"You can buy another time, tonight is on me."

I smiled at him. Whether he realized it or not, his company was a lifeline, pulling me out of a funk.

"Vodka and cranberry."

"You got it!" He yelled over the music.

John finally reached the bar and placed our order. I stood next to him and scanned the crowd. Gemma and Hendrix were already dancing, and Cade wasn't far away. I couldn't see who he was with over the sea of people, but whoever it was must have been short. I assumed he'd already picked out a girl to sneak off with. He seemed so casual about it all. Maybe I needed to learn a few things from him and do the same. There was a good possibility I wasn't in a bad mood at all, I just needed to get laid. The more I considered it, the more likely it seemed.

"Here ya go," John said, handing me two drinks. "Bottoms up so we can get on the dance floor."

"Thanks! To friends!" We clinked glasses. As he downed his shots, I drank both of mine a bit slower. Five minutes later and happily buzzed, I set my empty glasses on the bar, then John took my hand.

I giggled while he pulled me to the dance floor. The bass resonated through the club as we found our spot and danced to "Never Forget You" by Zara Larsson, but this version was on steroids.

Although John allowed an appropriate space between us, we were bumped and jostled until we were flush against each other.

We laughed and moved with the flow. I wasn't sure about him, but between the drinks and heat of the club, I felt almost euphoric. It was exactly what I needed, too. To forget everything and check my shit at the door.

After another half hour, John walked me over to the edge of the floor where Gemma and Hendrix stood.

"I'm going to grab some more drinks. You want the same?" he asked me.

"Yeah, thanks!" I said, dabbing the sweat from my forehead. Thank God I'd had the foresight to wear jeans and a cute short-sleeved shirt. I wasn't sure my deodorant was holding up anymore though, but I figured we were all hot and sweaty and no one would know the difference.

The DJ slowed down the pace, and Gemma and Hendrix snuggled up to each other not far from where I was standing.

"M'lady," Cade said, approaching me from the side.

My eyebrow arched suspiciously. "You want to dance?" I looked around but didn't see any girls with him. "Oh, dude, you already got laid, didn't you?"

"A gentleman never tells," he said, an ornery grin spreading across his handsome face.

Although Cade had worked fast and hooked up, I hoped for the girl's sake he wasn't quick to pull the trigger. Ugh. Why the hell was I even thinking about that? It was so not how I wanted to imagine him.

I laughed and took his hand. For some reason, he headed toward the opposite side from where Gemma and Hendrix were slow dancing.

Once we found a space of our own, Cade's hands gently trailed up my sides, then he positioned my hands around his neck and drew me closer. Even though I knew he didn't mean anything by it, it was still intimate, and a chill shot through me with his touch.

"Tight quarters," he yelled over the music.

I nodded. I'd spent the night next to Cade before, but this was different. We weren't sleeping. I'd also never realized how much taller he was than me. I barely reached five-five barefoot. He was at least six-one, which meant my head could rest comfortably on his chest.

I glanced around at all the couples making out in the darkness as the lights pulsated with the beat. Cade's hand caressed my back and slowly trailed up my spine. I suspected his move was partly alcohol induced and partly habit. He probably hadn't even realized what he'd done. But I noticed. My body definitely noticed. Holy crap. What was I thinking?

Someone bumped into me, and the narrow gap between Cade's and my body was now nonexistent. My boobs were full on smashed against him. The image of his rippled abs flashed across my mind while my body let me know it had other ideas next time I was in Cade's bed.

"You okay?" Cade asked, tightening his hold on me.

Embarrassed, I looked up to meet his gaze. I inhaled quickly when his eyes darkened and the strain against his jeans became obvious. Oh God. I swallowed and attempted to gain control of my now throbbing hormones.

"Yeah, it's just super crowded in here."

I swallowed again, my throat feeling parched, and dropped my attention to the floor, but his arms remained around me. My hands slid down to his muscular chest, and heat ripped through me. Fuck. This could not be happening. No way did I want to fuck Cade … but. My mind told me no, but my body had other ideas. I'd not been with anyone since Jeremiah in Louisiana. Months.

He adjusted his hips against mine, and a soft moan escaped me. Thank God no one could hear me over the music. There was no mistaking he was thinking the same thing I was.

Cade bent down next to my ear, his hot breath tickling my neck.

"You don't have to sleep alone tonight," he said.

My head snapped up, and I searched his face for any indication he was joking. Cade was always messing with me, but this wasn't funny. His amber eyes darkened, and his tongue darted out across his bottom lip. I wasn't misunderstanding his suggestion.

He wanted to play. With me. This was not a good idea in any way shape or form. Except … I needed to get laid. Bad.

Before I realized it, I was nodding. Crap. What had I agreed to? This had to be an alcohol-driven decision. Or was it? Cade was seriously hot, there was no denying it. And I'd known him for years. But no matter his reasoning behind it, the fact was he was a player. On the other hand, there'd be no danger of feelings getting involved, right? It'd be a hookup and that's it. Us. Playing. Naked. Heat swirled inside me, my core clenching with desire.

"My turn!" John yelled and bumped my hip with his, nearly knocking me over. He handed me my drink and grinned.

Cade scowled at him while John worked his way in between us. The music picked up, and Cade shoved his hands in his pockets and backed away. Before I knew it, John had his hand on my waist and was guiding me back toward Gemma and Hendrix.

"Hey," Gemma said, giggling. "I gotta pee!"

"Alright, I need a break anyway!" I yelled at her. "It's hotter than hell in here."

"Since you're going to the bathroom, I'll go with Hendrix to get some more drinks. Meet us back here, okay?" John asked me, gently squeezing my arm.

"Stay together," Hendrix said, eyeing us.

I took Gemma's hand and held it up for both of them to see.

"Happy? Sometimes you guys are worse than our body-guards!" I yelled before I tugged on Gemma, and we slowly made our way to the closest restroom.

"Dayumm," Gemma said once we'd emerged from the crowd, strolled down the long hallway, and into the ladies' room, which was surprisingly empty. She fanned her overheated cheeks.

"I know. I'm so hot." I placed my drink down on the sink as we each stood in front of a mirror. I grabbed us some paper towels and ran them under cold water.

"Eww, I do not smell good right now," I said, sniffing my pits. I handed a wet paper towel to Gemma and wiped off my face and the back of my neck. "Not to mention massive humidititties."

"What?" Gemma asked, giggling.

"Swoob."

I laughed while she stared at me with a puzzled expression.

"Boob sweat, girl. Yours aren't big, but I'm sporting a D cup, and the girls sweat." I pulled on the hem of my shirt, creating an air flow up my stomach and cleavage.

"Oh my God, that's hilarious." She dabbed her cheeks with the paper towel, then pulled her hair into a ponytail with the hair tie she had worn on her wrist.

"This night has been a lot better than I thought it would be," I said, peering into the mirror and removing the mascara smudges from beneath my eyes. "I never carry a purse when clubbing, but

I sort of wish I had some more makeup with me right now. Plus, a baby wipe would be nice to have and freshen up a bit. Guess it doesn't matter. We're going back out to sweat some more anyway."

"You look great," Gemma said. "Actually, the best I've seen you in a long time. You look genuinely happy." Her laugh filled the bathroom while she grasped the edge of the sink for balance.

I turned toward her.

"How ya feelin' there Gem-ma?" I asked, giggling. I didn't have to ask, I already knew she was super tipsy. She wasn't the only one. John had definitely kept the drinks coming.

"Let's just say Hendrix will be in a really really good mood tomorrow." She flashed me a mischievous grin.

"No deets! Please, he's my brother, and the last thing I want to know is ... anything about his sex life." I scrunched up my nose.

"Fine," she said, still grinning. "I'm happy you came with us tonight. You seem like you're doing better than you were earlier. I could tell you were in a funk."

"Yup. I was, but John and Cade have made sure I wasn't a fifth wheel tonight. It's been fun."

"They're good guys, even if they are sluts." Gemma giggled. "Geez, I almost forgot why we came in here. I've gotta pee!" She darted to an available stall.

"I'll wait in the hall," I called after her. I downed my drink and left the glass on the paper towel dispenser.

The bathroom door creaked open, and I made my way down the hallway. I spotted a good corner and leaned against it as I waited for her. Pulling my phone out of my pocket, I tapped in my passcode.

"You're so fucking hot!"

My head snapped up but before I could see who the voice belonged to, a solid body pinned mine against the wall. A mouth crashed down on mine, and my phone clattered to the floor. Panic surged through me while my arms flailed around, and I attempted to yell but was only met with a tongue in my mouth. I slapped my hands against the chest and pushed. Nothing. A hand grabbed my ass, and I attempted to scream.

A guttural growl echoed through the hallway as the stranger's body was suddenly ripped away from mine. Gasping for air, I looked up and attempted to sort out what had happened. Tears blurred my vision, but I could make out Pierce holding some guy by the back of his shirt.

"Oh, I've waited for this for a long, long time, my friend," Cade said, stepping around Pierce and in front of the guy.

I blinked hard. There was no way I saw this correctly.

CHAPTER 9

*W*hat the hell. Asher? What the fuck?

"Oh my God, I feel so much better," Gemma said strolling out of the restroom just as Cade's fist barreled into Asher's jaw.

Our screams echoed through the hallway.

"What the hell?" Gemma asked, her mouth dropping open.

"What are you doing?" I yelled at Cade as his fist hammered into Asher's stomach. "Pierce, make him stop!"

But Pierce continued to hold Asher while Cade whaled on him. I rushed to Cade and pulled on his arm before he could do any more damage.

"Stop! It's Asher!" My attention split between Cade, Pierce, and Asher. I cringed as blood oozed from Asher's most likely broken nose. His eye had already begun to swell shut, and his lip was split open.

Cade snarled. "You don't treat Mac like that. Ever. No lady deserves to be pawed at. Ever."

Asher whimpered and covered his nose with his hand.

"Come on," Pierce said. He jerked Asher around like a rag doll, then guided him to what I assumed was one of the exits.

"What the fuck just happened?" I sputtered. "Like, seriously, what the fuck happened?"

"Your prick of an ex is what happened," Cade said. His face twisted with utter disgust. "No one should ever treat you like a piece of meat, Mac."

I was too dumbfounded to argue with him. And I didn't disagree with him about Asher's behavior, but he didn't usually do crap like that. And what in the hell was he doing in Vegas anyway?

"I need to find him," I said.

"I'm going with you," Cade stated, his voice gruff.

"Um, thanks Cade, but I think you've done enough for tonight," Gemma said, her tone stern. "Tell Hendrix I'll be out front with Mac and Pierce, please. Let's go." She took my hand and led me through the club.

We barged through the door and into the night. Even though it was still hot, the temperature outside was much cooler than inside the crowded building.

I inhaled deeply and scanned the area.

"There," Gemma said, pointing across the parking lot.

We hurried toward Pierce and Asher.

"What the hell are you doing here?" I asked Asher. His eye had swollen shut now, but at least his nosebleed had stopped.

"We're going to give you a minute," Gemma said. She and Pierce backed away, their attention never leaving us.

"You've got some explaining to do," I demanded, my toe tapping against the asphalt.

"I have some explaining, Mac? Seriously? I kiss my girlfriend, and fucking Cade Richardson beats the shit out of me?"

A ball of anger erupted inside me.

"Girlfriend? No, I'm not in any way shape or form your girl-friend, Asher. And if that's the way you kiss your significant other these days, it's multiple levels of fucked up. I didn't know it was you! I thought some rando dude had attacked me!"

"Oh," he muttered, his eyes falling to his feet. He swayed slightly and leaned against someone's black Chevy truck for balance.

"Dammit. You're drunk," I said, disgust hanging on every word.

"I was really nervous about seeing you, so I had a few drinks," he slurred.

I turned away, unable to even look at him for a minute.

"Why are you here?" I asked.

"I saw the show and wanted to surprise you afterward. I miss you, Mac."

I rubbed my temples, exhaled, and turned back around.

"Did I not tell you to give me time to think things over? That we could talk when I got back from this tour?" I sadly shook my head, realizing there was nothing to think over. I knew what I had to do. "You've crossed a line, Asher and it can't be undone. We're finished."

"No, Mac, you don't understand. Wait ..."

I watched in horror as he fumbled around in his jeans pocket for something.

"Got it," he slurred.

Before it even registered in my brain, a bloodied and drunk Asher dropped to one knee in the middle of the club parking lot. The lights from the busy Vegas nightlife bounced off the diamond ring he held in his hand. I wasn't sure if my gasp or Gemma's was louder.

"Marry me, Mac. You deserve nothing but the best."

Fuck. My. Life. Before I had a chance to tell him there was no way in hell I'd marry him, and to get his sorry ass home, he teetered over, smacked the pavement face first, and passed out cold.

~

HONEST TO GOD, I wasn't sure who I was more pissed at. Asher, Cade, or Pierce for the crap he'd said to me earlier in the day.

Hendrix, Cade, and John joined us in the parking lot shortly after Asher face planted on the ground. I flipped Cade the dirtiest look I could muster. Eventually I'd want to know the full details of the fight, but I couldn't even deal with it right now.

Hendrix approached me while the guys hung back.

"I'm going to make sure he gets back to his hotel room in one piece. According to the key card in his jeans pocket, he's staying up the street," Pierce said to Hendrix.

"Thanks, man," Hendrix replied. "See you at the bus."

I turned my back on Pierce and Asher. I didn't want to see any more.

"That was a mess," Hendrix muttered, running his hand through his hair. I knew my brother well enough to know he only did that when he was on edge.

"No shit," I groaned.

"Let's get back to the home base. John requested an Uber since we're all a bit drunk. I think we've had enough excitement for the evening anyway. I'd prefer not to walk back and run into more."

"Good idea," I muttered. My brain shifted into overdrive and my fingers drummed against my leg as we waited for our ride. "I don't get it. Like, where does Cade get off beating Asher's ass? It's not his place."

"Mac," Hendrix said, placing a gentle hand on my shoulder. "From what Cade said, Asher had you backed in a corner, and you were trying to fight him off." He paused, his eyes softening. "I would have done the same thing. But there's another reason behind Cade's actions and I think you'll need to ask him about it after you've calmed down."

"What?" I asked, still pissed off to the max. "What in the hell could have justified what he did tonight?"

"Take a few deep breaths. It will all make sense soon, but give Cade the benefit of the doubt."

"Seriously? You weren't there. I mean, he smashed Asher's face in, Hendrix."

"I know. I saw him."

"So you're automatically on Cade's side because he's your band member? Like, it trumps what's actually right or wrong?" I asked, my tone sharp.

Hendrix's chin jutted up. Dammit. I'd stepped on his toes.

"You know me better than that, Mac. You know if I thought Cade was in the wrong, I'd deal with him."

I rubbed my forehead with the palms of my hands, the anger subsiding a little bit.

"You're telling me you think Cade had a good reason?" I asked, peeking through my fingers at my brother.

"I know he did. Listen, I realize he likes to party and sleep around, but there's another side to Cade. He's a really good guy. One of the best I know, actually. Give him a chance to explain, then whatever you decide about the situation, I'll let it go."

I dropped my hands. "You suck. Why can't you let me be mad for a while longer?"

A smile eased across Hendrix's face.

"Come here. It's been a crazy night." Hendrix pulled me in for a hug and placed a kiss on the top of my head.

"Thanks," I mumbled against his shoulder.

"Our Uber is here," Gemma announced, interrupting us.

I released Hendrix, and we all piled into the black SUV that had just pulled up.

"I need water." I slumped against the back seat as everyone settled in. John sat in front, which left the seat next to me open for Cade. He closed the door, and within sixty seconds the vehicle reeked of sweat and alcohol.

"Can we talk?" Cade asked softly.

"Later, I'm still mad."

Sadness flickered across Cade's face, but he left me alone for the rest of the ride.

Fifteen minutes later, we filed out of the car. Pierce was waiting for us at the entrance of the bus with a case of bottled water.

"Thanks, man," Hendrix said, taking some waters and passing them to us.

I took one, twisted the cap off, and poured it over my head.

Gemma choked on her water, stared at me, and laughed. Then she did the same.

"Pierce give me a few more, please," I said, water dripping off my chin.

It wasn't long before we were all soaking wet and laughing in the parking lot like a bunch of crazy people.

"I'll get some towels," Pierce offered, chuckling.

"Holy hell, did he laugh?" I asked everyone.

"Ha, yeah, it happens sometimes," Hendrix replied. "On a few occasions he's even gotten drunk with everyone. He's actually a pretty funny guy."

"What? When did this happen and where in the hell was I?"

"Home," Gemma said.

"He's an alright guy," John chimed in. "A little tough to get to know, but he's cool."

Cade remained quiet. I glanced in his direction while Pierce brought us towels. Cade was soaking wet, and I didn't miss how his shirt clung to his broad chest and shoulders.

My mind taunted me with images of his rippled abs, and the dusting of hair that trailed down from his belly button beneath his ... My body tingled as I recalled his earlier offer. It wasn't just the offer, but how his body had responded during our dance. I chewed on my lip and tore my eyes away from him. I was still pissed.

"It's probably best you all washed off out here. You guys smelled pretty bad," Pierce said, passing out the towels.

"Oh my God, I'm so embarrassed," Gemma said, hiding her face in the soft cloth.

"No one noticed, babe. We all reeked together," Hendrix assured her.

I couldn't help but laugh. It had been a jacked up night. My happy buzz had disappeared the minute Asher pinned me in the corner.

"I think we're going to go in," Hendrix said, wrapping his arm around Gemma's waist.

"Are you alright?" Gemma asked me.

"Yeah. I'm fine. I just need some time to think. I'll hang out here for a bit."

"I know Cade wants to talk to you, but I want to catch up tomorrow alright? And don't forget if you need me, wake me up."

I pulled her in for a big hug. "Thanks."

"Love you, best bestie," Gemma whispered to me before she stepped back.

"You too."

"You guys get some sleep. I'll stay with her," Pierce offered.

Great. Lucky me. Alone time with Pierce.

"Thanks," Hendrix said, and patted Pierce on the back while he and Gemma got on the bus. I wasn't sure how Hendrix remained calm around Pierce, but he seemed to genuinely like him even though he knew Pierce had feelings for Gemma. Maybe all the good Pierce did for us outweighed the fact he had feelings for her.

"Night," John said, giving us a little wave.

"Night."

An awkward silence hung in the air, and I peered up into the dark night. For a brief moment, I missed the Spokane sky with all of its magnificent stars.

"Can we talk?" Cade asked so softly I almost didn't hear him.

"Where? We have like no privacy." I shot a look of disdain at Pierce.

"There's a spot with seats and picnic tables right down the hill. It's softly lit from the lights in the city, too. That way Pierce can keep his distance and keep an eye on us at the same time."

"What about Hendrix and Gemma? He should stay here and protect them." I couldn't disguise the hint of hope in my voice. While I knew I should hear Cade out, I was kind of on overload at the moment.

"I know the place he's referring too. I'll be able to see the bus as well. Besides, Hendrix is a trained boxer. He can manage if anything happened," Pierce said.

I stared at Cade for a second, then nodded.

The guys were right, it was just down a hill from where the bus was parked. I glanced around at the benches and open grassy area. Since we would be here for a few days, this might be a good spot for me to have a few minutes to myself.

"I know you're pissed, Mac." Cade sat down on one of the benches. I sat next to him, leaving a sizable gap between us.

"What the hell, Cade? Was it really necessary to break Asher's nose?" I sputtered, my anger returning in full force.

His shoulders slumped forward, and his gaze fell to the ground.

"I know, Mac," he said softly.

"Know what?" I asked, confused.

His eyes traveled from the ground to my face, his expression full of sadness.

"I know why you and Asher broke up in high school."

I blanched. There was no way. Asher's dad had made sure it was kept quiet. Even my big mouth hadn't blabbed to anyone except Hendrix.

"I don't understand," I started.

"Mac, he told every guy on the football team he knocked you

up. He wasn't talking about it because he was upset, he was bragging about it."

"What?!" I gasped, my hands flying over my mouth.

"I'm sorry. Hell, I wanted to beat the shit out of him back then. I have no idea how he thought bragging about knocking up a girl was acceptable. Man, I don't get it. I mean, I wouldn't even do something like that."

"Wait." I shook my head. "There must have been someone else he was talking about. I wasn't the only girl pregnant that year."

"No, he said your name, plus you guys had been together for a few years, and everyone knew it. You got pregnant your senior year, right?"

A crushing ache ripped through my chest. How could Asher have betrayed me like that? A lump formed in my throat as the humiliation rolled over me.

Cade shifted in his seat and turned toward me.

"I'm not sure why, but he told everyone he knocked you up and his dad paid for the abortion."

A cry escaped me. He'd shared intimate details of my life with the football team. There was no telling who else they'd told. The cheerleaders? The dance squad? How many other people knew?

"Oh, God. It's why everyone stared at me like I was an alien after I went back to school. I mean, it wasn't that I was all that well liked in the first place. I just had a small group of friends, it was Hendrix who was popular. I guess I was so used to being talked about as the weird girl with ADHD it never even crossed my mind he would do that to me. Not to mention I was really fucked up after … after—"

"You don't have to say it."

"Did Hendrix find out? He would have told me if he had."

Cade cleared his throat. "I know Hendrix stayed with you after the, uh, the procedure, but if you recall, he had to leave for the boxing tournament the next day. Most of it went down when he was gone. I stepped in ... well, John and I stepped in and shut it down."

"John?" I cried. "Oh my God. He found out too?" I asked, horrified.

"Mac, we were trying to protect you. And if Hendrix had gotten into a fight, he'd have lost his boxing tournament. Not only was he fighting for the title, but there was a damned good scholarship, too. He couldn't blow it all over a fuckwad like Asher."

A single tear streamed down my cheek.

"I'm sorry you had to find out like this. When I saw he'd cornered you, and you were fighting to get him off ... I lost my mind. I'd waited a long time for the opportunity to beat his ass."

I nodded and dropped my head. The last thing I wanted was for Cade to see me cry.

"Does that mean you and John told Hendrix everything tonight?" I asked.

"Yeah. He fully supported me beating the hell out of him."

I barked out a laugh and wiped my cheeks. "I wouldn't have stopped you if I'd known." I shifted in my seat and finally looked at him. "You missed the best part, though."

"Yeah?" Cade's dark eyebrow rose in question.

"He proposed in the parking lot then fell over drunk. I mean he passed out cold."

Cade chuckled and smiled. "See, the dumbass can't do anything right."

My laughter trailed off as I tried to absorb everything that had happened in the last few hours and my anger began to waver.

"Earlier," I said. "Were you drunk or were you serious about tonight in your bed?" I blurted.

Omg. Really, Mac? I had intended to keep my big mouth shut for once. I figured if he'd been for real, he'd bring it up again. My anxiety cranked up a notch, and I sat on my hands. Cade couldn't see me shaking. "Besides, I thought you got laid earlier tonight," I said, giving him an easy out.

"Nah. I dunno. I ... just ..." He tossed his hands up in the air. "It didn't happen."

I nodded when our eyes locked, and butterflies fluttered in my stomach.

"I don't mess around with players," I stated.

Cade grinned. "I understand. I think it was in the moment ya know? I mean, you're fucking hot, but I get it. What guy wouldn't want you?"

Against my better judgment, my mouth gaped open.

"You think I'm hot?" I stammered. Cade had been one of the most popular and gorgeous guys in our high school. All he had to do was look at a girl, and she'd soak her panties.

"I've always thought so, but you and Asher were together during most of high school."

"And, I'm your best friend's sister."

"Correct." His lips pursed together.

"It's been months," I admitted. "I've not been with anyone since Jeremiah and I split up."

"I can't say the same," he muttered.

If I hadn't known better, I'd have thought he was a little embarrassed.

"Tell ya what," I said, my brain working overtime exactly like my hormones. "Let's play a little. No strings, no attachment. I need to get laid, and we already sleep together, so why not?"

"Mac, are you sure? You were just proposed to and found out what a douchebag Asher is."

I held up my hand to stop him. "I've been through hell over the last several months. I need some fun. But we need ground rules."

"Agreed," he said, the gold flecks in his eyes sparkling.

"No one can know, obviously. This is a casual fling. If this happens a second time, then you need to decide whether you want to whore around or be with only me for the rest of the tour. I'm not into pecker hopping, and ya know, I appreciate partners that aren't total sluts. Maybe partial sluts. Or maybe sign a contract you'll wrap your dick up. Hell, I'm going to shut up now."

He stared at me for a long minute. "Fair enough."

I hesitated. He'd agreed to some significant terms. He must be horny.

"No kissing. It's too personal."

Cade grinned. "You mean I can put my face between your legs and lick your pussy, but kissing is too personal?"

Holy Hannah. Just hearing him say it almost made me come on the spot. What in the hell was I doing?

"Those are the rules, or this playground is off limits." I gestured to my body and waited for his response.

His gaze lingered on my chest.

"Cade," I said softly. "If you answer me you can actually touch them."

"Huh?" he looked up, his pupils dilated.

"Are we in agreement? We'll try it once and see what happens?"

He stood slowly and attempted to discreetly adjust his jeans.

"Yup. You got it," he said a bit breathlessly.

"Good," I hopped up out of my spot. Cade followed me up the hill and toward the bus. "I'll see you in your bed then. And we have to be super quiet. Pierce knows."

Cade came to an abrupt halt, his mouth dropping open.

"Dammit. He won't say anything will he?" he asked, his voice full of panic.

"No. He doesn't care."

"You're sure?" Cade's face paled. I assumed he was considering the consequences for the first time.

"If Pierce were going to say anything, I wouldn't have agreed. Don't trip. He won't tell Hendrix. But I get it. We don't have to—"

Nerves fluttered in my stomach as I waited for his answer. Even though I'd put the offer out there, I was still nervous he'd turn me down, and my self-confidence was already in the toilet. It's not like I had any to begin with. I was just horny as hell. On the other hand, I knew what this could cost him. My foot nervously tapped against the ground while I waited to see if he was going to reject me.

CHAPTER 10

*C*ade stared at me silently.

"It's fine. Don't worry about it, Cade. I think the stakes are too high." I smiled, turned away from him, and continued to walk up the hill.

"No, wait." Cade grabbed my arm and whirled me around. "It's not that I don't want to, Mac." His eyes lingered on mine, and he twirled a piece of my hair around his finger. "I do," he whispered. His fingers slipped around the back of my neck while he bent down next to my ear.

"I've dreamed of what you'd taste like for a long time. How your pussy would feel wrapped tightly around my cock as I buried myself inside you."

Heat seared through me with his words and turned my entire body into jelly. I clung to his arm for support.

"I bet if I touched you right now, you'd come for me." His lips brushed against my neck, and I stifled a moan.

"Nope," I said breathlessly. "I'm going to make you work for it."

His hot mouth left my sensitive skin, and he glanced up to where Pierce stood guard.

"Let's go." He grabbed my hand and pulled me back down the hill.

"Where are we going?" I asked, giggling. I felt like we were running from the parental units.

Cade chuckled as we continued past the bench we'd sat on and to the bottom of the hill.

"I think we need more privacy than my bed will allow." He grinned. "Besides, I want to hear my name on your lips when you come for me."

"Oh my God. Are you always this forward?" I asked as he stopped on a grassy spot behind a large bush.

"If we're only going to do this once, then we need to make it good. I wish I had a blanket, but ..." He looked up at me. "Are you okay with the grass?"

I giggled. "Are you? Hell, you fucked a girl behind some trees before."

His face fell.

"Sorry. Rule number whatever it is. No mention of other sexcapades," I said.

His lips pursed together, and he nodded. "Good idea."

We stood there, staring at each other for a minute. Panic ignited inside me, memories of Brandon bombarding my brain. Could I have sex with Cade? Had Brandon stolen my ability to relax and enjoy a one nighter? I swallowed the fear down and in one quick movement, I removed my shirt and tossed it on the ground. Brandon Montgomery would not win. Ever.

"Damn," he sputtered, his focus landing on my black lace bra.

"Is that good or bad?" I asked.

He stepped forward, closing the gap between us.

"Good," he whispered. He guided my hand to his crotch where I could feel his growing erection through the rough denim. He grazed his fingers up my sides like he'd done at the club, but this time he didn't stop. He cupped my breast, his thumb tracing my nipple through my bra. I leaned into his touch, aching for more.

Fumbling with the buttons on his jeans, I hesitated, then freed his erection. I wrapped my fingers around his cock and moaned.

"No teeny peen here," I gasped. "Oh my God. I think you're the biggest guy I've had my hands on. Shit, I gave you a giant head, didn't I? I mean, the head on your shoulders, your ego, obviously you have a giant head. The one in my hand I mean." I groaned. "I know, hush, Mac, hush." I bit my lip in order to shut the hell up.

Cade's chuckle rumbled through his chest.

"Mac," he moaned while I stroked him. "You have no idea how long I've thought about this. Damn, you feel good."

He'd thought about me? Us? Sex? Of course he had. This was Cade.

He dipped down, his hot mouth gently grazing the swell of my breast. I inhaled sharply when his tongue darted across the thin material of my bra. He gently slipped the material away and exposed my nipples to the night air. A gentle breeze stirred across my skin as he stared at me.

"Lie down." His voice was deep and husky. He tugged on his shirt and pulled it over his head.

I released him and settled down on the ground. The grass was cool and soft beneath my skin, but I couldn't turn my gaze away when he stepped out of his jeans and boxer briefs. No wonder the girls were all over him. He was the most gorgeous guy I'd seen. His tan skin rippled with each movement, the muscles in his legs flexed slightly. For the first time since we'd agreed to screw around, I was nervous. He had so much more experience than I did. What if I was a lousy lay? What if I got nervous and froze? What if I called him some other dude's name? Dammit, what was I doing? But the second he wrapped his hand around his hard, thick dick my hormones took over. Suddenly, all I wanted was him inside me.

My fears calmed down as Cade towered over me, his hungry gaze roaming over every inch of my body.

"I'm trying to decide what I want first," he said, kneeling down next to me, his amber eyes locking with mine. He lightly traced his fingers down my stomach and flipped the button open on my jeans. Other than our heavy breathing, Cade pulling my zipper down was the only sound around us.

He tugged on my jeans and G-string, and I raised my hips up while he slid them down my legs. His eyes greedily traveled over my body.

My heart slammed against my chest with each second he devoured me with his eyes. No one had made me feel so wanted, so sexy. I'd never been this turned on before, either. Maybe it was the fact it had been a while, and with only a glance he'd reduced me to a quivering hormonal mess. All I wanted was to feel him inside me, but he was taking his sweet time and torturing me.

"Spread your legs," he ordered.

I did as he asked, entirely at his mercy.

He positioned himself between my thighs, his breath tickling my sensitive skin. If he didn't touch me soon, I'd explode from the sheer anticipation.

He ran his tongue up my wet core, and I arched off the ground.

"That's it," he whispered, right before he buried his face between my legs.

I whimpered with each tease and caress of his mouth against my throbbing center. His tongue swirled around my folds with expertise, and he slid a finger deep inside me.

"Cade," I moaned, fisting his short hair in my hands. "Jesus, what are you doing to me?" I bucked my hips up, moving with him.

"You taste so fucking good," he said, massaging my clit with his tongue. Heat swirled inside me, growing with intensity.

My legs tensed as he pumped his finger in and out of me and his mouth licked and sucked my sensitive skin.

"Ohh," I said, "Cade … I'm …" I panted. My hips jerked up as my entire body tensed and quivered against him with my release.

He gently kissed the inside of my thigh as my body calmed down, and I slowly returned to earth. He sat back on his heels, fumbled in his pocket for a condom, and rolled it on in one smooth move. I bit my lip, waiting for him. In seconds he was situated and ready. The feel of his hot skin sent ripples of pleasure through me.

"You still good with this?" he asked, his face serious.

"Yeah," I said, still a bit breathless. "Shut up and fuck me already."

Cade moaned softly, lifted up, and eased inside.

My breath caught in my throat as every magnificent inch of him filled me. I dug my fingers into his ass cheeks and wrapped my legs around his waist.

"Oh, God. It's definitely been too long," I panted.

Cade pulled out slowly, then slammed deep inside me.

"Oh my God," I said. "More."

Cade released a guttural growl as he pounded into me again and again. Pure lust swirled inside my body, and I raised up to meet him. My mind went blank, tonight's events flowing away like water. The only thing that mattered was how he was making me feel right now. I tightened my knees around his waist, rolled him over, peered down at him, and grinned.

"Perfect. Now I get to see those tits of yours bounce while I fuck you," he said and gripped my waist, lifting me up and down his long shaft. I reached behind me and placed my hands on his muscular thighs for support as he pounded against me.

"Does that feel good, Mac? Tell me what you want? Tell me how to fuck you."

No one had ever talked to me in bed like this, and I loved it.

"Yeah, you feel good." I shifted my weight and planted my palms on his chest. His hands moved to my tits, and I lowered myself down, guiding his mouth to my breast. I rocked against him while his tongue claimed me one nipple at a time.

I lost myself in his touch, then he flipped me over on my back and pulled out.

"Get on your hands and knees."

I did so willingly, missing his touch and the feel of his body immediately. Cade entered me from behind, then eased his hand between my legs. He rubbed my swollen clit while he picked up the pace, his other hand grabbing my hip for leverage.

I pushed back against him, driving him even deeper.

"Oh yeah. Your sweet little pussy is about to explode. I can feel you tightening around my dick."

"Fuck me, Cade," I moaned.

He thrust inside me until I couldn't take anymore, pure ecstasy coursing through me.

"Come with me, Mac."

He groaned, his body tensing with mine as we both released.

Shaking, I dropped to the ground with him still inside me.

"That was intense," he said and kissed the back of my neck.

"You can say that again."

He lifted off me, slipped off the condom, and tossed it into the bush.

"Omigosh. You just didn't."

He laughed and pulled up his jeans. I was almost sad when he buttoned the last one. The landscape had been magnificent.

I rolled over and sat up.

"Guess I should find my clothes."

An ornery grin spread across Cade's face.

"What?" I asked, suddenly self-conscious of my nakedness.

He sat up and reached for my hair.

"You have grass in your hair."

"Oh my God, you've got to check me and help me get my crap back together in case we see anyone other than Pierce."

Cade helped me gather my clothes, and within minutes we were as presentable as we were going to be.

We stood there and grinned stupidly at each other.

"I think I'll sleep better tonight," I said happily.

Cade wiggled his eyebrows at me. "You know where I'm at if you need any help."

I laughed. "Deal was one time unless you wanted to stop being a slut."

"Ohh," Cade said, stumbling backward and covering his heart with his hand. "So harsh."

"You're dramatic," I said, shaking my head. "Let's go back, but I'm sending you in first so you can manage any collateral damage. Like, if Hendrix is waiting for you."

"Man, you're ruthless."

"I am." We fell silent for the rest of the walk back.

"Well, this is goodnight," Cade said while we neared the back of the bus.

"I'm sure Pierce is around the corner." I leaned forward and spotted him walking around the bus. He must have kept an eye around the perimeter.

"Looks like he spotted us," Cade said, nodding in Pierce's direction.

"Ugh, I wish we didn't have to have a bodyguard. This is stupid." I waved at Pierce. He didn't wave back. "Anyway, you should go. I'll be behind you."

Cade nodded, then hesitated. "If you can't sleep, you know where I'm at."

"Sleep or sex?" I asked.

"Your choice, but I'm good with either. I mean, the sex was awesome, but if you need to sleep I get it."

"Thanks," I said softly. "I appreciate the distraction tonight."

"Me too."

I hung back while Cade walked up the rest of the hill and

disappeared inside the bus. I took my time and strolled toward Pierce.

"Hey," I said, stopping in front of him. "I wanted to say thank you."

"For what?" he asked, one eyebrow arching slightly.

"For pulling Asher off me tonight. For making sure he got to his hotel safely."

"It's my job."

"Ugh. Save me the bullshit. Yeah, maybe yanking him off me was your job, but you didn't have to make sure he arrived back at his hotel in one piece."

"True. Even though he's an idiot, I didn't want him to get mugged. Talk about an easy target."

"I appreciate it." I glanced at my shoes, then back up to him. "I don't know what to think of you. Like, you're totally in my business one minute and the next you're coming to my defense."

"What do you want me to say? Franklin assigned me to everyone during the tour."

"I'll tell you what I want you to say, Pierce. I want you to admit you care about us, and we're more than a job to you. I've seen how you look at Gemma. I know how you feel about her, but it's not only her. You continue to go above and beyond your *job*. No one asked you to have water for us tonight. It's what you do for friends. Ya know, because you care. Because your life would suck without us."

Pierce stared at me as I spoke.

"And our lives would suck without you," I muttered. "Even when you piss me off, I know you care. Only friends do that for each other, butt in when they're not wanted."

"You're right," he said quietly. "I've grown much closer to you all than any other assignment. It's —It's why ..."

"What? What is it?" I asked.

"It's why I asked to be reassigned."

CHAPTER 11

"*I*'m sorry, you did what?" I asked, my voice climbing up a notch. "No. No." I shook my head. How could he do this?

"Don't worry, my request was denied for the time being."

"Then why would you even tell me? Pierce!" Tears stung my eyes. What in the hell was wrong with me? I stared up at the sky, swallowing the ball of emotions that had lodged itself in my throat. "Dude, I'm sorry I threatened you at the park. There's no excuse for how I treated you. I was scared about not having the Xanax and Adderall to rely on. It wasn't really me talking."

"It's over, Mac. I just want you to be alright," Pierce replied.

"You can't leave us. We've all been through too much together. We don't trust anyone like we trust you," I pleaded.

"You could learn to trust someone else, Mac."

"I don't want to, and I know Gemma doesn't want to. Wait, does this have to do with her? I mean, seeing her with Hendrix? Is it too much?"

He answered me with silence.

"Fine. I know it's hard on you, but there's a bigger picture here. We need you. You're a part of this family."

"I'm not though, and at some point it will change, and you'll have to get used to it."

I bit my lip. "Not now. I can't handle any more changes. You know what we've been through. You know what Dillon and Brandon look like. Goddammit, you were there when Brandon released me and took Gemma at gunpoint!" A cry escaped me when the memories rushed back. After Brandon had released me, I'd stumbled across the parking lot and ran as fast as I could to Hendrix, Franklin, and ... Pierce. "It's been too much. Please. Don't leave us yet. I need to get back on my feet and feel safe before anything else changes."

"I'm here for now. I didn't realize it would upset you this much. I'm sorry. You focus on moving forward. I'm not going anywhere."

"Promise?" I asked.

"Yeah."

In the back of my mind, I'd never considered Pierce not being around. He'd somehow managed to wiggle his way into my heart and was now a permanent fixture in my life. He protected us and safety meant everything to me at this point.

Overcome with sadness and a multitude of other emotions, I flung my arms around him. The moment he returned my embrace, I burst into tears.

"It's going to be okay, Mac. I promise." He rested his chin on the top of my head and held me while I cried. I cried about Brandon, I cried about Asher, and I cried that my life was a fucking wreck.

After my snot fest, I wiped off my tear-stained cheeks with the palms of my hands and stepped back.

"Sorry. It's been a hell of a night. I found out Asher wasn't the person I thought he was."

"That never feels good," Pierce said, guiding me to the lawn chairs someone had set outside earlier.

I plunked down and sighed.

"When Cade first spotted Asher at the club tonight, he filled me in on Asher's previous treatment of you in school. We followed him, and that's when we saw he'd trapped you in a corner. I was all too happy to hold him as Cade got a few punches in."

Heat traveled across my cheeks. Everyone knew my business now.

"I had no idea. I mean, I knew people talked about me at school, but I never realized part of it was because Asher blabbed our business. I mean, why? What was the purpose of it?"

"Some guys think it proves they're a man when they get a girl pregnant," Pierce said, rubbing his jaw.

"That is the stupidest crap I've ever heard. I mean seriously, wouldn't getting a girl pregnant mean you were a dumbass? I realize accidents happen, but ..." I sank into my chair and stared up at the sky. "I guess it doesn't matter anymore. It's over. I'm not interested in being with him."

"I'm glad to hear it. You deserve better."

"See?" I said, peering at him. "Only friends say stuff like that to each other. And thank you. For the record ..." I hesitated and grinned. "I like you for the most part. I mean, I'd be happy if you stayed. In fact, I think I'll have a chat with Franklin and tell him you can never be reassigned."

A small smile pulled at the corner of his mouth.

I leaned toward him, my gaze never leaving his. "It will get better when the tour is over, and you're not in such close quarters with Gemma and Hendrix. When we get back home, we'll get you on Tinder. What do they say? You can't get over someone until you get under someone new? Something close to that anyway. You should try it. Besides, a smash and dash might help you loosen up a bit."

Pierce chuckled. "I appreciate your interest, but I'll be okay."

"Fine," I said, standing. "I'm exhausted, so I'm going to get some sleep. You should, too."

"Alright, let's get inside."

Pierce locked up after we entered the bus. Since it was almost two in the morning, everyone was quiet. I had no idea if they were sleeping or not, but I needed to have some space and sift through my jumbled thoughts.

My vodka cranberry buzz had nearly worn off, so I made my way to the fully stocked bar in the kitchen and downed a few shots of vodka. I shuddered as the alcohol traveled down my throat and into my belly.

Even though Pierce and I had bonded a little bit, I refused to look at him while I poured a third drink and downed it.

"Night," I said softly, setting the glass in the sink.

"Night," he replied.

I made my way to my bed, changed into my pajamas, and quietly rifled through my purse. I twisted the cap off my Xanax and shook one into my hand. I swallowed it with no water. Pierce's concern about my pill usage didn't phase me. The only thing I cared about was not having nightmares, and even sex with Cade couldn't fix it.

MY HEAD POUNDED like a son of a bitch the next morning. I stumbled out of bed a few minutes before noon and headed to the shower. Last night's events came crashing back as I stood underneath the hot spray.

Gemma would want a full update, but unfortunately, I was becoming more skilled at keeping secrets from her. A pang of sadness ripped through me. She was my best friend, my sister, but there was no way I could talk to her about Pierce or my night with Cade. I could tell her about Asher, though.

I leaned my forehead against the shower wall and groaned. What was my life becoming if I couldn't even confide in her?

Turning the water off, I reached for my towel, dried off, and dressed in a teal T-shirt and denim shorts. I brushed my hair out and decided against my typical braids.

The first thing I needed to take care of was Asher, which meant a text wouldn't do. I had to call him. He'd been so drunk last night I wasn't sure if my stern words had seeped through his alcohol addled brain.

I stepped out of the bathroom, my mind searching for the right words to tell Asher to fuck off.

"You look deep in thought," Gemma said, leaning against mine and Cade's bunk.

"Yeah. I was thinking I needed to call Asher."

"Come on, the guys are off gambling for a little while," she said, grabbing my hand and leading me to the living area. We plopped down on the couch and looked at each other.

"Fill me in," she said.

I rubbed my face, grateful the shower had helped relieve the pounding in my head.

"Yeah, you were in the bathroom at the club when it started," I said, glancing at her.

"That was insane. I mean I walked out, and Cade was beating the snot out of Asher."

A giggle escaped me. "Sorry. I wasn't laughing last night, but the more I learned, the more Asher deserved it."

"Hendrix told me about the pregnancy and how Asher spread it around school. Mac, I'm so sorry. Hendrix was livid. If Cade hadn't taken care of Asher, Hendrix would have."

I stared at the recliner in front of me, my mind whirling through the events.

"I know. I think the guys would have lined up to have a shot at him. Which, ya know, it makes me feel good they all care so much. But Gemma, I'm mortified. I get this was a few years ago, but I just found out last night. On top of everything else, I have to deal with that. No wonder John and Cade have always been so good to me. I mean, they irritate the ever-lovin' shit out of me, but ..."

"It's because they care. I wish I'd had them around when I was growing up. Granted, they never told you what happened with Asher, but it was because they wanted to protect you and Hendrix. Mac, they're really good guys. The more I've gotten to know them, the more they've grown on me. I've even stopped judging them for their one-night flings."

My heart stuttered. Would that mean she'd be cool with what Cade and I had done last night? Was *I* okay with what we'd done? Suddenly, my decision to sleep with one of my brother's best friends smacked me with full force. I felt the color draining from my face.

"Are you alright? You don't look so good all of a sudden."

I glanced at her, guilt washing over me. "Yeah. I dread telling Asher to go away. I hope like hell he listens. I don't need any more drama."

"Something tells me that after last night, Asher won't want to mess with you again."

I nodded. I'd find out soon enough if she was right.

"Hey, I've got to get to rehearsal. Do you want to come?" Gemma asked, standing and smoothing her navy-blue T-shirt.

"Nah, I'll hang out here and call Asher. The sooner I get it over with the better I'll feel."

"Let me know how it goes," she said.

"I will."

Gemma gave me a little wave and disappeared off the bus. It took me a minute before I realized no one was here. Not even Pierce. I wasn't sure if I was happy or nervous. Anyone could walk onto the bus. I jumped from my seat, locked the doors, and checked the windows. If anyone wanted in, I'd at least make them work for it.

I stared at my phone as I settled into the recliner and groaned. Dread tugged at me while I struggled to articulate what I wanted to say. Staring out of the window, my mind drifted to Cade and our sexfest on the grass. Would things be the same between us or had I screwed up our friendship? My body tingled in response. Sex with him had been off the charts. Maybe I'd been the lucky one, benefiting from all of his practice over the years. Not only had I never experienced multiple orgasms before, but I'd also never come during actual sex. Cade knew how to use his hips apparently. He repeatedly reached the right spots deep inside me. Heat swirled in my stomach, and I suddenly ached for him. Dammit. This. Could. Not. Happen. He was a one-time booty call.

Sucking in a deep breath, I forced myself to focus on Asher and tapped my phone screen. I chewed my bottom lip when it came to life and located Asher's phone number. Even though I knew it was over, my heart still ached for what could have been. His line rang three times before he answered.

"Mac?" Asher asked, hope in his voice.

Dammit. I was going to crush him.

"Hey. How are you feeling?" I asked, more out of politeness than actually giving a fuck. If I'd known he'd told everyone I'd gotten pregnant and had an abortion, I would have let him go a lot sooner.

"Like I've been run over by an eighteen-wheeler. Mac—"

"Don't," I said, cutting off whatever lame excuse he was about to offer me. Nothing he said could make up for his actions. "We're done. Don't call me, don't show up at my house, or school, or anywhere else. I know what you did, Asher. I know you told everyone at school that you got me pregnant. You even bragged about it."

He inhaled sharply. If there were any lingering thoughts of him having another chance with me, I'd just squashed them like a big ol' nasty bug.

"I'm sorry, Mac. I know it won't make up for what I did, but I was a stupid, scared kid. Unfortunately, I didn't realize what I'd lost until it was too late. The pregnancy, Rochelle, my dad ... I've not handled anything like a real man should have. I had no business showing up like I did last night."

Had Cade knocked some sense into him? I'd never heard Asher talk like this.

"Asher ..." I stared at my feet, debating how much I should say. Fuck it. When did I ever not say what I thought? "I'll always love you, and the pregnancy messed us up pretty bad. But there's nothing you can do to redeem yourself. We're broken."

"I know. I had to try one more time, though. I was nervous and scared last night and should never have shown up trashed. But I'm not the same guy I was in high school. Maybe one day you'll have an opportunity to see it." He blew out a long shuddering breath. "I'd give anything to go back in time and change it all. I would in a heartbeat," he said, defeat clear in his tone.

My stomach twisted in knots. Letting go of my past sucked. It wasn't even like Asher was a good choice for me. It was like an old pair of shoes, broken in and comfy but full of holes. There was no question it was time to toss them. "I need to go. Take care, Asher."

"I love you, Mac. I hope you find what you're looking for," he said softly, his voice cracking with emotion.

Silence filled the line. I pulled the phone away from my ear and tapped the end call button.

Tears streamed down my cheeks. I'd tossed my old shoes in the trash, and I'd realized it was the right choice, but it still fucking hurt. Somewhere inside me, even when we were with other people, I held onto the possibility of another chance with Asher. He had always been my safety net. With one phone call, I'd cut the cords.

I wiped my face with the hem of my shirt and eyed the bar. Everyone was gone, and God knew I needed a drink. Standing, I located the vodka and also spotted a smaller bottle in the back of the cabinet. It had been so well hidden to begin with, I doubted anyone would even miss it. Without giving it any more thought, I swiped the bottle and made my way back to my bed. Now, I'd have my own stash, and I wouldn't have to deal with prying eyes. After nestling it in between blankets and pillows, I returned to the bar. Three shots later, I sank back into the recliner and enjoyed the quiet.

A loud knock at the door tore me from my peaceful bliss. Dammit. I'd locked the door. It was probably Pierce or someone else checking on me.

I yawned and meandered to the door.

"Who is it?" I called.

"It's Cade. Let me in, Mac."

I opened the door and stepped out of the way while he hopped up the stairs and inside the living area. His Seattle Seahawks T-shirt stretched across his broad muscled chest, and his jeans hugged his thighs in all the right ways. My mind immediately wandered to what was underneath them. Flustered I was already picturing him naked again, I decided I needed to play it cool. We had an agreement, and even though it was true he'd be the perfect distraction from my constant thoughts of Asher and Brandon, I couldn't use him like that. We were friends.

"Thought you were at practice," I mumbled, pretending to be a little perturbed he'd interrupted my alone time.

"I am, but my guitar string broke, and I forgot to pack an extra in my case," he said, his eyes slowly traveling down my body. "And I wanted to know how you were doing after last night." His voice was low while he stepped toward me, and a trace of his woodsy aftershave tickled my nose.

"I'm fine. You?" I asked, hoping I was playing it off as no big deal.

He moved closer. I wondered if his heart was hammering as hard as mine was at the moment.

"I've got a few minutes before everyone will expect me back … and we're alone," Cade said, softly.

"Are you suggesting what I think you are?" My core clenched with anticipation as I leaned against the wall, pretending his presence wasn't having a major effect on me.

"Last night was amazing. It's all I can think about," he whispered in my ear.

My back arched and my breasts grazed against his chest. He was right, we had a rare opportunity, and no one would ever know if we had a quickie.

His warm mouth brushed against my neck and his hand slipped under my T-shirt, skimming my stomach. I shuddered at his touch. I needed this. I needed to forget about all the crap in my life, and Cade could give me a temporary reprieve.

I hooked a finger in a belt loop on his jeans and tugged his hips into me. He was ready to go, and even though my brain said no, my body had already told it to shut the hell up.

"I wish I had more time," he said, flipping the button on my shorts open. He shimmied them along with my G-string over my hips, and I quickly kicked them to the side. He dropped to his knees, trailing hot, wet kisses down my stomach and the inside of my thigh. He paused and glanced up at me, his eyes heavy with desire. His hands dug into my waist as his mouth claimed me.

"Dammit," I said, threading my fingers through his hair. He lifted my leg and placed it over his shoulder, never missing a beat. I moaned and leaned against the wall. His tongue danced over my clit, and in record time he'd brought me to the edge, then stopped. I let out a soft cry as his mouth left my throbbing core.

He wiped his lips with the back of his hand and removed a condom from his pocket. My attention never left him while he stepped out of his jeans, his cock bobbing free.

"Your tight little pussy had me messed up all day," he said, rolling on his protection.

"I'm not going to apologize." I peered at him through my eyelashes as he slowly stood up.

"Turn around," he ordered.

I faced the wall next to the recliner and spread my feet apart. I released a soft moan as he rubbed the tip of his dick along my slick folds.

"Jesus you're wet. You missed me too, huh?" In one swift motion, he slid inside me.

"No," I panted with every thrust. "I was thinking about Asher," I said. I wasn't really lying, but I couldn't let Cade know he'd gotten into my head. It was enough that he was inside me again even though I'd said only one night.

His pace quickened with the mention of Asher's name. I wasn't sure if he was angry I'd mentioned another guy or he was trying to fuck Asher out of my mind, but I wasn't complaining.

Cade shifted his hips, sending ripples of pleasure through me. My palms flattened against the wall while I pushed back against him.

"Harder," I said, glancing back at him. His tongue darted out over his lower lip, and his fingers dug into my hips. "That's it. Fuck me, Cade."

"Say it again," he panted.

"You like that?" I asked, smiling. "You want me to tell you how good your huge cock feels inside my pussy? Do you want me to tell you I thought about you before you showed up and it's why I'm so wet? All I could think about was your mouth all over my body, and you pounding into me."

"Dammit, Mac. You're going to make me come."

I groaned when he slipped his hand between my legs and gently massaged my clit.

"You like my mouth right there?"

"Yes," I gasped. "Holy hell ... Cade ..." My body tensed, my climax building in intensity until I exploded.

"Ahh," he groaned as he thrust deep inside me. "So. Fucking. Good." He buried his face against my neck, shuddering as he let loose a muffled yell and then stilled.

I collapsed against the wall as he finished.

He leaned forward, raised my shirt, and placed a gentle kiss along my spine.

"Maybe I can focus in practice now," he said softly and pulled out of me.

"Sorry," I said, turning around and stepping back into my shorts. "I didn't mean to mess up your music."

Cade wrapped up the condom in some tissue and tossed it in the trash. He definitely looked more relaxed than he did a few minutes ago.

"Not your fault I can't think straight today. Well, it might be," he said, flashing me a grin.

"Ugh, help me open the door and windows, it smells like sex in here, and if Hendrix shows up …"

Cade nodded and hurried to the back of the bus. I snatched the air freshener off the shelf in the bathroom and sprayed a little.

"Is it better?" I asked, giggling. "I don't know why this is funny."

Cade chuckled and ran his hand over his dark hair. "Yeah, I think so. I'd leave the windows open for a few minutes even though it's hot as fuck outside."

"I will. Did you get your guitar strings?"

"Huh?" Cade asked, glancing around our bunks. "Yeah, I almost forgot what I came back for." A shy smile eased across his face while he glanced at me.

"Well duh, for me. Helloo," I said, giggling.

Just then the door opened.

"Hey man," John said, hopping onto the bus.

"How's it going?" I asked, hiding the air freshener behind my back.

"I'm on my way back now," Cade said holding up the package with his guitar string.

"We were wondering if you stopped along the way and

hooked up with some chick or something. Hendrix sent me to find you."

A flush traveled across my cheeks. "Gotta pee," I muttered and disappeared into the bathroom. The moment I closed the door behind me I heard John ask why all the windows were open. Cade professed total ignorance and said they were open when he got here.

Their voices trailed off, and I listened for the click of the door. They were gone.

Holy Hannah. That had been a close call. If John had been a minute or two sooner, we would have been caught.

CHAPTER 12

*A*fter the band performed and greeted fans that night, we all piled back on the bus. We were finally leaving Vegas and on our way to Arizona, New Mexico, and then off to Colorado. The week would be full of rehearsals, practices, and long drives.

Although I'd tried to sleep in my own bed that night, my thoughts raced with all the drama Vegas had offered. Asher, Cade, and the best sex of my life.

"You awake?" I whispered loudly. John's soft snores carried through the small sleeping area while I waited to see if Cade would respond.

"Yeah, come on," Cade replied.

I tossed my covers off, scrambled up the ladder, and into his bed.

"You're getting good at catapulting over me," he said, grinning.

"Thanks, I'll be sure to enter the Olympics for hot dude hopping," I said dryly.

"You think I'm hot?" Cade asked, rolling over on his side to look at me. The muscles in his arms and chest flexed with his movements.

"No, you're a troll. But no guy has ever gotten me off as fast as you can, so I put up with you."

Cade's chuckle filled the small space.

"Shh, you'll wake up Pierce," I reminded him.

We settled into a comfortable silence for a minute.

"You were drinking today," Cade said, his expression gentle.

"We drink all the time," I replied.

"I guess so. It's normally after a show is all."

"Not in the middle of the day?" I asked, arching my eyebrow at him.

"Mac, I'm not judging. I'm the last person on earth to judge anyone. I just wonder what's going on in that mind of yours sometimes."

I searched his face, but all I saw was sincerity. Maybe he really was concerned.

"If I invited you inside my head, you'd take off running in seconds. It's dark, Cade. I'm not a good person. I don't think good things, and I'm judgy as hell."

I bit my thumbnail, afraid to see his reaction.

"I honest to God hope someone gets a hold of Brandon in prison and stabs him. I hope he dies a slow horrible death for what he did to Gemma and me. Not to mention all the other girls," I said.

"Would it make you feel any better if I told you I also hoped the same for him? And I can tell you John does, too. Even Hendrix and Gemma have weighed in on the topic. You shouldn't feel bad about it. Getting rid of Brandon would mean one less evil bastard walking around on the planet in my opinion."

"Really?" I asked. Good to know I wasn't the only one who had those thoughts. "I'm scared to go out by myself anymore. And I truly believe I'd be able to sleep again if he disappeared for good. Ya know, I mean he haunts me everywhere I turn. I just want to move on with my life. I'm not sure I'll be able to, though."

Cade's arm moved out from under his blankets, and he took my hand in his. His touch was gentle, different than earlier in the day when we were fucking like bunnies in the springtime.

"When I got older and realized Mom needed me to take care of her, it was really tough to deal with. I hated her, actually. The last thing I wanted was to be tied down, fully responsible for her and Missy. But as soon as the thought formed in my mind, I felt lower than a piece of dog crap on the bottom of a shoe. I knew foster kids at school who would have given their left nut to have a mom, sister, and a safe place to live."

I traced his long slender fingers as he talked.

"It's super tough for a kid to step into a parental role, for any reason. You probably felt like you didn't have a life. When Hendrix was thirteen, Franklin's alcoholism was at its worst. But you can't force an addict to get clean. My mom had already given up trying and we left. But Hendrix stayed for a while, hoping he could get through to his dad. It didn't work. When Hendrix came to live with us he was a mess. He was angry and depressed, but his music saved him. Was it like that for you? Your music I mean?"

The gold flecks flashed in his eyes while I waited for his answer.

"Yeah. It kept me from getting into even more trouble."

I couldn't stop my grin. Cade was always pulling a prank on someone in school or getting into some kind of predicament.

"Have you ever thought of doing anything other than performing? Or is this your life like it is for Hendrix?"

"As long as I can sing and play … I'm good. It's all I've ever wanted to do."

A pang of sadness twisted inside my stomach. I wanted that as well. Something I loved so much it kept me sane no matter what else was happening in life.

"You and Hendrix are lucky," I said, shifting on my pillow. "It's hard when you don't know your place or where you belong."

I stifled a yawn, growing sleepier by the second.

"You'll find it, Mac. I promise," Cade whispered, right before I drifted off to sleep.

~

EARLY THE NEXT MORNING, I slipped back into my own bed. Minutes later I heard the bathroom door open and close. Even though I suspected it was Pierce, I really needed to be more careful. Pierce already knew I slept in Cade's bed more than my own, but I didn't want him to know any real details. A nagging thought tickled my brain. I hoped he didn't feel obligated to say something to Hendrix or Gemma. He wouldn't do that, would he? He'd always stayed out of our personal business unless it came down to safety. I chided myself, rolled over, and pushed the thought back down.

An hour later everyone was up and ready to find a place for breakfast.

"Welcome to Phoenix," John said, stepping off the bus.

I cringed against the heat and sunshine as I followed him and Hendrix.

"Geez, is it hotter here than Vegas?" Gemma asked, pulling her hair into a ponytail.

"I'm going to start carrying deodorant in my purse," I mumbled, patting my bag with my secret stash of vodka and pills.

"At least we'll be inside most of the time. I wanted to sightsee, but this heat is brutal. I think I'll pass."

"There's a park with a big pond and water fountain over there." Cade pointed to the right of us.

"It looks pretty, maybe I'll check it out later. For now, it's breakfast for me and then I'm staying for your rehearsal," I said.

"Oh cool. You'll get to see what Hendrix and I have been working on."

"A new song?"

"You'll have to wait and see," he said, elbowing me gently in the side.

I shot him a nasty look. If we were going to keep up appearances, I had to give it right back to him.

"You two are like a brother and sister," Gemma teased.

I inwardly cringed. That comparison was all kinds of wrong. Yeah, we were friends, but we'd had sex, and in most states banging your brother or sister was illegal. I shuddered at the thought.

"That bad, huh?" Cade said, laughing.

"You weren't thinking the same thing? Like, that's seriously illegal."

"What's illegal?" Gemma asked. "All I said was you two are like brother and sister."

Cade's face paled with my slip.

"Oh, haha. No, I thought you said something else. Never mind. All these late nights and lack of sleep are getting to me, and I'm not making any sense over here," I said.

Gemma stared at me skeptically. "You're still not sleeping?" she asked softly.

"Some nights are tough," I whispered.

She took my hand and squeezed it as we followed Hendrix and the guys into the diner, the smell of fresh pancakes and bacon immediately taunting me. My stomach growled in response.

We seated ourselves at a table in the back of the restaurant, and twenty minutes later biscuits, gravy, and flapjacks were in front of me.

I took a bite of biscuit and gravy and moaned.

"Heaven," I said around my mouthful of food. "But still not as good as Ruby's breakfasts."

"Right? I think one of the things I miss most when we're on tour is not stopping by Franklin's for meals. Ruby's cooking is amazing," Gemma said.

"I know. I'll probably gain ten pounds when we get back home."

"You and me both," she said smiling.

The rest of the conversation was filled with the band's schedule and what time we needed to roll out of here to reach New Mexico. A gentle graze across my knee stopped me short. My eyes cut across the table to find Cade leaning forward as far as he could. His hand slid beneath my knee, and he lightly caressed my bare leg. I shivered visibly, which sent my fork clattering to the floor.

"You alright?" Gemma asked.

"Yup," I said, "Just got a chill for a minute. I'm fine." I flashed my best smile at her while I shot Cade the evil eye for teasing me under the table. What was he doing?

When everyone's attention had turned to Hendrix again, Cade gave me a wink and mischievous smile.

"Later," he mouthed and licked his lips.

My panties were wet in seconds. How could he do that to me? Besides, the deal was one time, and we'd already broken it yesterday afternoon. No more. Plus, I'd told him that if he wanted to be with me, he needed to let me know he was going to stop visiting other girls' playgrounds. So far, he hadn't given me his decision. Apparently he was going to push a little and see what he could get away with. I'd have to talk to him.

"Maybe," I mouthed back.

Cade's face fell, and he slumped back in his chair, folding his arms protectively across his chest. Why was he acting like I'd hurt his feelings? For a moment I almost felt bad, but we had a deal. I wasn't going to sleep with someone who tapped everything with a pulse. I had self-respect, but my hormones overruled it sometimes.

Forty-five minutes later we had finished eating and arrived at the concert venue. John held the door open for us as we filed into the back.

"I swear every time I walk into a new place for a concert, I panic a little. I've never gotten over the tornado at the concert in Louisiana," Gemma admitted.

"I was thinking the same thing. It's almost like Deja vu or something." My attention quickly darted to Hendrix while I recalled the long recovery he'd gone through after the tornado had nearly killed us all at Cane's River Center. Thank God Gemma had acted quickly, or I'd have been sucked up into the vast whirlwind.

At least Cade and John were back in Washington when it happened. Shaking the memories from my mind, I took a deep breath and glanced around at each of my friends. We'd come a long way in a short time.

We stepped out onto the stage and stood quietly as we scanned the rows and rows of empty seats.

"You guys ready?" Hendrix asked, running his hand through his hair.

"Yeah, man, let's do this," John said, taking his sticks out of his back pocket and settling in at the drum set.

"I'm so excited," I said, bouncing up and down and clapping my hands. "I'm going to go have a seat. I can't wait to hear your new song!"

I hopped down the stairs two at a time and plopped down in a front row chair. A few of the technical and lighting crew joined the band on stage. Cade grabbed his guitar case from one of them and Hendrix did the same. Gemma sat at the piano and gave me a tired smile.

Cade slipped the strap over his shoulder and strummed his electric guitar. I nearly laughed as I remembered Marilyn's comment at an earlier concert about how she'd like him to strum her. Well, if I ever saw her again, I would be more than happy to let her know his fingers were even better on my body than on his guitar.

The band played a few songs and adjusted to the new acoustics of the auditorium. They sounded better with each performance, if that were even possible.

An hour later, Gemma joined me in the front row.

"This is going to be so amazing," she said, grinning. "Cade has talked about this for a while."

"Talked about what?" I asked and leaned over to her.

"Watch and listen," she said, motioning to Cade and Hendrix on the stage.

Cade walked toward Hendrix, and quietly conversed with him. What were they doing?

They nodded, then returned to their own microphones. Cade strummed his guitar, the sound filling the auditorium as it resonated through the speakers. And then he began a song I'd never heard before. Hendrix moved back and played bass and John continued on the drums.

Cade's silky tenor voice enveloped me as he began to sing.

I gaze into your deep brown eyes, hypnotized.

And nothing else seems to matter, it all fades away.

I think about your touch, and the way I feel when I'm with you.

His eyes fell on me, our gazes locking. Mesmerized, I remained still. Our focus never left each other while his amazing voice penetrated every fiber of my being. My entire body tingled as he finished the song.

The taste of your lips I can't ignore.

But it's your heart that makes my life worthwhile.

I'll show up for you, and we'll hold onto each other

No matter what we go through.

"Oh. My. God," Gemma whispered and jabbed me with her finger.

"What the hell?" I asked, rubbing my arm and breaking free from my Cade daze.

"Is there something going on between you two?" Gemma asked, her expression full of questions.

I frowned and glared at Cade, who was now busy talking to Hendrix about tweaks in the performance. What had just happened? Was the song about me or had he simply gotten nervous and used me to stay focused? That was probably it. He couldn't have stared at Gemma or Hendrix would have thought he had a thing for her. As far as I could tell, Cade didn't have a thing for any girl.

"What? Don't be ridiculous. You do realize what a player he is, right?" I asked.

"Yeah, but the way he looked at you ... and wait a minute." She wiggled in her seat so she could see me better. "Cade has only disappeared a few times during this tour, nothing like before you were with us according to Hendrix." Her stare intensified as she searched my face for any sign her assumptions were correct.

I swallowed hard. At least two of the times Cade had disappeared, he'd been with me.

"Nope. Don't forget we've known each other since high school. Remember the first time you performed solo? You focused on one thing to calm your nerves. He knows I support him, and he sure as hell couldn't look at you while he sang. Hendrix would have pushed him right off the stage." I swallowed hard, hoping my logic would deter her from further questioning.

Gemma giggled. "Maybe you're right, but something about those lyrics, Mac. I remember what it felt like when Hendrix sang to me the first time. There's nothing like it."

"Well, I wouldn't know. No one has ever written or sung a song about me."

"How did it sound out there?" Cade asked, interrupting our conversation.

"Great!" Gemma called. "I think we need a little bit more bass though, it's a smidge heavy on the guitar during the chorus. It needs more balance."

"Alright, thanks. Mac?"

Butterflies fluttered in my stomach with his question. Why would he even care about my opinion? All I really wanted to know was who he had thought about when he wrote the song. A million girls had brown eyes, but I couldn't ask him now. "What she said." I smiled and pointed at Gemma.

The guys laughed and ran through the song again. This time, although Cade's eyes landed on me occasionally, he focused toward the back of the auditorium or walked the stage. I inwardly sighed, grateful I wasn't the center of his attention this time. But the more he sang the lyrics, the more I had to squash the hope he'd written the song for me.

CHAPTER 13

*a*fter rehearsal, I joined everyone on stage.

"So you're singing tonight?" I asked Cade.

"Yeah, I'm nervous as fuck, too. As you know, I've always sung back up to Hendrix."

"You got this, man," Hendrix replied, slapping Cade on the back. "Listen, Gemma and I are going to get out of here for a while and check out Phoenix. We'll meet you back here at six. Pierce will be with us, so Cade, watch out for Mac please."

Dammit. If Hendrix had any idea how Cade was watching out for me ... I hated to think what that would mean for Cade.

"Yeah, no problem," Cade responded.

"I'm tired as hell, and I'm headed back to the bus to crash out," John said, stretching his full six-two frame to the ceiling.

"Don't be late," Hendrix said, grinning.

I got the impression John had overslept a few times.

The moment Hendrix and Gemma walked off, Cade shot me a look and nodded toward the back of the stage. Good, we needed to talk.

The auditorium was eerily quiet after everyone had left. I followed Cade behind the curtain and down a long, partially lit hallway. He grabbed my hand and led me to a dressing room, flipping on the light switch.

"It's mine tonight, so I figure since I'm assigned to protect you …" The flecks of gold in his eyes sparkled.

I glanced around at the dressing area, my eyes landing on the big plush brown leather couch along the wall. The area was small but cozy.

He guided me to the couch and pulled me down next to him. My heart hammered against my chest. What was my problem? I'd known him for years, and now my nerves decided to go nuts?

He leaned back against the arm of the seat and stared at me.

"Did you really like the song?" he asked softly.

"If you're nervous, you shouldn't be. Your voice is amazing. I've never heard you sing by yourself, and I had no idea how good you are. Omigosh, you were totally holding out on everyone. I mean, Hendrix knew obviously, or he wouldn't have you sing with him at all …" I stopped myself before I went any further.

"Mac, it's not what I asked." A frown line deepened in his forehead while he waited for me to answer.

"Why is my opinion important to you? You've been singing for a long time," I said, trying to dodge the question. Although I wanted to know who the song was about, I was also afraid to hear the answer.

He slid over to me, only an inch away, his handsome face growing more serious.

"Did you like the song?" he asked me again.

My insides quivered. I wanted to skip this conversation, rip his clothes off, and savor every inch of his body.

"Yes, I loved it, but who did you write it for?" I blurted. I looked away, unwilling to see his expression. "Sorry, that was rude and none of my business."

"Look at me." His thumb gently caressed my cheek, and I had to remember Cade was seriously skilled at moves like this. Soft, tender ... The ones that made girls slip right out of their panties without a second thought.

I dared a look at him.

"It's for you, Mac. I wrote the song for you." His shoulders visibly tensed as the words left his mouth.

Holy. Fucking. Shit.

"I ... I."

"I wasn't sure how you'd take it," he admitted.

A bit lightheaded with his confession, I simply stared at him. I didn't understand. What was he saying? I took a deep breath.

"Alright. Cool. I mean it's actually really cool. Gemma said there's nothing like it when a dude writes a song for you. Well, a hot dude. An ugly dude, meh, yeah, not so much. But when he's hot, and the girls are literally creaming themselves just watching you play. Then it's a big deal because—"

"Mackenzie," Cade whispered, brushing his thumb gently across my lips. His eyes flashed with longing as his gaze dropped to my mouth. "I want to kiss you."

Too stunned to disagree, I didn't respond.

He leaned in, his fingers trailing down the side of my cheek. His warm lips grazed mine ever so softly, lingering for one sweet moment. Cade leaned his forehead against mine, cupping the back of my neck with his hand. I peered up at him, speechless. He knew my kissing rule. He knew what it meant to me, so what was he up to?

He gently tipped my chin up as he kissed me again. His mouth parted slightly, and his tongue tentatively touched mine. I moaned against him, then my brain switched off, and my hormones took full control.

Cade leaned me back on the couch, his mouth never leaving mine. I ran my hands along his back while he settled between my legs. Tugging at his shirt, my fingers danced across his skin.

He broke our kiss and smoothed my hair.

"You kissed me," I whispered.

"Yeah," he said quietly, nipping at my bottom lip.

"You called me Mackenzie," I said.

"I did," he said, smiling. "I have a confession," Cade said, still playing with my hair.

"Alright." Normally I was always down with a good confession, but this one had my stomach in knots.

"My feelings are changing."

I frowned. What? He didn't want to be bunk and fuck buddies anymore?

"What do you mean exactly?" I asked, trying not to freak out. Over the last few weeks, I'd gotten used to having him around. I needed him. He was the gatekeeper to my nightmares and anxiety.

"Ever since high school ... I've always cared about you, I've always thought you were gorgeous. I even find your babbling endearing."

I attempted to remain calm, and not roll him off me onto the floor, then make a mad dash out the door. Not only was he freaking me out, but he needed to get to the point. My heart had literally stopped beating, waiting for what he was going to say next. Was our arrangement over?

"You were with Asher, though. Then when you guys broke up, the band had started taking off and I figured you weren't ready anyway."

"Cade? What are you trying to tell me?"

He inhaled deeply. "I have feelings for you, Mac. I have for years. And over the last few weeks, having you next to me at night, our whispered secrets, the mind-blowing sex ... It did me in. I don't want to be with anyone else. I want a chance with you."

I scrambled out from underneath him, my mouth gaping open. Shutting it, I chided myself for most likely making him feel bad.

"Sorry, I didn't mean to react like that. I—. Dayummmm. Like really? No, I'm sorry," I said, slapping my hands on my cheeks and sitting up. "I had no idea. I really thought you were simply being a good friend and, ya know, we had convenient sex. Cade … I've never looked at you other than my brother's best friend and a man whore."

The color drained from Cade's face the second the words left my mouth, and I quickly grasped his hand.

"No … I'm sorry, it's true, but then … after my nightmares, when you allowed me in your bed, all the walls came down. You didn't even try to get me out of my pajamas. Well, at first anyway," I giggled nervously. "Sorry. I'll try to stay on track here. I saw you differently. It was like for the first time in the years we've known each other I had a glimpse of the amazing guy you really are behind the sex and partying."

"You did?" he asked.

I didn't miss the beat of hope in his voice.

"Yeah, I did. Cade, I don't know what this means. I'm not sure where I am emotionally from one day to the next, but I can say my feelings are changing for you, too," I said. A little stunned by our conversation, I realized I'd admitted my feelings to him and myself for the first time.

His eyes widened, and he grabbed my hand in between his. Electricity traveled through my body.

"Can we see where this goes?" he asked.

I paused while memories of Asher and Jeremiah ran rampant in my mind. The lies, the betrayal, the heartache. Could I try this? Would Cade revert to his womanizing ways? Was this another compulsive moment in my life that would end up in a big ass disaster?

"Listen, to clear the air. There's not been anyone else since you were in my bed the first night," Cade said.

I literally gaped at him.

He gently closed my mouth. "I'm serious. The last person I had a smash and dash with as you call it was at Multnomah Falls a few weeks ago. It's only been you since then."

How in the hell was I supposed to digest all of this? Cade Richardson, one of the most popular guys from my high school days, lead guitarist and singer, a guy almost any female wanted to screw, was into me?

"What about Hendrix? You can't risk your career for me. No one is worth sacrificing your passion for. Especially me."

He shook his head adamantly. "Don't ever say anything like that again. I've spent a lot of time thinking about it, and you're worth the consequences," he said.

"Okay," I said, shyly.

"If you're in, Mac, I'll talk to Hendrix. I think he would want us to be honest. I'm willing to take the chance if you are."

I nodded, trying to sift through everything he'd said to me. "So, is this like … are you asking for a committed relationship or? I'm a little bit confused. Well, I mean, I sort of get it, but I think some clarity would help. I'm sorry, I'm rambling, I'm trying to figure everything out, and I talk even more when I'm nervous."

Cade leaned in and kissed me gently.

"I'd like to see where this goes, but I heard what you said. Besides, I don't want to be with anyone else. I promise," he said.

"Umm, I think that's committed, Cade."

"Call it whatever you want. If you'll have me, I'm all yours."

I slipped my hands around the back of his neck and pulled him to me.

"Yes," I whispered and kissed him.

"Yeah?" He pulled away slightly and searched my face for reassurance.

"Don't break my heart, Cade. I'm seriously fragile right now. Besides, Hendrix will be the death of you, and even the thought of it breaks my heart."

His fingers danced down my cheek, down my neck, and over my left breast. He flattened his palm and rested it over my heart.

"I'm here to protect it, not break it."

He moved his hand from my chest and gently threaded his

fingers through mine. Before now, Cade would have taken the opportunity to feel up my tit, but he didn't. This was new territory, but so far, I liked it.

I nodded and grinned. "Yeah, if someone has to make an honest man out of you, then it might as well be me." I laughed.

His lips brushed against mine, and he leaned me back onto the couch.

"You're all mine," Cade said softly, his breath tickling my ear and causing a shiver down my spine.

Every ounce of my being loved hearing those words roll off his tongue. All worries and fears quickly melted away as he tugged my shirt over my head, and he covered my collarbone and chest in gentle, tender kisses. He was in no hurry this time, and neither was I.

"You're so beautiful," he said, gently sliding my bra straps off my shoulders. I arched into him as he moved his hands around my back, undid the clasp, and moved the material out of the way.

His tongue massaged my nipple, and I moaned, gently raking my nails up his back. He leaned up and tugged his shirt off, then covered my body with his. We were skin to skin. Although we'd fucked a few times, this was different. His eyes flickered with a mix of desire and emotion.

He leaned to the side, his fingers skimming down my stomach to my jeans. He flipped the button open and eased them over my hips, his attention never leaving my body. I kicked my jeans to the floor, and he gently parted my legs.

"I love touching you, feeling you quiver when you're about to come," he said softly. His thumb danced across my clit, and I arched into his touch. "Nice and slow for me babe."

His fingers spread me apart, and he slipped one finger inside me slowly. I latched onto his arm for support. His mouth teased my nipple while he moved his finger in and out of me. I whimpered and raised my hips to meet him. I wanted him hard and fast, but he wasn't having it.

Cade scooted off the couch and removed his jeans. He rolled on a condom and wrapped his hand around his shaft as his gaze traveled from my core, up my stomach, chest, and finally my eyes.

"I need you inside of me," I whispered.

He settled over me, guided his cock to my entrance, and paused. In one slow motion, he eased inside. Every magnificent inch of him filled me.

"Cade," I whimpered.

"Does it feel good, babe?" he asked, moving his hips in a circular motion.

"Yes," I panted. I dug my nails into his ass cheeks while he continued. Our bodies found the perfect rhythm, and for the first time I felt as though I truly saw all of Cade. All of his fears, vulnerabilities, kindness, and all the love he had inside him. And it rocked me all the way to my soul.

CHAPTER 14

J spent the rest of the afternoon naked and in Cade's arms. Nothing I'd ever experienced before compared to this moment. Safe, accepted, comfortable. Neither my relationship with Asher nor with Jeremiah had even come close. It was funny how I'd thought I'd loved them both, but maybe I was in love with the idea. I didn't know. What I did know was that I was in different territory, and I thought Cade was worth the risk. Hopefully, I was right.

Cade slipped his arm around my waist as we exited the dressing room.

"I don't want to go back yet," he admitted while we walked down the hallway.

"Me either, but you have a performance in a few hours."

He stopped mid-step and turned toward me. "You'll be there, right?" he asked.

"In the front row, hanging onto every word," I said sliding my hands around his neck.

"I can't believe you're really here with me, Mac." He shook his head in dismay. "Those years you were with Asher ... watching how he treated you, how you hung onto his every word, broke me. But now you've realized what I knew all along, that he doesn't deserve you. You stood up to him and demanded to be respected. You amaze me with your kindness and strength. I'm so proud of how far you've come, but I'm even prouder to call you mine."

He tilted my chin up with his finger and brushed his lips against mine. Heat swirled in my stomach as our mouths parted, and our tongues tangled. His fingers grazed the back of my neck, then speared through my hair.

"Thank you, and I'm elated to be next to you. Never in a million years would I have thought you'd belong to me, and I wouldn't have it any other way."

He kissed me slowly, passionately.

"If we don't stop, I'm going to take you back into the dressing for a quickie," I said, breathlessly.

Cade's chuckle rumbled through his chest before he backed away.

"Tonight, I'll take care of you," he said, twirling a strand of my hair between his fingers. "By the way, I love your braids, but I like your hair down even better."

"Yeah?" I asked, suddenly shy. I loved that he noticed the little things, and for the first time in forever, I felt like someone really saw me for me.

"We better get going. I need to get back to the bus and here by six. I need to make sure John is awake, too." He grinned, took my hand and led me out of the auditorium. The minute we were in public, we dropped each other's hands and kept a safe distance between each other. It sucked on every level possible.

AN HOUR AND A HALF LATER, Cade and I were shooting each other nervous glances backstage. Not only was he worried about singing, but I suspected our little secret as well as knowing he had to talk to Hendrix were also weighing heavily on him. They certainly were on me.

I excused myself and ran down the back hallway to the women's bathroom. My anxiety had kicked into overdrive the second I'd seen Hendrix. He was going to blow his lid. Not to mention my best bestie would be furious with me for hiding my new relationship with Cade.

I hurried to a stall, closed the door behind me, and rifled through my purse. I twisted the cap off the vodka and took several drinks. I grimaced as it burned down my esophagus and into my stomach. Leaning my head against the stall door, I wondered what was going through Cade's mind. Was he regretting everything he'd said to me earlier? Had he realized I wasn't worth the risk of losing his career and best friend?

I inhaled sharply and quickly regretted it. The bathroom wasn't typically the best smelling place to breathe deeply, and this one was no exception. I tilted the bottle up and took a few more drinks before I replaced the lid and tucked it back into my purse.

Slipping out of the stall, I dampened a paper towel and blotted my face. I knew my makeup would melt off shortly, but I wanted to look my best as long as I could.

"Suck it up, girl. You know your brother is going to lose his shit, but you and Cade are adults. It will be alright. Everything will be okay," I said to my reflection, but deep inside, I wasn't sure if it was the truth.

Hendrix's voice echoed down the hallway as I hurried back to where they were backstage. The band was running over a few minor changes before the performance when I stepped behind the curtain. I scanned the area, noting all the security backstage, but I didn't see Pierce.

"Anyone have any questions?" Hendrix asked, his attention bouncing between John, Cade, and Gemma.

They all shook their heads. It seemed like everyone was a bit more nervous than usual. I wasn't sure how they did it honestly. The second I strolled on stage, I'd full on faint.

"Hey, how ya doing?" Hendrix asked, walking over to me.

"Good," I said, smiling. "Where's Pierce? I don't see him anywhere."

"We have more than enough security tonight, so I gave him the night off. Hopefully he'll get drunk and laid," Hendrix chuckled. "He works so much I think he forgets how to have any fun."

I giggled. "The crowd is really ramping up out there," I said, peeking through the curtain.

"Yeah, I know. The first little bit out there in front of that many people never gets easier, but once we start playing it all falls into place."

"Yes, it does, but Hendrix is right, this part never gets easier," Gemma said, slipping her arm around Hendrix's waist. He leaned down and kissed her. My focus bounced to Cade and found his attention was also on me. He glanced around before giving me a subtle wink. Maybe he was still okay with his decision.

"Alright, let's do this," Hendrix said, motioning for everyone to gather around him.

We all moved our arms around each other and grinned. The energy in the auditorium was insane.

"Let's give it—"

Hendrix's cell phone vibrated loudly, cutting off his words. In quick succession Gemma's, then mine, John's, and Cade's phones sounded. Our arms dropped as we all fumbled for our phones, frowning. How weird was it they were all going off at the same time? Was it Franklin? Was there an emergency?

Gemma gasped, her hand flying to her mouth as her phone clattered to the floor. I tapped the screen and waited for my message to load.

"Mac," Hendrix said, his expression growing alarmed.

Suddenly, I heard my voice come from Cade's phone.

"Mac, don't look," Cade said, attempting to grab my phone, but I dodged him.

Gemma ran toward me, but it was too late. I'd seen all I needed to.

My mouth hung open when I saw the video had already gone viral. How? How had this happened?

Everyone stared at me, their faces filled with disbelief and pain.

Without a word, I darted off the back of the stage, down the hall, and out the back-auditorium door. The stale, hot air took my breath away. I had no idea where I was going, but I couldn't stay there and deal with the way my friends and family had looked at me.

Tears streamed down my cheeks as I hightailed it through the parking lot and in the direction of the bus. I had no intention of going there in case Pierce was hanging out. I couldn't look at anyone right now anyway.

I hooked a sharp right and recalled the park and water fountain Cade had pointed out earlier in the day. It was nearing dark, but I would be able to hide there for a while.

Within minutes, my feet were pounding across the soft grass to my destination. A large palm tree stood on the far side, and I slipped behind it. Sobbing, the soul-shattering truth of what I'd seen on my phone brought me to my knees. That son of a bitch had gotten to me again.

A MILLION THOUGHTS rushed through my mind as I recalled the video someone had released of me when Brandon had me in captivity. Although I knew he was behind it, I wasn't sure how he'd set it up. He'd apparently had someone on the outside prepare and send it.

My chest ached. Everyone who mattered to me had seen it at

the same time. I'd never even told my therapist about what Brandon had done to me, and now the entire world knew.

The bitter sting of the violation settled deep inside me as I leaned against the trunk of the tree and drew my knees up into my chest. The sky burned a brilliant orange, then the sun set, leaving me in darkness, but I didn't care. I grabbed my purse and pulled out my bottle of vodka. I downed as much as I could stand without choking it back up and waited for the alcohol to numb me. How in the hell would I ever be able to look at my brother again? Or Cade? He wouldn't even want to touch me after what he'd seen.

Oblivion wasn't coming fast enough, so I scrambled through my purse again and located my bottle of Xanax. I rolled the bottle in my hand, weighing my options. My pulse pounded wildly while I realized I'd never be free from Brandon. I'd never be free from what he did to me, the pain and the constant fear. Nothing helped. Not Cade, not the alcohol, or the pills. Nothing could make this right again, except one thing.

I glanced at the bottle, eyeing how much vodka I had left. It was enough to wash the handful of Xanax I had left down.

Glancing at my phone, I was shocked to realize I'd been out here for a few hours. I assumed the concert was over and Hendrix and the group would be searching for me. I'd probably screwed up Pierce's night off, too. If I was going to end this miserable excuse of a life I had, I needed to do it before they found me.

I placed the vodka bottle between my legs and twisted the Xanax lid off. There should be enough to do the trick and end it all. Dumping them into my hand, I stared at them through a blurry, tear-filled haze. The vodka had done its job, but now it was time for me to do mine. I inhaled sharply and mentally told everyone I loved goodbye.

"Mac?"

Startled, my hand bounced, and the pills spilled onto the grass. Dammit!

"Mac," a gentle voice came from behind me again.

I squeezed my eyes shut, hoping he'd keep going, but he didn't.

"Mac," Cade said, kneeling down next to me.

"What?" I whispered. "Please, leave me alone."

"I can't. You scared the hell out of us. We've been searching everywhere for you. It finally occurred to me I'd pointed this place out earlier to you."

I turned away from him. There was no way I wanted him or anyone else to see me this fucked up.

The grass rustled as Cade settled in next to me, his shoulder touching mine.

"Holy fuck." Cade grabbed the now empty pill bottle from my hand, his eyes wide with fear. "Did you take them all?" He was breathless, his voice panicked.

"No," I muttered, pointing to the ground where I'd dropped them when he startled me.

He blew out a heavy sigh, leaned over and removed the vodka bottle from between my legs, then stared at me.

"I didn't know," he muttered. "I didn't realize you were struggling so much. But babe, listen, ending your life isn't the answer," he said, choking out the last words. "Come here."

Before I knew it, Cade had pulled me into his lap. His muscular arms wrapped around me like a safe cocoon. He wasn't going to let me go. Laying my head on his chest, the tears returned, and he rocked me while I cried.

"I can't do it anymore, Cade. I'm not as strong as Gemma. Day after day I fight to get up and show everyone I'm alright, but I'm not and now … now the video is out, and everyone saw it. The horror on your faces when you all looked at me," I hiccupped. "Do you know what Brandon said after he forced himself in my mouth and came all over my face? He said I wasn't even worth fucking."

Cade's chest heaved, and he tightened his hold around me.

"He's a bastard, Mac. He lies, he torments, and he's evil. You can't believe anything he said to you, because all he wanted was to hurt and break you down."

"But he did." The tears rushed down my cheeks even faster, and I fisted Cade's shirt, clinging to him.

"I'm here. Please promise me you won't give up. Please, I just got you," he whispered into my hair. "I don't want to lose you again. First it was Asher, then Jeremiah. Promise me, Mac. Talk to me on the really rough days, but don't let Brandon win. Don't let him take you away from everyone who loves you. Don't let him steal your dreams and future."

I sat silently, listening to the soothing yet pleading words flowing from Cade's heart.

"I can't put my happiness on your shoulders, it's not right," I mumbled.

"You're not. I'm simply holding your hand until the darkness passes, and I promise you it will."

I tilted my chin up to him. The alcohol had definitely hit me hard on top of the sudden and intense emotions from Brandon's video. For whatever reason, I never remembered a video camera, but I suspected he'd used his phone. Maybe I'd been so terrified I never realized he was recording my assault, or my brain shut it out.

What I didn't miss was the gentleness and support in Cade's eyes. My heart stuttered back to life as I leaned up to kiss him.

"I'll try," I said.

He tucked a strand of hair behind my ear and kissed my forehead.

"Do or do not. There is no try," he said, imitating Yoda.

I barked out a laugh and smacked him gently on the chest.

"You need to tell your family, Mac. You need some additional support."

My stomach clenched with the thought. Franklin would make me come home right away if he knew I had been seconds away from swallowing a bunch of Xanax.

"I can't, Cade. I'll never be allowed out of the house to see you if they know."

"We can keep this near attempt between us, but only if you promise me you'll tell them how you're feeling."

"I have a therapist, I'll tell her."

Cade shook his head adamantly. "No, you need to tell your family ... or I will."

I gawked at him. "You'd tell?" I asked, the pitch in my voice climbing.

"Only if you don't. They need to know, and you need their love and support. I can't take this lightly. Your life is too important to me."

"Fine. I assume Franklin knows about the video by now anyway, so he'll have everyone stick to me like a fly on a cow patty."

Cade laughed at my southern expression.

"That's Gemma's fault for making me spend time in Louisiana."

A twinge of panic rushed through me, and I slapped my hands over my face. The mere thought of Franklin or even Hendrix seeing what Brandon had done to me nearly crushed me. How in the hell would I be able to look at them again? They'd literally seen me with Brandon's dick shoved in my mouth.

Cade's phone buzzed, and he shifted me off his lap so he could remove it from his pocket.

"Yeah," he said.

I could hear Hendrix on the other line.

"I've got her. Yeah, she's a mess, but she's going to be alright."

His eyes searched me while the words left his mouth. He wanted an answer. I nodded.

"Excellent. I'll let her know, and we'll meet you at the home base shortly. I'm not sure she will be up for talking much tonight, though. I'll have to leave it up to her."

He paused. "Yup. See ya in a bit."

Cade ended the call and shoved the phone in his pocket.

"Good news, Hendrix talked to Franklin, and he called in some favors. The video is down. I realize a lot of people saw it, and there's nothing we can do. But no one else will be able to view it now. That part is over."

I nodded and wiped my tear stained cheeks.

"Thanks," I whispered, my voice cracking with emotion.

"I know you don't want to see anyone, but we should get you back," he said, stroking my hair. "The minute everyone is asleep, you come on up to my bed."

"Okay," I said, dread washing over me. Maybe I wouldn't have to talk tonight, but tomorrow we'd be driving to the next city, and there would be plenty of time for conversation. Maybe it would be better to get it over with. I wouldn't know until I saw everyone.

Rising slowly, I stepped back and allowed Cade to stand as well. He slipped his arm around my waist and pulled me against him.

"We're going to get through this together," he said. He leaned down and kissed me gently before he laced his fingers through mine and walked me back to the bus.

Cade's hand never left me as we walked up to the steps to where an anxious Hendrix, Gemma, John, and Pierce were waiting for us.

CHAPTER 15

"Mac," Gemma said, running toward me and flinging her arms around me. "I was so worried about you. Are you alright?" she asked, releasing me and searching me for any telltale signs of what I was really feeling.

"I'm fine."

Cade cleared his throat from behind me, reminding me of our agreement.

I squeezed my eyes closed for a moment and opened them again.

"No, I'm not fine."

Gemma took my hand and dragged me to the couch. Hendrix's gaze followed us as he sat down in the recliner on the other side of the small room. John, Pierce, and Cade remained standing against the wall and bar. I glanced at Cade, and he nodded.

My knee bounced while I attempted to form the right words. Saying it wasn't easy, but it would be just as difficult for them to hear.

"Hendrix," I said, "I'll tell you guys everything, but you can't tell Franklin."

His forehead creased, and he clasped his hands together. "I can't agree to anything yet, Mac."

I nodded. "Fine." I leaned back against the couch and sucked in a deep breath. "I don't know what else was on the video, but everyone saw enough ... You ... you got a clear picture of what Brandon did to me. Ever since that night ... It ... I think he broke me," I choked out my last words.

Pain etched across my brother's face, and Gemma linked her fingers through mine.

"I have horrible nightmares if I can sleep at all, and I think I see him everywhere I go. I'm terrified he'll show up and hurt us again." Even though I couldn't articulate it in front of John and Cade—Hendrix, Gemma, and Pierce knew it was more than Brandon. But John and Cade couldn't find out about the society. I looked at Gemma and continued. "Unfortunately, instead of getting better, things have gotten worse. In order to sleep, I've been mixing Xanax and vodka, plus ..." I groaned. "I have a stash of edibles."

Hendrix's eyebrows knitted together but he didn't say a word. He merely ran his hands over his hair and waited for me to continue. But I knew him well enough to know he'd have a lot to say to me soon enough.

"Pierce actually confronted me while we've been on the road. He noticed a few times I was drinking during the day. I know you're disappointed in me, but I can't deal with it anymore." I turned toward Gemma. "I don't know how you did it. How did you get through the depression and the terror that they might find you again?"

"Mac," she said gently. "I wouldn't have without Ada Lynn. She was with me every day."

Tears pricked the back of my eyes with the mention of her name. I'd forgotten that Ada Lynn was the only person my bestie had to turn to after her own trauma. At least I was fortunate enough to have everyone here. "I miss her," I said quietly.

"Me too," Gemma replied. "This is what I can tell you. It will get better, but only if you talk to us. We love you so much. I know exactly what you're going through, but we're not the only ones. There are support groups for rape victims, your therapist, you can stay with Hendrix and me anytime you need us. I'm sure Franklin would be fine if you wanted to tour with us longer as well. I mean, you can take online classes. We can work it out. You're not alone in this. Not by a long shot. Once you realize it and let us in, that's when you start the healing process."

"She's right," Hendrix agreed. "But for now, as we're working through everything, no more drinking or pills. If you want to stay with us, that's the deal."

"No drinking at all?" I complained. "Hendrix, alcohol isn't the problem, it's the pills with the it."

Hendrix stood and stared at me. "Mac, I'm only going to say this once. First, your behavior is dumb as shit for transporting edibles over the state line. It's a federal offense. Do you realize the situation you put us all in?"

"Oh my God. I'm sorry. It never crossed my mind, Hendrix. I'm so used to living in a state where it's legal. Please, you've gotta believe me. I wouldn't do anything to hurt you or the band on purpose."

Hendrix's shoulders relaxed a little. "Now you know. Don't ever do it again. I want you to hand it all over—pills, edibles, everything. And as an extra measure, I'm going to search your stuff. Since you're prescribed Adderall, I'll give you the daily dose and watch you take it. I think you should give it a chance. It might really help, Mac. As far as the alcohol, you can drink as long as we're all together."

Fuck. I'd just been grounded by my brother. My leg bounced up and down as I realized my Xanax days were over. Not only had they spilled all over the ground in the dark, but I was out of refills. Even if I wanted more, my therapist had been clear she wouldn't refill the prescription early. But for the first time since

I'd started popping the pills, I wanted to stop. I'd almost ended my life, and it's not what I wanted. I was just desperate to make the pain and fear go away.

"I'll take care of it in a few minutes, Mac. I need to speak with Cade first." Hendrix turned to Cade, his jaw tensing and their gaze deadlocking.

Crap, he must have seen us holding hands. In our defense, it'd been a fucked-up night, and Cade had been supportive. But from the anger on Hendrix's face, he realized there was more going on.

"Outside," Hendrix said gruffly.

Cade didn't argue as he opened the door and walked down the steps. Hendrix followed, paused, and whispered something to Pierce. I swallowed down my fear while I watched Hendrix disappear. Pierce stood in front of the door, blocking anyone from joining the guys outside.

"What the hell?" Gemma asked, jumping from her seat. "What's going on?"

I grabbed her arm.

"You might want to sit down for this," I said, guilt ripping me in two for not telling her sooner.

Confusion danced across her features while she stared at me.

"You're fucking with me, right?" Hendrix yelled, his voice carrying through the parking lot.

I hopped out of my seat and made a beeline to the window.

"No, man. I wouldn't do that. Not over this," Cade's voice wasn't as loud as Hendrix's, but he was obviously trying to make a point. Although I knew Cade was worried how this would play out, his voice remained even.

"Do what? What in the hell are they arguing about?" Gemma asked, her cheeks flushing with alarm.

"Cade and I are together," I blurted.

Slowly, she turned toward me. But before she could say another word, a loud thud smacked the side of the bus.

We scrambled to see what was going on, but from what I

could tell the guys were directly underneath the window and we didn't have a clear view.

"You and Cade, huh?" John asked from behind me.

Reluctantly, I turned to look at him. It was hard seeing that I'd disappointed my friends.

"When?" Gemma asked. "Wait, the song. Ohh, I was right, wasn't I?" Her brows arched up with her realization.

I tossed my hands up in surrender. "I didn't know at the time you mentioned it. He told me after rehearsal."

"You son of a bitch," Hendrix yelled.

"Pierce! Let me out," Gemma said, running to the door. "He's going to hurt Cade."

"I don't doubt it," Pierce said dryly. "I can't let you or anyone else out. Let them deal with it. Once they do, it will most likely be over."

"If we're lucky," Gemma said, glancing at me.

My shoulders slumped forward in defeat. What had Cade and I been thinking? Inwardly I groaned as I realized I'd lost my damned pills in the grass. I sure as hell needed something to take off the edge right about now.

Knots formed in my stomach with each additional sound of the guys' punches. I sighed and sank into my seat, hiding my face in the palms of my hands.

"I know you're my best friend, but goddammit, I've been in love with her for years," Cade snarled.

My head snapped up. Had I heard him, right?

No one said a word as they stared at me. Even Pierce raised an eyebrow.

Why hadn't he told me? We could have gone to Hendrix together. If Cade had been honest, it might have gone smoother. Hendrix understood what it felt like to not be with someone you loved. But now, he most likely felt betrayed by both of us, which compounded the situation. By the look of it, Gemma was definitely upset too.

Eventually, Hendrix's and Cade's voices quieted. As hard as I strained to hear them, I couldn't make out anything they were saying. Nausea seesawed in my stomach.

"Did you know?" Gemma asked, sitting down next to me.

I shook my head. How had this night turned into shit? This was supposed to be Cade's big night and first solo performance of the song he'd written for me.

"He only admitted he had feelings for me earlier today. He never said anything about ... about ..." I couldn't finish as a tear streamed down my cheek.

"Being in love with you?" She placed her hand on my back and waited for my response.

"Yup," I squeaked.

"Mac, why are you crying?"

"Because this is fucked up, and I shouldn't have found out this way. Cade and Hendrix should not be beating the hell out of each other in the parking lot, and instead of everyone being mad at me ... Why can't they be happy we're together? I need something good in my life right now, and I wish everyone could support us."

Gemma released a slow sigh. "We need some time to adjust is all. Cade has been such a player. I really think it's why Hendrix is so pissed. And I suspect he's also disappointed Cade didn't ever confide in him. They're best friends."

"I know. I'm no better," I said, peeking at her.

"Did you want to tell me?" Her eyes filled with sadness.

"Omigosh so so so bad. But I couldn't tell you and ask you to keep it a secret from Hendrix. That's why I didn't say anything. It had nothing to do with me not wanting to tell my best friend. It was the position I would have put you in. Please, Gemma. Please try to understand."

Gemma paused for a moment. "Mac, I do understand. I really do. It was a tricky situation, and it sounds like you two are brand new, so you're trying to figure out where this is going. If you recall, I didn't tell Ada Lynn about Hendrix for several months.

The only reason you knew is because you were right there through it all."

"Really?" I asked, a small amount of relief spreading through me.

"Yeah. You and I are good." She gave me a quick hug and smiled.

John cleared his throat but didn't say anything, and I looked over in his direction. I couldn't get a good read on his thoughts.

"Do you think Hendrix will ask Cade to leave the band?" I asked, my fingers nervously drumming on my leg.

"What?" Gemma exclaimed. "No. Is that what you two are worried about?"

"Well, yeah. I mean, we all know Cade's activities up until now haven't been what Hendrix would want for me."

"I wish you would have talked to me. Hendrix might be pissed, but they'll work it out. You know Hendrix is overall a really fair guy. He and Cade go too far back, and they're more than friends. They're family. Just like we are," Gemma said, soothingly.

"You think?" I asked, cringing with the thought of Cade losing his career.

"If there's even a murmur of something, I'll let you know, and we'll take care of it together. Our guys can be a bit hard-headed sometimes, but I think everyone will adjust to the changes. Plus, Hendrix knows what it's like to fall in love. All he wants is for you to be with a guy who loves and cherishes you. If Cade's the guy to do it, I'm in. You have my full support."

"Really? You mean it?" I asked, gratitude swelling inside me.

"You do remember you're the reason Hendrix and I are together, right?"

I laughed softly. "I might have encouraged it a little."

"It's been a hell of a night, and everyone is on edge after the video and your confession concerning Cade. On top of it, we all found out tonight he's in love with you. I think we need a few days to settle down. Not to mention you need to process the information for yourself. It's a big deal. I seriously doubt he'd planned for you to find out this way, either."

"I've been sleeping in his bed," I confessed, my leg bouncing with yet another confession tonight. "The first night on the road the nightmares started again. Cade made sure I was okay and told me I could sleep next to him." I fiddled with the hem of my polo shirt, then glanced at her. "He never even tried anything, Gemma. He promised I was safe and to get some sleep."

"That sounds nothing like Cade," John chimed in. "Dude must be whipped." A slow grin eased across his face. "I knew something was going on with him, but I didn't realize you were the change. I should have known, but I've had my head in the music and the tour. If you got this guy to settle down, Mac, it says a hell of a lot about what an amazing girl you are. Don't ever doubt it," John said, shoving his hands in his pockets.

"I think I'd have to agree with John," Pierce said.

Gemma smiled and squeezed my hand. "We all love you, Mac. No one could ever replace you."

I smiled shyly, overwhelmed with their kindness.

Just then, the door clicked and opened.

CHAPTER 16

"Holy hell," I said as Hendrix entered the living area first. His hair was a mess, and he had a good size knot and gash on his cheek. Cade walked in behind him, his eye already sporting a shiner.

Gemma folded her arms across her chest and stared at them both, her foot tapping against the carpet.

"Are you two finished now?" she asked, displeasure clear in her tone.

My mouth hung open as I shot her a look. Hendrix looked over at Cade and back at us.

"Yeah. We're done," Hendrix replied.

"Told you," Pierce said, attempting to hide his grin.

I heaved out a sigh and slapped my palm against my forehead. Why did dudes have to be Neanderthals to work their issues out? My gaze landed on Cade, and he gave me a reassuring smile.

"Let's get you cleaned up," Gemma said, taking Hendrix's hand. "We're going to get some sleep, and we can talk in the morning, Mac."

"Thanks," I said, my attention focused solely on Cade. I

approached him, my anxiety over the situation creeping up a few notches. "Are you alright? We … we heard some of what was said."

"Oh." He pursed his lips into a thin line and stared at his feet. After a moment, his eyes found mine. My stomach flip flopped. Even with a black eye, Cade was hot as hell. "I'm not in a rush, Mac. I know my feelings are ahead of yours, but you're worth the wait."

I flung my arms around his neck and buried my face against his chest. He placed a soft kiss on the top of my head and wrapped me up in the safety of his strong arms.

"Well, I've had enough entertainment for tonight. I'm off to get some sleep," John said, waving at us before he strolled down to the beds and disappeared behind his curtain.

"I'm going to clean up my eye, and I'll meet you in my bed. Everyone knows, so there's no reason to sneak around anymore."

I hesitated for a minute. "I'm relieved they know. I'm sorry you and Hendrix found it necessary to beat the hell out of each other, but at least it's out in the open. I felt like complete crap hiding it from them."

"Me too," he said, taking my hand in his. "Let's get some sleep."

NEITHER OF THE guys looked as bad as I'd assumed they would the next morning. After the evening's drama fest, we all slept in until almost noon.

The conversation was light while we gathered around the table at a local diner for breakfast. Thank goodness the café wasn't crowded. After the release of Brandon's video and the knowledge it had gone viral, I wondered if every person that looked at me had seen it. It was difficult enough knowing the people I cared about saw it, much less strangers. Even though Cade and Hendrix appeared back to normal for the most part, the previous evening weighed heavily on me. Not only had Cade caught me before I attempted to end my life, but constant images of Brandon bombarded me as I had lain awake all night.

"You alright?" Cade asked, pulling out a chair for me. I hadn't missed the protective expression Hendrix threw Cade's way and neither did Gemma. She smiled and gently rubbed his back while they sat down. She gave me a discreet wink, and I inwardly heaved a sigh of relief. For whatever reason, Gemma believed in us, and I loved her for it. I needed my bestie right now.

"Yeah, I've got a lot on my mind," I said, gazing up at him.

"I can't promise you cherries and rainbows, but we'll get through it." He placed a kiss on my cheek, then busied himself with the menu. Although Hendrix and Cade said they'd work things out, I'd not had a chance to talk to my brother yet. My heart ached with the thought we were growing apart. There was a time we confided in each other about everything. But since he'd been on the road, things were changing. I couldn't let that happen.

I grabbed my phone out of my purse, my fingers dancing across the screen.

I'm sorry I didn't tell you. Please don't be mad at me. I can't stand it. I already miss seeing and talking to you like we used to. Please, promise me Cade won't pull us apart.

I stared at it and hit send. Hendrix's phone vibrated against the table, and he picked it up. His poker face was solidly in place, and it was impossible to figure out what he was thinking.

My phone buzzed with a response. Chewing my bottom lip, I read the message.

Honestly, I figured something might be going on, I just wish you'd come to me first. I'm more concerned about the pills. I should have been there for you. It broke my fucking heart to hear you talk about it last night, and all I could think about was how I'd failed you. Unfortunately,

Cade took the brunt of my anger and frustration, but he did it for you. That tells me he's for real, Mac. He has his issues like we all do. And for the record, nothing in this world will tear us apart. You're stuck with me.

A ball of emotions erupted inside me, and I released a small cry. I covered my mouth with my hand, willing the tears away, but it wasn't happening.

"Babe?" Cade asked, confusion flickering in his eyes.

Unable to say anything, I squeezed his hand, stood up, and excused myself. Pierce followed me outside and into the parking lot. He kept his distance, though, which I appreciated.

"Mac," Hendrix said, approaching me.

Without another word, Hendrix wrapped his arms around me while I snotted all over his black T-shirt.

"I'm sorry I wasn't there for you. You and Gemma are my entire world. I couldn't stand it if anything ever happened to you. What the son of a bitch did ..." Hendrix's words trailed off as my body trembled against him. "I love you, little sister," he said.

"I love you, too. I was terrified you'd hate Cade or me. It was wrecking me on top of everything else, and I lost my shit. I haven't been using pills and edibles very long. I promise."

"It's alright. Everything's out in the open now so we can work through it."

I shuddered with my last tears and pulled away from him.

"Thank you ... for not giving up on me."

"Never," he said, smiling at me and tapping the end of my nose with his finger.

Relief washed over me, and I began to settle down. Whether he realized it or not, my brother and our relationship was every-thing to me.

"Omigosh, I'm fucking starving."

Hendrix chuckled, and slid his arm around my shoulders, pulling me against him.

"Nothing like a little stress to make my sister hungry, huh?"

I giggled. "Yeah, I think some unlimited pancakes are in order."

Wiping my cheeks off the best I could with my hands, I attempted to pull myself together before Cade saw me.

"I think I'm going to sneak off to the bathroom and freshen up before I join everyone at the table," I said while Hendrix opened the door for me.

"See ya in a minute, then."

I hurried across the diner and down the hall before Cade even spotted me. It was strange I cared. It was even more strange we were together after knowing each other for years, but he was what I wanted. At least I was clear about one part of my life.

Pushing the bathroom door open, I turned the faucet on and let the cold water run. I splashed my cheeks and dried off with a paper towel. Peering into the mirror, tired brown eyes returned my stare. At least Cade and I were no longer hiding our relationship, and I was no longer carrying around secrets that were impossible to manage on my own.

A few minutes later, I slipped back into my seat and took Cade's hand.

"Hendrix ordered for you," he said, smiling gently. "I forgot how much you can eat when you're stressed out."

Heat traveled up my neck and cheeks, and I fidgeted in my chair.

"You used to laugh about it, but I don't think you considered that one day we'd be dating and you'd be buying me dinner."

"Sucker," Hendrix said, snickering.

The diner filled with laughter as the realization fully dawned on Cade. His focus cut over to me, and a silly grin eased across his face.

"I have a good job, I can afford it," he said and smiled proudly.

"Do you remember when you used to get the box of fruit loops, throw one at a time at me, and I'd catch them with my mouth? You and John thought it was seriously entertaining. Poor Mom. She always came home to a wrecked house when you guys were over. Which was like every day," I said, giggling at the memory.

Hendrix laughed and leaned back in his chair. "Janice wasn't too happy about the mess we made, but she was pretty cool about it."

Our food arrived, and Cade took a bite of his pancake. "Hell, we could all eat, and no matter what, your mom always stocked food at the house for us. Since I'm grown, I probably should give her some money for all the waste. I mean, we had multiple food fights when she was working."

"Gem-ma! They haven't changed," I said. "They just do it in public now, too."

Everyone burst into laughter while we reminisced over breakfast, and shared stories with Gemma. And for the first time in years, I felt like I was finally where I belonged.

The sound of Hendrix's phone interrupted our boisterous conversation. He leaned over, reading the name that popped up on the screen.

"It's Franklin. I'll be right back," he said to us. He tapped the phone and raised it to his ear.

"Hey, Dad."

Fear bubbled up inside me. Although I had assumed we'd hear from him today, I dreaded talking to him about the video. Even though it was offline, Franklin wouldn't let it go. He'd track down the source and use any means necessary, then he'd go in for the kill. He was one hell of an attorney unless he was drinking. Not to mention he had very powerful connections across the country. I'd never want to fuck with him, that's for damn sure. But when he was on my side, life seemed a little better.

I glanced over at Pierce, who had a protective eye on us as well as Hendrix outside. To my surprise, he pulled out his cell phone and took a brief call. His body visibly tensed when my brother strolled back inside.

Hendrix rubbed his jawline, his eyes locking with Pierce's. He turned to us, stood at the end of the table, and hesitated.

Shit. What was going on?

CHAPTER 17

$\mathcal{U}$nfortunately, I'd seen the same look on Hendrix's face in the past, and it wasn't good. Not even close.

"Babe?" Gemma asked, touching his arm. "What's going on?"

"We need to get our food to go. I can't talk here," he said, scanning the few people in the restaurant.

Uneasiness pulled at me. Was this news about Brandon? Had he been released on a technicality? Was his father following us? My thoughts sped into overdrive as we gathered to go boxes and quietly left the restaurant.

Hendrix slid his arm around Gemma, and Cade laced his fingers through mine. His thumb stroked the back of my hand while we all walked quietly.

"This is bad," I whispered, looking up at Cade.

"I'm right here. I'm not leaving your side. Whatever is going on, you're not alone."

My heart galloped into overdrive as we all filed onto the bus.

"Let's go, Mike!" Hendrix yelled toward the front. The engine roared to life, and we eased forward.

"What's going on?" I asked, placing my hands on my hips. "Hell, I didn't even know Mike was on the bus. Fuck. It is Mike, right? I mean we didn't get hijacked, or something did we? Pierce? Did you look?" I ran up to the front and poked my head around the corner of the driver's seat. "Omigosh. All of this is freaking me the fuck out. You're lucky you're you, Mike."

Mike gave me an alarmed look and returned his focus to steering.

"Sorry, sorry. It's been a bad few days," I muttered, backing away.

I clung onto the bar and furniture as Mike turned out of the parking lot and onto the road. What bothered me more than me trippin' was that my brother hadn't stopped me.

When I finally reached Cade, he pulled me into his lap and tucked a strand of hair behind my ear. Hendrix hadn't let Gemma go, either. They were wedged together in the recliner.

Hendrix swallowed visibly, repositioned Gemma in the chair, then stood. He leaned against the bar and crossed his ankles while his blue eyes focused on each of us, then landed on John and Cade.

"It's not public knowledge but Pierce is ... although he's employed with Westbrook's Security firm, he also consults with the FBI on some cases. Dad employed him a little over a year ago, but the FBI was also tracking Gemma and her father. Pierce was a part of the team. When Gemma moved from Louisiana to Spokane, well, they realized her father's connection with the Dark Circle Society spread across the country and led directly to Brandon and his father, Dillon." Hendrix's jaw visibly tensed as he paused.

"Dude, the FBI?" Cade said, shock flickering across his features. "I knew you were a bodyguard, but this is an entirely different level. And why now? I mean, why is Hendrix telling us this now?"

"It's a good question, and I'll get to it in a minute," Pierce said, picking up where Hendrix had left off. "Dillon Montgomery's grandfather was one of the founding members of the Society, instrumental in building it to what it is now. Dillon worked alongside his grandfather for years before the old man died. The Society is a carefully orchestrated operation. The victims are typically related to a member—daughter, niece, step-daughter. Makes it easier to plan an assault if they know when the girls might be alone and vulnerable."

Horror danced across Cade's expression.

"So Brandon was a part of it too? I thought he was arrested for the rapes on the college campus." For the first time, he was learning the entire story. Which meant there was a new development. Otherwise Pierce and Hendrix wouldn't be supplying the information.

I peeked over at John, but he remained quiet with his hands shoved deep in his pockets. From the looks of it, he was chewing on the information. It was a lot to handle.

"Pierce was with us that night ..." Gemma's words trailed off. "The night Mac was kidnapped. He coached me on how to take Brandon down when I traded myself for Mac."

"Mac? You knew all of this?" Cade asked, the color draining from his handsome face.

"I'm so sorry, Cade. We weren't allowed to discuss any details. The FBI worked with a judge and sealed all the information except about Brandon's arrest for kidnapping and assault. The media was forbidden to release most of the footage they had, including images of Pierce. He's still working the case. It's not really closed like the public was led to believe."

"So all this time on the road, Pierce has been more than your bodyguard, he's working a huge fucking case?" Cade shook his head in disbelief and looked at Hendrix. "Dude, I just thought your dad had enemies because he was an attorney and super rich. I had no fucking clue this was so big." His focus bounced from Hendrix to Pierce then settled on me. "Your nightmares," he said, his voice hovering above a whisper. He clutched my hand, and his shoulders slumped forward with the weight of this new reality. "You're not safe yet. This isn't over."

Tears streamed down my cheeks.

"It's not over for any of us, and now you and John are caught up in it. I'm so sorry, man." Hendrix rubbed his forehead then nodded at Pierce.

"Although he wore a disguise, facial recognition picked up Dillon's location today. He was a few miles from our cafe this morning."

Gemma and I gasped in unison.

"He has the balls to show up in public?" My anxiety increased with each word.

"Unfortunately, he's eluded the FBI since Brandon was arrested. You have to remember Mac, these people are sneaky and highly intelligent. The reason their operation has existed for so long is because they're skilled at staying invisible," Pierce said.

"But why? Why did we have to run? Couldn't you have waited around the corner for him and shot the son of a bitch in the head or something?" I asked.

Pierce attempted to hide his grin, and Cade gently rubbed my back.

"I'd love to take the son of a bitch out, but the society is huge. We need him. He and Brandon are the only connections we have that are part of the actual operation at the moment. They're more valuable to us alive than dead."

No longer able to sit still, I hopped off Cade's lap and paced the small living and kitchen area.

"Well can I at least torture him? I mean, between Gemma and me, I'm pretty sure we could get him to talk. I'd want to come up with something more than pulling a few teeth or fingernails out, though. Even waterboarding would be too good for him. Maybe a few needles in his eyes?" I tapped my finger against my chin while I entertained different scenarios.

"No shit," Gemma agreed. "I'd be happy to help. In my opinion, these people aren't human. I mean, how can someone harm children like they do and not be classified as an animal?"

Cade sank back in his seat and dragged his hands down his face. My insides cringed with regret. Life had been filled with so many secrets lately, and I hated it. It had to be over the top nuts to learn you were inside a federal investigation.

"I have questions," Cade said.

"I'll do my best to answer them, but some of the information I can't share," Pierce replied, folding his muscular arms across his chest.

"Why are you including John and me now?"

"Because you're in danger. We realized there was a chance Dillon would show up during the tour, but we needed to flush him out. It's no secret what the band's schedule is. Now we know for sure he's coming back. There was also the possibility he'd left the country and had gone into hiding."

"Too bad he hadn't literally gone underground and suffocated," I hissed.

"Fuck," Cade said. "Are we going to stop touring? I mean I get it, but I'm the sole provider for my family. I need the money for medical expenses for my mom, and I have a sister to support."

"We have to keep going," Hendrix replied. "If we stop now, it will send Dillon back into hiding. We can't change anything we're doing at this point. We hightailed it out of the restaurant today because Dillon was so close. Franklin had called, and while we were talking, he received information Dillon was close to us. Usually it would come from Pierce or his higher-ups, but since it was urgent, Franklin was notified. It was a coincidence we were already on the phone together when his contact called."

"When Hendrix walked back into the restaurant, I was also notified to move you all out," Pierce said.

"Fire," I muttered under my breath, still plotting revenge. My thoughts ran full speed ahead about how to inflict the most torture on Dillon and anyone else associated with him.

"We'll get him, Mac. But it's not cut and dry," Pierce said.

"Well, one bullet would be pretty cut and dry. Plus, cheap ... I mean it's a few dollars compared to hundreds of thousands if the bastard rots in jail. He gets housing and food the taxpayers have to cough up. What in God's name is right about any of this?" I asked, fisting my hands together in frustration.

"I agree with Mac, but I also know he has others that work alongside him and multiple people are primed and ready to step up and take over the society if something happened to Dillon. Then we'd be at a disadvantage again. We'd be starting from ground zero," Hendrix added.

"Exactly," Pierce said.

"What happens now?" Cade asked.

I stopped my pacing and sank back down on his lap.

"Additional security is on the way. The concert venues will have multiple undercover agents and bodyguards. This doesn't mean you can walk around unaware or go anywhere alone," Pierce explained.

My body went limp, and I buried my hands in my face. "Does this mean Calvin will join us? I have every intention of telling Dad about Cade and me, but it should be a conversation I have, not my bodyguard." I dropped my hands and leaned against Cade's chest.

Pierce actually chuckled.

"So not funny, dude! Like can't you do something with him?" I pleaded.

"There won't be any more security on the bus, Mac. Hendrix is a championship boxer, Gemma is trained in self-defense, you have me ..." Pierce stopped, clearing his throat. "And—

"And me."

My head snapped up, and my jaw dropped open."

CHAPTER 18

"*I*s anybody on this bus who they say they are?" Cade asked, jumping up so quickly he nearly dumped me on the floor. He grabbed my arm and placed me on the couch.

"I work with the same agency as Pierce," John admitted, rubbing his lightly stubbled chin.

Hendrix's brows knitted together in disbelief. "How?" he asked. "Dude, I've known you for years. How would you have snuck it by me?"

Too stunned to speak, I remained still and listened. This crap just kept getting better.

Cade crossed his arms over his chest and anger flashed across his expression.

"I'd considered the military, but I wanted to stay close to home and the band was picking up. When Westbrook's Security approached me, it sounded like a great fit. They recruited me right out of high school. My dad was a sergeant in the Marines, a drill instructor. He managed the family like we were his troops. Insisted I learn to handle and shoot firearms properly and trained me himself in self-defense. He was tough. I was young enough to blend in on a college campus and continue to be friends with you guys. Apparently the firm is short on guys my age which made me more valuable. Remember all the trips I took with my family to visit my grandparents and how we were gone for weeks at a time? I was training."

"You used your grandparents to lie to us? Dude, totally harsh," I sputtered.

John shrugged. "I did what I was told. I was learning and working on small assignments. It was when they realized I was touring with Hendrix ... that's when I was also assigned to keep you guys safe."

My eyes narrowed at him. "You knew." I stood with my hands on my hips. "You knew about Cade and me. And now that I think about it, you were pretending to snore and be asleep, weren't you?"

John's forehead creased. "Yeah. I knew about you and Cade. At first I wasn't too keen on the idea, and I let my personal feelings get in the way of my assignment and protecting you guys."

"The club ... you stuck to me like glue when you saw Cade and I dancing together."

"I'm sorry. I've known him for a long time, and until recently I thought you deserved better, Mac."

In one smooth motion, Cade stepped forward and clipped John in the jaw.

Before he could get another swing in, Hendrix and Pierce grabbed Cade and pulled him away from John.

"For God's sake, you guys have got to stop this. We're all adults, aren't we? I mean, everyone is shocked, and I even understand you feel betrayed, but there is a way bigger picture here. John, thank you for keeping us safe," Gemma said. "But for right now. I'm done. I'm at maximum capacity for any more drama. I can't deal with it right now." She whirled on her heel and hurried toward her bedroom.

At least she had a place to go. All I had was my curtain and two bodyguards.

Cade rubbed his knuckles and glared at John.

"Listen, guys, it's been a hell of a last few days. Gemma, Mac, and I have been dealing with this for a while so we're a little more accustomed to how quickly life can change. But here's the deal. First, we're a band and this is our career. I can't have us fighting. I include myself in that. We either figure out how to move forward and stay friends, or ... I'm canceling the tour, and I'll look for a new guitarist and drummer. There's a much bigger picture here than us. Mac and Gemma are at risk. Brandon hurt them both. Now I'll be goddamned if I'm going to let it happen again. Not to mention the thousands of young girls who have been viciously raped by this society. We can either stick together, remember we're family, and be a part of the solution instead of the problem, or we're done. It's your decision." Hendrix's lips pursed as he gave a disapproving look at Cade and John. "I'm going to spend some time with my girlfriend. I'll need your answer by the time we reach New Mexico tonight."

Pride swelled up inside me. That was *my* awesome brother. He was a take charge kind of guy, and I adored him for it. He even admitted he'd been a part of the problem.

Cade turned to me slowly and held out his hand. I took it, and he led me to the bunks. We quietly climbed into his bed and shut the curtain. I don't think either of us wanted to discuss what had just happened, but we needed some time to wrap our heads around it all.

Silence filled the bus, and my mind raced a million miles an hour. I'd rarely seen Hendrix give someone an ultimatum, but he'd not had any other choice. Shit just got real.

I rolled over onto my side and looked at my him. A part of me was astonished Cade Richardson, reformed playboy, was my boyfriend, and the other part was in awe. Never in a million years would I have thought we'd end up together, but I loved every minute with him.

"Are you okay?" I asked softly.

"Honestly?"

"Always," I said, placing my hand on his chest.

"I don't know. Life took a huge unexpected turn, and I'm not sure what to do with it yet."

A lump formed inside my throat. Had he regretted his decision about me?

"Does this … does this mean you don't want to be with me? I'd understand. It was a huge concern I'd had in the first place. I shouldn't have agreed, it was too much to risk—"

Cade's mouth crashed down on mine, silencing my fears. He rolled me over on my back and pulled away.

"You're the one thing I've done right. I've got a lot of regrets, but not us. Not you." His amber eyes softened while he spoke.

"What do you regret?" I asked, making sure my voice was low enough no one else could hear us.

"A lot. I regret the women and meaningless sex, Mac. I was chasing highs, trying to fill a void."

"What void?" Suddenly, I found myself wanting to reach inside him and heal the pain that was so evident in his face.

His lips brushed gently against mine.

"You. The space inside my heart that was only for you."

My breath caught in my chest. No guy had ever said anything like that to me before. All this time I'd wanted someone to cherish, value, and love me. I wanted to belong and be loved for all my good and all my crazy. And the thing was, it'd been in front of me all this time. Emotion swelled inside me.

"Too much too fast?" he asked, smoothing my hair.

"No. I'm glad you told me." I traced his jawline with my fingertips, taking in every beautiful thing about him. His heart, his protectiveness, and his willingness to be so transparent with me.

I wrapped my hand around the back of his neck and pulled his mouth down to mine. Our lips parted, and his tongue caressed mine. My body ached for his touch, but there was more to it this time.

"I want to make love to you, babe. We have to be seriously quiet, though."

I nodded. There wasn't a single part of me that wasn't craving him on every level.

He rolled off of me, positioning himself on his side. His hand slid underneath my shirt, lingering at the edge of my bra. I lifted up slightly and unhooked the clasp, pushing it through my sleeve and placing it next to me.

"Since we don't have much privacy, I'm not going to take your shirt off." He lifted my top, exposing one of my breasts. He took my nipple between his teeth and sucked it into his mouth. My eyes fluttered closed as I surrendered to his touch and everything else faded away.

Tugging on his shirt, I ran my nails along his muscular back. The heat of his skin sent shivers down my spine.

His fingers lightly trailed down my stomach, only stopping long enough to unfasten my shorts. I wiggled out of them, tossing them next to my bra.

"I know it's tough being quiet, but ..." His thumb danced across the thin fabric of my panties. "I want to take my time and savor every inch of your beautiful body."

How in the hell could I possibly argue?

I chewed my bottom lip while he slowly slid his fingers across my core. He traced my entrance, and I moaned softly into the pillow.

"You're making me so hard it hurts," he said softly against my ear.

I reached for the waistband of his shorts, and he quickly moved my hand.

"Not yet." He moved my panties out of his way and eased a finger inside me.

"Cade," I mouthed, attempting to not yell his name out loud as he slipped another finger inside me.

He scooted down in the bed and trailed soft kisses down my stomach. I gasped as he left the inside of my body.

Cade slid my panties over my hips and tossed them to the side. He glanced up at me and smiled while he settled in between my legs. With the anticipation of his mouth and his hot breath against the inside of my thigh, I was afraid I wasn't going to be able to stay quiet for long.

He gently spread me apart, his tongue running along my wet center.

"So good," he whispered. His mouth found my clit, and he eased his fingers back inside me.

My hands dug into his shoulders while he sucked and licked me. I lifted my hips, moving against him. Desire swirled deep inside me as he continued. Maybe it was the fear of getting caught or maybe it was the fact I knew his true feelings for me, but I couldn't get enough of him.

In record time, my entire body tensed and shuddered with my orgasm. Bunching the blankets between my fingers, I somehow managed not to scream his name.

I whimpered when his mouth left my body.

"Shhh," Cade warned with a smile as he removed his shorts and reached above my head to grab a condom from his stash between the mattress and wall. My attention never left him as he rolled on the protection. Hovering above me, he placed a gentle kiss on my mouth. He lowered his weight on top of me, his cock at my entrance. But this time, his eyes never left mine as he eased inside me. A spark ignited while he moved inside me, our gaze remaining locked. With every thrust, my walls crumbled. With every kiss, he claimed a little bit more of my heart. And with every breath, I willingly gave him more of me.

CHAPTER 19

There wasn't a single moment we weren't on high alert, but New Mexico's concert had gone smoothly, with no threat from Dillon or anyone else.

Cade, John, and Hendrix had settled their differences as well. None of them wanted to leave the band or lose their long-time friendships. And after some consideration, Cade understood John's predicament about working with Pierce. It was a bit odd knowing John was a badass bodyguard, but I felt safer with two of them. Maybe I could swap him out with Calvin on a permanent basis.

Mike had parked at a Wendy's, and everyone had gone inside to order. I'd chosen to hang out with my brother for a few rare minutes alone.

"We go back home after this last stop in Denver, huh?" I asked, plopping down next to him on the couch. He'd been tapping a pencil against his notebook, staring at a blank page.

"Yeah. Sometimes the shows go by really fast, and other times it seems like we're gone forever."

"Well, it's been a month," I replied. "It doesn't feel like it, though. I'm sort of sad it's over for now."

Hendrix placed his paper and pencil down and gave me his undivided attention. "I think it will be good for us to be home for a while. We need to see Dad, and it'll also give you and Cade some time to go on a real date." He grinned and nudged my arm with his fist. "How are you guys doing?"

I raised my eyebrow at him. He and Cade were best friends, I knew how this worked.

"He hasn't told you?"

"Some, but it's different coming from a guy. I need to know how my sister is doing with everything."

I stretched out across the couch, propped my feet up on his lap, and grinned. He always knew what to say to me.

"It's been different, but good if that makes sense. I mean, right out of the gate I found out he was in love with me. Realizing someone is ahead of you emotionally ... well, I felt a little pressure at first. But then ... I remembered all the fun times we had together in high school, all the times he and John were there for me and by my side. Over the years he's always been there, but in the shadows."

"You were also with Asher," Hendrix said, laying his arms across my ankles.

"I have a confession. I always thought Cade was hot. I mean every girl in the school and the surrounding areas did. All I heard was about how gorgeous you and he were. I tuned it out because I was in a relationship. However, the other night I remembered when Asher and I broke up for a while—it was Cade I was interested in."

"Really?" Hendrix asked, surprised.

"I know I never told you, but what girl doesn't have a crush on one of her brother's best friends? It was a moot point though. Asher and I were only broken up for a week, junior year. And when I ended it for good, after the abortion, I was in no place to be thinking about guys and dating. Before I knew it, I was in college, Gemma showed up, then we were living in Louisiana.

Never in like a million jillion years did I ever think Cade had even paid any attention to me other than as your little sister. I brushed it off as my unrequited high school crush."

"Are you saying you've had feelings for him all these years, too?" Hendrix asked.

"I wasn't in love with him, but yeah, the feelings were there." I chewed my bottom lip. "I guess when you're all intertwined in a relationship that may or may not be healthy for you, you lose yourself. It's like you become so entangled with the other person, you don't know where you start or stop anymore. I lost track of what I wanted, and what was important to me. Who was important to me. I couldn't even see what was right in front of me any longer. Does it make sense?"

"Yeah, I've seen it happen with other couples."

"Me too. The thing is, I didn't realize it had happened to me when I was with Asher. I no longer knew who I was as an individual outside of our relationship."

"And now? I realize you and Cade are just starting out, but how do you feel?"

"He already knows who I am. For the first time in my life, other than with you, Franklin, and Gemma ... Hendrix, I don't have to hide who I am. He's seen it all over the years, and he loves me anyway. Without the constant fear nagging at me, I've been able to settle down and get to know him in a new way." I wriggled my eyebrows at him and giggled.

Hendrix tossed up his hands in surrender. "I realize in the past we've talked about sex and our relationships, but now that we spend a lot of time with each other's significant others, those images don't leave my brain. So please, we can talk about anything else, but not those details."

I snickered. "Fair enough. I sure as hell don't want to hear about your head between my bestie's legs. I mean, we all know it's where your mouth has been, but I don't want to know how good you think she tastes or whatever shit you might want to share." I blinked furiously as I realized I'd actually spoken out loud instead of to myself.

Hendrix coughed into his hand, attempting to hide the flush across his cheeks. He was incredibly difficult to embarrass. I almost wanted to give myself a high five.

"Yeah, those things we don't need to discuss," he said, clearing his throat.

"Agreed."

"Do you think Franklin or my mom will have a conniption fit when they find out Cade and I are together?"

"It's hard to tell. Sometimes I think I've got Dad figured out and he reacts the complete opposite, but at least they know Cade."

"Yeah, it's part of what I'm worried about," I said, rubbing my forehead with the palm of my hand.

"You have to keep in mind they don't know Cade like we do. Dad knew Cade played around some, but Dad was our age once, too. He doesn't really know the extent that Cade partied, and it's a good thing."

"True, but he has heard some of the stories. If he thinks there's a problem, you know he'll talk to Mom."

"Yeah, he will, but it's because he really sees you as his daughter, Mac."

"I get it, but it would mean a lot if he and Mom supported us."

"Part of it's up to Cade. He's going to present himself differently in some ways. It's up to him to prove he's grown up and ready to handle a relationship with their daughter."

I twirled a strand of hair around my finger. Even though I'd done alright without the Xanax, I missed it. A lot. It wasn't until the night I'd dumped the pills into my hand that I realized how much I'd depended on them to stop me from constantly reliving the events of my kidnapping. But things were changing for the better.

"And for the record," he said, drumming his fingers on my sandals, "I think he's up for the task."

I couldn't hide my grin. "It helps that you believe in him."

"I see a big difference in him since you've been with us on tour. I've never seen him serious about anyone before. From what he says, he's waited a long time to have a chance with you, and I think he's terrified he's going to blow it to hell."

"Really?" I asked, frowning. I didn't want him to be worried about it. I knew what the constant fear of fucking up felt like, and there was no way I wanted it for him.

"If you're getting serious about him, Mac, you might want to think about how to reassure him a little. If you're still figuring things out, then take your time. I thought you might want to know where he's at."

The door opened, and everyone filed back onto the bus. The smell of fries and burgers filled the small space, and my stomach growled with anticipation.

"Thanks," I said to him. I lifted my feet off his legs and joined everyone at the table to eat.

∼

WE ROLLED into Denver early the next morning. The band was scheduled to play two nights in a row, which left a little bit of time to sightsee. Cade would be performing solo, and this time I wasn't going to miss it.

Since Dillon had been spotted in Arizona, we stayed in pairs. Most of the time we all stayed together, but there were times Cade and I grabbed a few minutes alone.

The group had gathered on the Red Rocks Amphitheatre Stage, and I settled into a seat a few rows back. As they warmed up, Pierce eased into the chair next to mine.

"Hey," I said, surprised he wasn't at the stage standing guard. Glancing over my shoulder, I spotted a few additional security guys up the hill. "The view of the rocks is breathtaking. I've never seen anything like it," I said. "I bet the acoustics will be kick ass, too."

"It's what this amphitheater is known for," Pierce said.

The band started their warm up, and I sighed. "I've loved touring, but in a way, I'll be happy to be home. I guess …"

"You'll still have security at home, but I do have some good news for you."

I turned in my seat, facing him. "Yeah? I could use some of that right now."

"Calvin has been reassigned."

"What?" I slapped my hands over my mouth, realizing I'd yelped.

Pierce chuckled. "I figured you'd be happy about the information."

"Well, wait. He didn't get fired, did he?"

"No, just a different assignment."

"Hmmm. This means I'll have to break in someone new, huh?"

Pierce shook his head and smiled. "You know we're not dogs, right? You don't get to break us in or train us."

"Omigosh. It's not what I meant." I slumped in my chair and stared at him. "I'm sorry it came across wrong. At least as far as you go, you're family, and I'd never think of you in any other way."

Pierce's expression softened for a moment. "Thank you. I've grown pretty fond of you all as well."

"Wait," I straightened in my seat. "Is it John?" I asked, unable to hide the excitement in my voice.

"No, there's too much history for him to remain with you guys. After this, he'll be reassigned if he wants to continue."

"Fuck. Does Hendrix know?" I asked.

"No, and neither does John so keep your mouth shut."

"Why would you tell me?" I asked, puzzled.

Pierce's intense gaze landed on me. "Because I trust you, Mac."

I blinked a few times. He looked serious as hell.

"Holy crap. Thanks." I beamed at him.

"You're welcome." He returned his focus toward the stage.

"So, it's definitely someone new."

"He will be new to you, not to the security firm."

"Well spill already. What's his name? Where's he from? What's he like? Is he hot like you? I mean even Calvin was hot, but he was a total wuss and tattletale. I mean, don't they teach people not to tattle in grade school? Do you think he missed that day?"

"You talk a lot," he said, raising his eyebrow at me.

"Tell me something I don't already know. And so do you. You're stalling. Cough it up, dude."

He smirked and watched me squirm in my seat with anticipation.

"Pierce," I said, grabbing his arm and pulling on it. "You're killing me over here."

He answered with a soft chuckle and patted my hand.

"His name is Zayne."

I dropped my hold from his enormous bicep.

"Huh, interesting. Is he more like you or Calvin?" It wasn't as though I knew a ton of bodyguards to compare them with.

"I'd say me. He's pretty no-nonsense, an honorable, and loyal guy. I personally recommended him. We've worked together in the past, and I know your family well enough to know who would or wouldn't work well by now. He won't report your business to Franklin unless you're in danger somehow. You'll have some of your privacy back."

I flashed him a big grin, relieved and grateful for the information. Although I was ready to head home in some ways, I'd dreaded dealing with Calvin. He'd be the first to snitch me out when I snuck Cade in my room for the night.

Cade's strong tenor voice rang through the speakers, and I stood slowly, hanging on every word he sang.

But it's your heart that makes my life worthwhile.
I'll show up for you, and we'll hold onto each other
No matter what we go through.

Hendrix had stepped back, allowing Cade to own the stage. Gemma sang backup next to John. She'd never stood next to him before. I wasn't sure if they'd made the change because it sounded better vocally or if they were positioning her next to John for security purposes. A part of me wondered if he had a gun hidden nearby. Pierce was always packing.

Cade played the chorus, and every part of my body hummed. His eyes landed on me while he continued to sing, and I didn't move a muscle. This song was for me. Every lyric he'd written was for me. This hot, sexy, guy loved ... Me. The truth traveled straight through my soul.

The second Cade finished and set his guitar down, I scrambled over the few rows of seats in front of me, jogged up the stairs of the stage, and ran straight to him. He laughed as he picked me up, and I wrapped my legs around him.

"I love you," I whispered in his ear. "I am mad crazy in love with you, Cade Richardson."

He stilled, and I drew back from him a little.

"Say it again," he said, searching my face.

"I love you," I said softly.

He tilted back, careful not to topple us over, and let out a whoop that rang through the stage. "She loves me!"

Giggling, I glanced around at my brother, Gemma, and John. I buried my head in Cade's neck, hiding my embarrassment, but at the same time I was thrilled he was so happy he wanted to yell it at the top of his lungs.

He twirled me around and kissed me passionately. Lost in his touch, I was completely unaware we were still in front of everyone.

Hendrix cleared his throat, and we broke our kiss. I peeked behind Cade, expecting to see Hendrix looking irritated, but my brother was full on grinning. Gemma had moved over next to him, her expression filled with excitement.

"Before you say anything, I'd like to remind you that you laid a few hot kisses on your girlfriend in front of a live audience. In fact, it was so steamy I'm pretty sure some babies were made when people got home," I said to Hendrix.

Cade set me down and took my hand. "I think they call those searing kisses. They set everyone around them on fire."

"I'll never forget them, either," Gemma said. Her cheeks flushed slightly as she looked at Hendrix.

"Hell, none of us will." I laughed and peered up at Cade.

He slipped his arm around my waist and pulled me against him.

"I hate to break up the new couple, but we need to finish rehearsal so the first band can have the stage for a while tonight.

"Sorry, I'll go sit back down," I said, raising on my tiptoes to kiss Cade one more time.

I literally bounced across the stage, down the stairs, and back to my seat. Pierce was nowhere to be found.

CHAPTER 20

"*I* love you," Cade whispered, nuzzling my neck. We'd snuck off to one of the dressing trailers after rehearsal. Thank goodness the door had a lock on it, which meant we could get one hundred percent naked.

"I love you, too."

He unbuttoned my dark green shirt and slid it slowly over my shoulders.

"Mmm, nice. I like this bra. Navy blue is a good color on you, but I think it will look better on the floor." His focus landed on the swell of my breasts, and I inhaled slowly while he unfastened my bra and the material fell away from my body.

He bent down and placed his cheek against my sternum. My fingers weaved through his short, soft black hair.

"I could stay here and listen to your heart all day."

"Yeah?" I asked.

"It's because I know it belongs to me. I've waited so long, Mac."

"I'm sorry. I didn't mean to make you wait." I leaned down and kissed the top of his head.

"This is better. Your decision about Asher is final. If we'd gotten together any sooner and he'd wanted you back, I'd have lost you. I don't think I could have handled it."

My heart stuttered with his words. No one had ever loved me so completely. The more time I spent with Cade, the more honest and vulnerable he became with me.

"I'm yours now, babe," I replied.

He placed gentle kisses across my chest and down to my breasts.

"These are the best things God ever made," he said, cupping them.

I giggled. "Lucky for me you're a tit guy. God knows they're big enough."

He took me in his mouth, teasing my nipple. His hands traveled down my bare back and slid into the back of my running shorts, caressing my ass cheeks. In one smooth motion, he pulled my shorts and G-string down. I held onto his arms while I stepped out of them. Tugging on his T-shirt, I slipped it over his head and tossed it into the pile of clothes that were accumulating on the floor.

"I'm also a pussy guy," he mumbled, trailing kisses down my belly, over my hip bone, and between my legs. I gasped as his tongue danced across my clit.

"Oh God," I gasped. He stopped seconds later, and my lower lip stuck out in a pout.

"What's wrong?" I asked.

"Nothing. We have some space and we don't have to be quiet." An impish grin eased across his face.

He stood, shedding his shorts and boxer briefs. There was nothing pretty about the male anatomy, and the females were even worse. But when you were really attracted to a guy, and in love with him too, their peen was the most magnificent thing ever.

"They should use your dick as a mold for vibrators," I blurted.

Cade laughed and took my hand. "I'm glad you're happy with the equipment."

"Very. One hundred percent customer satisfaction over here."

Cade lay down on the floor, his erection pressing against his stomach. I sighed, ready to be filled with every inch of him. Not to mention I could scream his name, and no one was around.

"Come here." He took my hand and guided me until I was standing over his face. "Sit down," he ordered.

My eyes popped open wide. I'd never sat on a guy's face before.

"Are you sure?" I asked. "I mean, can you breathe? Will you die of pussy asphyxiation? What if I'm coming, and I have no idea you're struggling? Then I've killed my boyfriend, and the magazines will all read 'Star guitarist suffocated by girlfriend's twat.' It's not how I want us to be remembered. They'll probably think I'm deformed or something. Like one of my lips was too big and plugged your nose."

"Mac!" Cade said firmly, talking over me and putting an end to my anxiety fueled ramble.

"I'm sorry. I'm so sorry. New things scare me." I sank down on his stomach, my shoulders sagging with embarrassment, frustrated with myself.

"Then we don't have to do it, but for the record I like it. I'm also strong enough to toss you off me if there were some problem, but I swear you're not going to hurt me."

"You're sure?"

"I'm positive." A grin spread across his handsome features. "Don't apologize for rambling babe. I've known you for years, and I'm used to it. I also know it's worse when you're stressed."

"I'm so used to apologizing, Cade."

"No more. I mean if you've done something wrong sure, but don't apologize for being you. Just remember, I fell in love with who you are. All of you. I'm well aware you struggle with ADHD, but it's not what I see when I look at you. I see an amazing, smart, funny, loyal, beautiful woman. You're full of fire, and you're all heart at the same time."

"Cade," I whispered. "You're going to make me cry."

"I don't want to do that unless they're tears of happiness."

I nodded, unable to articulate what I wanted him to know. I reached for his hand and placed it over my heart. Closing my eyes, I imagined he could feel everything I felt at the moment; love, gratitude, belonging, and safety.

"When everything in my world turned so hopeless, you were the light that broke through the darkness." I peered at him, my heart racing with his touch.

Cade swallowed visibly. "I've loved you for a long time. There's nothing I wouldn't do for you. When the days are dark, I'm here. We don't have to talk, just snuggle up to me, and let me love you."

I kissed the palm of his hand, then slowly moved down his body. My core rubbed against his throbbing cock.

"Cade? I guess I should have asked this before we had unprotected sex, but I wasn't thinking beyond wanting you inside me ... have you ever gone bareback with another girl?"

He placed his hands gently on my hips. "Mac, I know I've been around, but I've never once had unprotected sex. I've also gotten tested every six months. I realize my previous behavior was risky, but I'm clean—"

Before he could say another word, I slipped my hand around him and slid him inside me.

"I'm on the pill," I whispered, feeling every bare inch of him slide inside me.

His eyes fluttered closed while he raised his hips up and released a slow moan.

I leaned forward, placing my hands on his chest. "I wanted to be the first girl you had sex with without a condom. We've both been with other people, but I want to cherish our time together in new ways we've not experienced before."

"Jesus, Mac." He thrust upward, digging his fingers into my hips. "You're my first," he said, panting.

"Cade," I whimpered, leaning back and rocking against him. "You feel so good."

He sat up, and I wrapped my legs around his waist.

"I love you," he said, kissing me slowly. His tongue swept across mine and we found our rhythm.

"I'm sorry, Mac," he mumbled. "I'm used to wearing a rubber. You feel so good, I can't hold on." He bucked up, clinging to my hips as he released deep inside me. He eased his finger between our bodies and massaged my clit, still moving inside me even though he'd already come.

"I want to watch you, Mac. I want to feel you clench around me and call my name. Tell me you're mine," he said, still hard inside me.

"I'm yours," I said, rubbing against him. "Don't stop. I love you." Sheer ecstasy coursed through my body as I climaxed. My nails dug into his back and time literally stopped.

In that moment, I completely surrendered to him. I gave him every part of myself and embraced him in return. For the first time in my life ... I felt complete.

"Wow, we perform tonight and then we're headed back home tomorrow. I can't believe it," I said to Gemma. We had chosen to take a break on the bus before returning for the concert. The guys were drinking a few beers while Gemma and I sat on the couch. I'd made a strong screwdriver with Hendrix's watchful eye, but my bestie had decided against any alcohol.

"I'm ready. I love performing, but I know it won't be our last tour, either. I miss my little cocoon with Hendrix and dinner at Franklin's house in the evenings. Plus, you and I have multiple places where we can talk in private at home." Hendrix and

Gemma had their own place, but Franklin's was still home to them.

"God, I miss you guys living there, too. I know I see you all every day now, but you've been busy with rehearsals and performances. Sometimes I wish I could rewind time to before Ada Lynn died, and we were all together again at Franklin's."

"I know. Me too," she said, grief flickering in her bright blue eyes.

"Tonight," I hesitated, "is the first concert where I can say I'm Cade's girlfriend."

Gemma smiled at me. "It's great when we're all together and we don't have to share our men with the world, because man … sometimes I turn into a catty bitch when those girls rub their boobs on Hendrix. Everyone knows we're together and they do it anyway."

"Dammit. I'm going to have to beat the hell outta some skank hoes, aren't I?"

Gemma laughed. "I sure as hell want to sometimes, but Hendrix takes care of it really fast. I'm sure Cade will do the same."

An ache spread through my chest. What if he didn't? What if he still portrayed himself as a player for the attention?

"It'll get easier. The more Cade proves to you he's serious, the less you'll stress. Maybe …"

"Ha, thanks, Gemma," I replied. "I guess it's one of the consequences of falling for a famous singer, huh?"

"Yeah, but in my defense, I had no clue who Hendrix was when I fell in love with him. You, on the other hand, had full disclosure."

"Ha! Yes, I did." I wiggled my eyebrows at her.

She giggled. "How's the … ummm, well … we discussed sex with Jeremiah, so I guess Cade isn't off limits?"

"Are you asking me about his penis?" I asked, fighting off a fit of giggles. Gemma was the most conservative person I knew when it came to sex, but it had to do with her past. Although I wanted to encourage her to talk to me, I also knew it was a sensitive topic for her.

The poor girl turned fifty shades of red.

"Well, not his … parts necessarily," she coughed into her hand, glancing at him. "But is he good? Are you happy? I mean … ya know, does he take care of you first? Or is it all about him?"

I barked out a laugh, managing to gain everyone's attention. Cade raised his eyebrow, flashed me a smile, then returned to whatever the guys were discussing.

I wiggled in my seat and faced her. "I can't explain it, Gemma. In every way possible he's the most generous guy I've been with. I don't mean just in bed, but with his words, his actions, his vulnerability. I never had that with Asher or Jeremiah. Maybe we were too young and naïve, I don't know, but this is different. It's like I love him from a different part of myself."

She grabbed my hand. "Mac, when it's the real thing it's almost unexplainable. I'm so so so happy for you guys," she said, flashing me a huge smile. "No one deserves it more than you."

I pulled her into a big hug and held onto her with everything inside me.

"I love you, bestie," I said.

"I love you, too, Mac."

There was nothing better in the world than having a best friend by your side when you fell in love.

CHAPTER 21

$\mathcal{T}$he stadium had sold out both nights. My heart sank a little that we were on the next to the last night of the tour, but I was also ready to have Cade to myself. At the same time, I'd be returning to the city where Brandon had kidnapped and assaulted me. I was literally split in two about returning.

Since I was part of the band, so to speak, I always had first row tickets. It was fun pretending I was a groupie for a few hours, too. It wasn't public knowledge Cade and I were together like Gemma and Hendrix. Not that it mattered. It seemed like some girls always enjoyed the challenge of trying to steal someone else's guy. Although I hated that petty bullshit, it would also test Cade's loyalty. I'd see first-hand how he handled the overzealous fans, and if his feelings and everything he'd said to me were for real.

The band spread out across the stage and opened with their most popular, upbeat song. The crowd immediately hopped to their feet and started clapping and dancing.

"Holy hell, they're so fucking hot!" The girl next to me said a little breathlessly. "If you had your choice who'd you fuck? I mean, one night with any of them, who would it be?"

Even though I knew it was part of the deal, my body bristled.

"I don't know. They're all drop dead gorgeous. What about you?" I asked while jumping up and down and keeping the beat to the song.

"Cade. Definitely Cade. I mean, Hendrix is super-hot, but I'm not into the long-haired dudes. John is pretty hot too, but Cade is delish. I'd drop on my knees in a heartbeat and suck his dick. I have every intention of doing exactly that too. I have VIP tickets," she said with a condescending smirk.

I stood still, my eyebrows knitting together with her words.

"Did you know he has a girlfriend?" I asked, eyeing her.

"Who cares? These guys don't. They'll cheat on their wives or girlfriends. All it takes is a good hand job." She laughed like she had an inside secret.

"Really?" I said, jealousy rearing its ugly head.

"Yeah. They don't care or respect anyone. It's all about their dicks."

"I'm Cade's girlfriend," I stated firmly.

"What?" she said, blinking a few times as though something was in her eye.

"I'm Cade Richardson's girlfriend," I repeated.

"Oh my God. You had me going for a minute. You're hilarious. We both know Cade wouldn't touch the likes of you."

I sighed. Any further conversation with this girl was a waste of time. She wouldn't believe the truth if it slapped her upside the noggin. Gemma was right, this fight was up to Cade and how he handled the fans, but it still didn't stop me from verbally sparring with her.

"I'm not kidding. I'm his girlfriend," I repeated.

Her eyes traveled over me skeptically.

"No way," she said, waving me off like I was a pesky bug.

"I have neither the time nor the crayons to explain this to you. Catch up, girl," I said. "There's more to these guys than you're giving them credit for."

"What a bitch," she replied, sneering at me.

We'd see who the bitch was once we were all backstage. Maybe I'd block her at the door along with her friends.

SWEATY AND TIRED, I made my way to the VIP room where my friends were.

"Hey," I said to Pierce. He nodded and let me in.

"Hey, babe," Cade said, greeting me the second I stepped into the room. He wrapped me in his arms and kissed me.

"You were amazing," I placed my hands on his chest and peered up at him.

"We sounded good?"

"Better and better," I replied, trailing my hands over his stomach and slipping my fingers into the back pockets of his jeans.

Pierce opened the door, and the fans rolled in. I stepped back, but Cade grabbed my hand. I frowned at him.

"I want you next to me. Then there's not a single doubt in your mind how I handle the ladies."

"Cade, are you sure?" I asked. I might not like it, but he also had an image to maintain with his fans, so even though I wasn't ecstatic about it, I was alright with a little flirting.

He pulled me into him and laid a searing kiss on me. "Soon, the entire world will know I'm yours."

My heart melted on the spot.

"Oh, you weren't kidding?" I turned to see the girl that had been sitting next to me in the front row. Her eyes were filled with disbelief as she glanced from me to Cade.

"No, I was serious," I smirked, then walked away and let Cade do his job. I'd allow the skank to fangirl over my boyfriend. At some point, I'd have to learn to trust him like Gemma did Hendrix.

I leaned against the wall and folded my arms over my chest while he took pictures with gorgeous girls and signed autographs. I wasn't sure how Gemma dealt with it. What helped was watching the girls' faces when Cade mentioned he had a girlfriend. Some of them pushed anyway, and I snickered more than once when they realized he wasn't going to give in.

Several hours later, I had a little more confidence about Cade's and my relationship. Pierce ushered the last few fans out of the room, and we all visibly relaxed.

"Let's get the hell out of here," Hendrix said, wrapping his arm around Gemma. "We've got one more night, so let's get some sleep and make it a hell of a show."

We all high-fived, then dragged our exhausted asses back to our temporary home on wheels.

I snuggled up to Cade in his bed and released a contented sigh. Even though I'd had to deal with a fangirl who wanted to get in my boyfriend's pants, overall it had been a good night.

"You did an amazing job on your solo," I whispered, snuggling up to him in his bed. I traced my fingers across the smooth muscles of his chest while we talked.

"Thanks. I couldn't have done it without you," he said, placing a sweet kiss on my forehead.

"It's strange being on this side of you. I don't mean in your bed, but as your girlfriend versus just a friend. I know it sounds weird, but I might have gotten a bit pissed at a girl in the audience. I'm not sure how I'm going to deal with all of this. To me, you're Cade. I've known you for years. I mean, you're the guitarist in a famous band, too, but you're still Cade," I said, hesitating. "And, well, *my Cade?*"

He shifted in the bed and rolled over toward me. "Don't you

doubt it for a minute. You're mine, I'm yours. Don't you think I go a little nuts when I see guys ogling you? You have no idea how many random dudes I've wanted to murder during this tour. I don't want anyone else. I realize the only thing that will prove this to you is time, but you own my heart, Mac."

My lips brushed across his, and I kissed him gently. "I'm scared," I admitted. "I've given you everything I have, and you can snap me in two within seconds."

"Oh babe, I don't want you to be scared. Anytime the doubt creeps in your mind ... remember, I've loved you for years. If anyone can bring me to my knees and destroy me, it's you."

"I don't want to break you, Cade, I want to be the person who brings you to life in a way you've never experienced before. I want to complement and support you. I want to be the yin to your yang. Ha. Sorry, that was totally cheesy." I rolled my eyes at myself.

Cade shook his head. "No, it wasn't. I feel the same about you. I love you so much."

I rested my hand on top of his. "I love you, too," I whispered, staring at him. "I'm going to miss this most of all when we go home."

"Me, too," he said. "We'll figure it out, though."

"Promise?"

"Promise," Cade said, reassuring me.

THE DAY FLEW by with preparations for the performance. The clear, brilliant blue sky and warm temperatures that hovered in the upper eighties were perfect for an outdoor concert.

We all gathered on stage and Hendrix discussed last-minute changes with the band. Cade slipped his arm around my shoulders, and I nestled into his side as naturally as if he'd been made for me. "I think I'll hang out backstage tonight. Well, behind the curtain anyway," I said to Cade. "I don't feel like hearing the girls talk about which guy they want to screw." I wrinkled my nose and crossed my arms over my chest.

"It's tough," Gemma agreed, strolling leisurely across the stage toward us. "Some fans are nice about it when they realize we're in a relationship, but then there are the others who honestly don't give a rat's ass. Those are the ones I want to smack as hard as I can."

"I'll help," I muttered.

"Are you jealous?" Cade teased, a mischievous grin easing across his face.

My eyes narrowed at him. "How would you feel if some guy approached you and asked what my name was?"

"No big deal." He shrugged.

"Uh huh. And what if this guy then talked about how much he'd like to take my shirt off and grab my tits? Oh, and bury his big dick in me."

Cade's jaw visibly tensed with my words.

"Well said, Mac," Gemma said, snickering slightly.

"I have to hear similar comments about Gemma, and it sucks," Hendrix said, joining us.

I glanced around for John, but he and Pierce were over to one side of the stage, speaking quietly. I assumed it was security stuff for the concert. It was still strange to know John had worked for the same company as Pierce and kept it secret for the last few years. To me he'd always be the same ol' John I'd known in high school, though.

Pierce and John joined us a few minutes later.

"We're all ready," Pierce said to Hendrix. "We have security around the perimeter as well as in the crowd."

"Thanks, man." Hendrix patted John on the back and smiled at him. "I have to admit it does feel better knowing you're more than our drummer."

"I literally have you guys' backs," John said, laughing.

"I don't know about the rest of you, but I'm ready to wrap up and head home tomorrow. I miss Franklin, too. He's the only parent I have left," Gemma said.

Hendrix slid his arm around her waist. "He called me earlier and wished us luck on the last performance. He has a nice dinner planned for us tomorrow night at his place."

"Do you want to come over?" I asked, glancing up at Cade.

"I'd love to babe, but I need to spend some time with Mom and Missy."

I chewed my lip in disappointment. We'd been in our cocoon for so long, I'd forgotten about his responsibilities.

"But I'll be over as soon as Missy goes to sleep. I've decided to keep the caregiver."

"Really?" I asked, bouncing up and down clapping. This meant he'd have more freedom for us to spend time together.

"Yeah. Mom and Missy really like her, plus it allows me to have some time for practice, and most importantly you."

I pushed up on my tiptoes and gave him a quick kiss.

"I'll talk to Franklin before you come over then. I'm not sure how he'll react, but I think he will settle down once he sees we're serious and not playing around."

Cade traced his fingers down my cheek, his eyes softening. "No more playing," he said.

"You two are perfect for each other," Gemma said, walking across the stage and moving the microphone stand back. "It's too bad you guys didn't figure it out sooner."

"I wouldn't have been ready," I admitted. "I was still hung up on the idea Asher would grow up. I think if people realized we can't change someone else, we'd be better off. I mean, I don't know what I was thinking. It would have been so much easier if I'd taken his words and actions at face value."

"Mac, I think it's a huge lesson everyone has to learn."

"Yeah. It would have saved me a shit ton of heartache for sure if I'd figured it out sooner."

Hendrix looked at his phone while the first audience members showed up.

"Guess we'd better get ready." He took Gemma's hand, and a sad smile pulled at the corner of his mouth. "It's been a great tour; let's give them a show they'll never forget."

AN HOUR LATER, I hugged my bestie, brother, John, and my boyfriend for good luck. I smiled as they strolled out on stage and waved to the audience. The crowd went wild, and I was grateful we weren't inside an auditorium. The noise would have been deafening.

"Hello, Denver!" Hendrix yelled into the microphone.

"Are you ready to get home?" I asked Pierce, who was standing next to me side stage.

"Yeah. I think we all are. Touring night after night can definitely take its toll."

The band began their first song, and I peeked over at Pierce. He was in full work mode, but without his sunglasses.

"We should find you a girlfriend or someone special when we get home. You're always working, and you've got to have some fun, too."

"I don't have time. This job takes up every minute of every day," he responded without looking at me.

"Does it help that we're friends and not just a job? I mean, don't you get lonely?"

Pierce shifted his weight from one foot to the next, his attention continually scanning the crowd and area around us.

"I've always been a loner, Mac. This life fits me well."

"Oh. If you ever change your mind, I'm sure we can get you a date. I mean, you're hot as hell, make good money, and how old are you?" I asked.

"I'm twenty-six."

"Ah hell, you're only four years older than I am. For some reason, I always think you're older. It must be the constant stoic expression you wear so well." I wondered what Pierce had been like as a kid and if he ever relaxed even when he was off duty. Hell, we didn't even know anything about his background. Maybe one day I'd get some real deets.

"Thanks," he replied dryly.

Pierce and I stood in silence and enjoyed the band's next few songs. My pulse raced when I realized it was almost time for Cade's solo. No matter how many times I heard it, my insides turned to jelly. Each time he sang it, he owned another piece of my heart.

Cade's attention drifted over in my direction and he mouthed I love you. I blew him a kiss, beaming at him. The last thing I'd ever expected when Hendrix had asked if I wanted to spend a month on the road with them was to fall in love with my brother's best friend. But I had. Hard.

The lights in the outdoor arena shut down and the curtain closed. The stage crew scurried around and prepared for Cade's song.

"I never get tired of hearing him sing," I said to Pierce.

A worry line creased Pierce's forehead as the curtain opened, and his focus darted across the stage. John raised his glow in the dark drumsticks then tapped a rhythm on the rim of his snare drum.

Pierce's hand went to his earpiece, and before I could ask him what was wrong, a rapid popping sound rang through the arena. Pierce dashed out from the side stage and jumped in front of Cade as the spotlight singled in on him. Cade stumbled backward, then dropped to the floor. Pierce's body jerked and he tumbled to the stage while John ran in front of Gemma, but it was too late. She staggered back, grabbed her side and collapsed. To my horror, Hendrix fell to the floor next and my shrill cry ripped through the night. Terrified screams rang through the audience. Too stunned to move, I stared in disbelief as everyone I loved lay still on the stage.

CHAPTER 22

*V*iolent trembles traveled through my body as my addled brain pieced together the situation in front of me. Although I was side stage, I had no idea where the shooter was, and I sank to my hands and knees. There was no way to tell if the shots had stopped either because the auditorium echoed with screams and shouting.

Dropping to my stomach and lying flat, I slithered on my belly across the stage until I reached Cade, who lay crumpled up next to Pierce. The bitter taste of bile filled my mouth, and I willed it down as my heart thumped against my chest. Everyone I loved was now motionless on the floor. Were they dead? In a split second, had I lost everything important in my life? What the fuck had happened?

"Cade," I called through my tears, scrambling forward. A pool of blood was quickly collecting next to him on the floor. "Baby?" I cried. "Hang on," I said, grabbing his hand. "Pierce? Are you okay?" I called in his direction. "Goddammit, Pierce, please help me!"

A groan escaped from him, and a flicker of hope ignited in my chest. "Pierce? I need your help! Are you alright?"

"Mac, I'm fine. The bullet hit my vest." He rolled over on his stomach and grimaced.

"He's bleeding," I said, near hysterics. I peered through the semi-darkness and sat up slowly.

Pierce cautiously glanced around and crawled toward us. "Stay down, Mac."

I flattened myself against the cool stage floor, my eyes never leaving Cade.

"Is he going to be okay?" I asked. "I don't know where he's bleeding from." I held up my hands, staring blankly at Cade's blood that now stained my fingers bright red.

"It looks like a chest wound," Pierce replied, raising up enough to tug his shirt over his head and revealing his bulletproof vest. "I need you to stay calm. We have help on the way, and the entire arena is full of security and paramedics. He's going to be okay." He wadded up his shirt, placed it over Cade's chest, and pressed down.

Tears flowed down my cheeks as I stared at my boyfriend. How could this have happened? He'd just told me he loved me, and the next second, he was bleeding out on the floor.

"Listen to me. Mac!" Pierce yelled at me over the noise and hysteria of the crowd. I flinched and looked up at him. "I need you to get to the others and check on them."

Fuck. I'd seen Gemma, Hendrix, and John drop like flies. Were they alive?

"Stay low and be careful," he ordered.

I wiped my cheeks and crawled as quickly as I could to Hendrix.

"Hendrix," I said near his ear. "Hey, it's Mac. Can you hear me?" Hendrix's eyes fluttered and slowly peeled open.

"Are you alright?" he asked, his voice so soft I almost couldn't understand what he was saying.

"I'm fine. Help is on the way, but you need to be still, Hendrix. You've been shot."

"Gemma? Is she alright?" he asked, his tone thick with fear.

"I'm on my way to her, now." I squeezed his hand reassuringly. I wasn't sure who I was trying to console more, Hendrix or myself. "I'll be right back."

I worked my way to the back of the stage where Gemma and John lay unmoving. Tears blurred my vision, and I blinked hard, attempting to stay focused.

"Gemma! Gemma!" I searched frantically to see where the blood was coming from. There was so much. Suddenly, my chest tightened, and nausea swelled in the pit of my stomach. I couldn't see the rise and fall of her chest. "No, no, no. Best bestie, you have to be alright."

"Pierce!" I screamed. "It's Gemma! I don't think she's breathing," I hiccupped, sheer panic coursing through me. Where were the paramedics and why the hell was it taking so long to get here?

Fear flickered across his face as he continued to apply pressure to Cade's wound. "Check for a pulse, Mac! On her neck or wrist."

I took her limp hand and flipped it over. Nothing. I couldn't find it.

"You listen to me right now, Gemma Thompson. If you kicked Brandon's ass, you can survive this. You're a strong person. You're fine. Do you hear me?" I placed my first two fingers on her neck and held my breath.

CHAPTER 23

"*I* got it!" I yelled at Pierce and Hendrix. "Gemma's got a pulse!" Even though I'd found a pulse, it was weak. Not a good sign. I had no idea where she'd been shot.

"Now John," Pierce ordered. Thank God he had training for these types of situations. My brain had completely blanked out.

I held onto Gemma's fingers and my focus traveled to John. My other hand flew to my mouth as a small whimper escaped me. John's blank eyes stared at me, his mouth gaping open. A fresh bullet hole had torn through his forehead. He was gone.

"Mac?" Pierce asked.

I turned toward him and shook my head. It was John's blood all over the floor.

The next minute, everything around us was a flurry of activity as the EMTs swarmed the stage and loaded Hendrix, Gemma, Cade, and John on gurneys. Pierce ran over to me, his attention landing on John while the EMTs pulled the white sheet over his body.

"Goddammit," Pierce muttered and pulled me to him. I shivered against his body, my brain scrambling to make sense of the bloody scene in front of me.

"Are they going to make it?" I hiccupped.

"They're all fighters, Mac. Let's get to the hospital. You're not to move out of my sight, do you understand?"

I nodded numbly, my legs threatening to give out as I stumbled to keep up with Pierce.

"Hang on," he said, swooping me up in his arms. "This will be faster. I think you're in too much shock for us to move as quickly as we need to."

Pierce followed the EMTs, my boyfriend, and my family down the back stairs and to the ambulances.

Without a second thought, Pierce hopped into the emergency vehicle they'd loaded Gemma in.

"I'm her bodyguard, and this is her sister," he said to the EMT. They nodded, closed the door behind us, and the wails of the sirens filled the night.

~

OVER AN HOUR HAD TICKED by agonizingly slowly while Pierce and I waited in the emergency room. The shrill cry of a baby filled the bustling room, and I attempted not to chew my fingernails down to the quick while we waited for some news. I fought back an overwhelming urge for a few Xanax. Dammit. I needed something to help me through this. Why the hell had I ever admitted my prescription use in the first place?

Frantically, I reviewed the night's events, the ball of anxiety growing inside me. I inhaled sharply and willed myself to remember why I'd stopped the pills in the first place. I loved Cade. I loved my family, and for the first time in my life, I was beginning to love myself. The desire for the pills eased, and I turned my attention to Pierce.

"What happened, Pierce? I thought we had extra security. I thought the place was locked down!" My tears had been nearly nonstop since I'd watched my family drop like rag dolls.

"We were trying not to tip off Dillon, waiting for him to make a move. My guys had him in their sights and then poof, he was gone." Pierce shook his head and stared into the distance. Defeat and anger flickered across his otherwise stoic expression. "I should have insisted the show be canceled as soon as he showed up in town."

"How many of our loved ones are we going to bury, Pierce?" I asked, the pitch in my tone rising. "We've already lost John, what if no one is left?" Sobs shook my shoulders, and I curled into the chair. Pierce wrapped his arm around me, and I clung to the clean T-shirt an EMT had given him. His original shirt was now soaked in Cade's blood.

"You can't think like that, Mac. They're strong. They're all going to pull through." He took my hand and held it tightly. "I talked to Franklin and he'll be here shortly. It's a two-hour flight from Spokane and he was already on his plane."

I nodded, the rush of fear and intense emotions making my head pound with each movement.

A reporter's voice on the TV pulled my attention toward it. I pointed to the caption scrolling on the bottom of the screen. 'Shooting at the Red Rocks Amphitheatre Stage.'

"Hendrix Harrington, Gemma Thompson, John Cooper, and Cade Richardson of the band August Clover were shot earlier tonight while performing at the outdoor arena this evening in Denver, Colorado. At this time, we don't have confirmation as to the number of injuries or fatalities. Shortly after opening fire on the band and audience, the alleged shooter was located at a nearby building. He'd apparently taken his own life."

I bolted out of my chair. "No! Now we won't know anything," I said, crumbling down in my seat again.

"Mac, you have my word I'll find out who was behind this, and I'll personally take them down."

I peered at him through swollen eyes. "Promise?"

"Yeah," he said, taking my hand in his. "I suspect it was someone hired by Dillon, but we can't confirm it yet."

Although my body was exhausted, my mind raced on overdrive with a million thoughts. Not one of them was good. What would my world be like without Hendrix and Gemma if they didn't survive? I didn't think I could make it without them. And Cade. What if I was the only one that lived? How would I deal with it?

"Mackenzie Worthington?" A female doctor asked, approaching me.

I hopped out of my seat, my chest tightening while I waited for an update. Pierce stood silently by my side.

"I'm Doctor Lynn. Hendrix and Gemma are fine, you're welcome to come on back."

"They are?" I cried. "They're not going to die?"

A soft smile eased across her face, reaching her large brown eyes.

"That's correct." She patted my shoulder reassuringly.

"Did you hear that, Pierce?" I asked, unable to hide my excitement.

"Yeah, it's great news." He released a breath, reached for my hand, and gave it a tight squeeze.

We followed the doctor down the hallway to where Gemma and Hendrix were.

"They're in the next to last cubicle," Doctor Lynn said.

"Thank you," Pierce replied to her.

The room was overflowing with patients and their families, and a woman's wail reached my ears. I spotted Gemma's red hair immediately and burst into tears. Oh my God, they were alive.

Tugging on Pierce's hand, I hurried toward them as fast as I could maneuver through the people without being rude.

Hendrix and Gemma's faces lit up with huge smiles at the sight of us. I was about to tackle them for a hug, but Hendrix held his hand out, halting me from throwing my arms around them.

"Slow down," he said, pointing to his arm in the sling. "I've got a shoulder wound, but overall I'm fine."

I wiped away the tears and my attention darted to the large blood stain on Gemma's shirt.

"It's only a flesh wound," she said, pulling me in for a hug. "It hurts like hell, but I'm fine. We're fine."

I released her and hugged Hendrix gently.

"Why were you unconscious?" I asked Gemma, sniffling.

"I hit my head on the stage and it knocked me out. I'm exhausted, but I'm going to be okay. I promise. The bullet nicked my side, but it's only a minor injury." She slipped her shirt up enough for me to see the bandage.

"What the fuck?" I gasped, my hands flying to my mouth.

"Try not to worry, Mac. They gave us some antibiotics and Tylenol 3. At least the pain is better."

"You're both really alright?" I asked. My body trembled with an overload of emotion, and Pierce slipped his arm around my shoulders for support.

"Yeah, we really are," Gemma assured me. Even though she wanted to appear strong, I didn't miss the grief and fear in her eyes.

Pierce's gaze fell first on Gemma then Hendrix.

"I'm sorry." His voice was thick with emotion. "I should have been there to protect you."

"You did," Hendrix said. "If you hadn't, I think we would have lost Cade. At least he's still fighting."

"Omigosh, I don't understand. It all happened so fucking fast," I said, wringing my hands together. "One minute Cade was about to sing his solo, and the next everyone was lying motionless on the stage. Pierce stayed with Cade so he wouldn't bleed out, and Gemma, I couldn't find your pulse," I hiccuped. "You scared the ever-living shit out of me. Then I found it and ..."

My sobs picked up momentum, and I fought to control them enough to deliver the horrible news. I took a deep breath.

"John," I whimpered. "When I saw his face ... I knew he was gone. How? How could this have happened?" I asked, biting my bottom lip.

"He's gone?" Hendrix asked, the blood draining from his face.

"No," Gemma whispered, shaking her head in disbelief. "What happened?"

"I ... I."

"He was shot in the head," Pierce said quietly, his voice filled with grief. "I'm so sorry."

Hendrix laid his head on Gemma's shoulder, his body shaking as he sobbed. I stepped forward and wrapped my arms around them both as our tears flowed.

"Mac!" Franklin's voice boomed through the room. I whirled around, ran toward him full speed ahead, and threw my arms around him.

"Dad!" I cried against his chest. He kissed the top of my head, and I released him, dragging him over to his son.

"Hendrix ... Gemma ..." Franklin's voice trailed off as he assessed the situation, tears brimming in his eyes. Gemma and Hendrix stood, and Franklin gently wrapped his arms around all of us. I wasn't sure how long we stood there, clinging to each other and crying.

Eventually we released each other, and Gemma and Hendrix sat back down on the bed and chair.

"I'm so sorry about John," Franklin said, grief consuming his expression. "I'm going to see what I can learn about Cade's condition. I'll notify his mom and sister when we know something. I'm concerned about how his mother will handle it, so I'd like to wait."

I watched him as he approached the desk. I chewed nervously on my thumbnail, waiting.

Franklin's conversation was too short to have found out anything useful. He returned to us, sighed, and sank into the chair next to me.

"He's in surgery. The bullet lodged itself in his chest. It barely missed his heart. All we can do is wait."

A sob escaped me, and I tucked my knees under my chin, rocking back and forth. He had to make it. He had to come back to us. Franklin smoothed my hair as I cried and waited for me to calm down.

"Do you know anything else about the shooter?" I rubbed my head and stared at the floor.

"I spoke with my FBI contact on the way here. They identified him as Michael Conway. He's from Ohio and has a record for multiple rapes and an attempted murder. He's not been linked to Dillon yet, but I suspect either Dillon hired him, or Michael was a part of the society."

"I'll find out," Pierce said, his hands clenching into fists. "Dillon has hurt this family for the last time." His expression darkened as his attention traveled over all of us.

"You can't blame yourself, Pierce," Franklin said. "The lights were out, and the shooter had a high-powered scope. There's nothing you could have done. He fired quickly, and there was no way you and John could have covered everyone at the same time."

My heart skipped a beat with the mention of John's name. The image of his lifeless eyes and gaping mouth haunted me. How could someone be alive one second and gone the next?

"He died protecting me," Gemma said, choking on her words. "He must have seen Hendrix drop and moved in my direction, but he lined himself up with what I assume was a headshot meant for me. Now he's gone, and all I have is a surface wound."

I gasped, my hands flying over my mouth. Worry lines creased Hendrix's forehead while he grabbed her hand and kissed it.

"Why would someone want to kill you?" I asked, my attention bouncing from Gemma to Franklin.

"Because you and she both have to testify at Brandon's trial, Mac," Franklin said in a hushed tone.

CHAPTER 24

"Fuck," My gaze found Gemma's. "Why didn't you say anything sooner? I guess I'd blocked it out and forgotten about it until a trial date was set."

"I'm sorry, Mac. I wanted to shield you from any more stress for as long as I could. You were already having nightmares and terrified. I couldn't add to it until we had a date," Franklin explained.

"We have a date?" Gemma asked, her voice barely above a whisper.

"Yeah, but we'll discuss it later," Franklin said.

Pierce leaned forward in his chair. "We suspect Michael was hired to take Mac and Gemma out so they couldn't testify. You two are the only eye-witnesses against Brandon. And Gemma, you're one of the few people who have ties to the society through your father. That's another reason they want you out of the way." He rubbed his hands together, anger flickering across his face.

Dammit. I'd been so wrapped up in my own nightmare, I'd not considered much beyond trying to get through each day without having a panic attack. I realized Franklin didn't want to scare us, but this was beyond fucked up. Dillon had put a hit out on us. A mix of fear and anger swirled through me. I glanced at Gemma. She held my gaze for a moment, her cheeks flushed. I suspected we were thinking the same thing. We were in serious danger.

"Do you have any more tours scheduled, Hendrix?" Franklin asked.

"Not yet. We'd planned to record in the studio before the next set of dates."

Franklin rubbed his chin, deep in thought. "We're tightening security for all of you. There are a few weeks until the trial, so I'd feel better if you all stayed at my place."

Hope fluttered to life in my chest. Even though it was only for a few weeks, we'd be together again.

"I realize you and Gemma would prefer to stay at your own house, but I want security as tight at possible. Plus, I might actually sleep at night."

"Dad," Hendrix said, his gaze landing on Franklin's. "I love Gemma, and I made a commitment to love and protect her. If this is best for all of us, I'm good with it." He paused and looked at Gemma. "Are you in, babe?"

She squeezed his hand and nodded. "Yeah. I want to stay close to Mac, too. Thank you, Franklin."

"I have to take care of my family, and right now the only way I can is under one roof. We've replaced Calvin with a new guy named Zayne, too. He and Pierce know each other, so I think he will be a good fit."

Gemma's brow discreetly rose with the news, and I nodded at her before I returned my attention to the conversation concerning the security.

"Another bodyguard will replace John when we arrive in Spokane," Pierce added. "His name is Vaughn. We'll all work perimeter security as well as being assigned to one of you.

"I'm really sorry about John," Franklin said, his voice trailing off. "I'll always be grateful for what he did to save my family."

Tears streamed silently down my face as I remembered him licking my cheek and teasing me when I'd arrived at the bus the first day of the tour. Now. He was gone. Forever. He'd given his life to save my best friend. When would all of this insanity end?

"Excuse me, are you Cade Richardson's family?"

Franklin stood, not correcting the doctor.

"He's a strong guy. He made it through surgery fine, but he's looking at some significant recovery time. Cade's a lucky young man. The bullet nearly hit his heart."

A small whimper escaped me, and I squeezed my eyes closed, attempting to control my emotional rollercoaster. Turning to Pierce, I grabbed his hand. "You got to him in time, dude."

Relief washed over his face, and he nodded. "I couldn't have done it without you, Mac."

"You stayed with him. You saved him," I said. Overwhelmed with gratitude, I flung my arms around Pierce and hung onto him. "Thank you," I whispered hoarsely against his chest.

I straightened up and looked at the doctor. "When can we see him?"

"He's really groggy, but as long as you promise not to stay long, you can see him now."

My attention landed on Hendrix, and he stood slowly. "Please let me tell him about John," he said, glancing around to all of us.

I nodded. There was no way I wanted to deliver the news.

We followed the doctor down the long hospital hallway to Cade's room. As eager as I was to be with him, I hesitated, suddenly afraid to see how badly he'd been injured. I peered cautiously around the door. His chest was bandaged, and his face was almost as white as the gauze. He turned his head, a loopy grin spreading across his beautiful features when he saw us.

"Hey, babe," he said softly.

I ran into the room, but then dialed my enthusiasm down a notch. I couldn't fling myself on top of him.

"Hi baby," I gently touched his cheek. "You made it back to me," I said, my voice cracking from the weight of my emotions.

"I've waited this long for you, I'm not going anywhere now that you're mine," he said. "Are you alright?" His brows knitted together, and his eyes traveled over me.

I nodded, grabbing his hand and kissing it.

Franklin cleared his throat behind me, and I cringed. I'd been so relieved to see Cade, I'd forgotten Franklin was with us. I flashed Franklin a sheepish smile and turned my attention back to Cade.

Hendrix approached Cade and a sad smile pulled at the corner of his mouth.

"Hey man, I can't tell you how good it is to see you awake and talking," Hendrix said, his eyes growing misty.

"You too." Cade nodded at Hendrix's arm, then his attention landed on Gemma's bloodied shirt. Pierce and Franklin waited patiently behind us. "I'm assuming you guys got shot, but you're here and alright so I'll take it." Concern flickered across Cade's face. "Where's John?" he asked.

Even though he was drugged up, he was still aware enough to realize his other childhood friend wasn't in the room with us.

Hendrix grimaced and his lips pursed together. "Cade," he started.

I chewed my bottom lip, attempting to not interrupt Hendrix. This wasn't the time for me to blurt out whatever crap was flying through my mind.

"He didn't make it, man. He jumped in front of Gemma. He saved her life, but he sacrificed his own." Hendrix's voice trailed off, his shoulders tensing while we waited for the news of John's death to fully sink in.

Cade looked confused as he searched each of us for any indication it wasn't true.

"No way," he whispered in disbelief. "No fucking way. He

can't be gone." He released an agonizing moan as reality crashed down on him.

His head hung down, and he gripped the railing of the bed so hard his knuckles turned white.

"Aggghhhh!" he yelled, tears streaming down his cheeks.

A dark-haired nurse bolted through the doorway and to the side of his bed.

"Get back, all of you." She shooed us away and injected something into Cade's IV. His agonizing cries turned into whimpers, then he fell silent and his eyelids grew heavy.

The nurse turned to us, anger flashing in her expression.

"He's fresh out of surgery, what in the world was so important?" She placed a hand on her hip, her eyes narrowing at each of us.

"His best friend was shot tonight as well," Franklin said, stepping forward. "But he didn't make it. He sacrificed himself to save this young lady." He nodded at Gemma.

Her expression softened. "I'm really sorry. You're the band that was performing tonight, aren't you?"

Hendrix and Gemma nodded. "Cade's our guitarist," Gemma added. "John, our drummer was the one who ..." Her body trembled and Franklin wrapped a protective arm around her.

"It's been a horrific night. We weren't going to tell Cade yet, but he was lucid enough to realize John wasn't in the room with everyone else."

The nurse pursed her lips. "I see. Well, he'll be asleep for some time. His body needs to heal, so maybe you all can come back later."

She wasn't asking.

"We can go check in at the hotel up the street," Franklin said. "I'll need to call his family, too."

"I want to stay," I said, peering at Franklin. "Cade and I are together, Dad."

"I saw." He didn't ask me a million questions or argue, he

simply nodded. "I'll have hospital security positioned at the door. We're not leaving you until they arrive, though."

"Thank you." I sank into the chair next to Cade's bed and took his hand in mine.

∼

"Mac?"

My eyes fluttered open. At some point, I'd drifted off to sleep while waiting next to Cade.

"Yeah, baby. I'm here." I leaned forward in my chair. "Are you in pain?"

"Not really," he said, his tongue darting across his chapped bottom lip.

"You weren't hurt?" he asked, searching me for any signs.

I shook my head. "I was too far to the side of the stage. Pierce was hit when he knocked you out of the way. Well, if he hadn't, you wouldn't be here with me right now. The bullet almost got your heart." A tear snuck down my cheek, and I wiped it away self-consciously. "I'm relieved you're going to be alright," I whispered, my voice shaking with emotion. "I love you so much."

He gave my hand a gentle squeeze, the gold flecks in his eyes darkening. "I love you, too. I don't know what I'd have done if you'd been hurt."

"I was the only one who wasn't," I said, guilt washing over me. "But it's not that they weren't looking for me. Fuck. I ummm—. We'll talk about it later."

"You're still in danger," he stated, his brow arching.

"Ya know, it's just another day in the life of Mackenzie Worthington. No biggie." I attempted a grin and waved him off.

Cade chuckled and cringed, grabbing at his chest. "I'm not sure why I thought it was funny."

"Because you're on good pain meds."

"My mom," he said, swallowing visibly.

"Franklin talked to the caregiver and your mom. They're alright. You're alright. The doctors said you'll need to hang out here for a few days, then we'll fly home on Franklin's plane."

"No commercial flight, huh?"

"Yeah. It's nice. You can lie down and sleep if you're tired. I'll be next to you. And, uh, Franklin knows we're together. I didn't go into any details, but he heard us talking and stuff."

"How'd he take it?" His forehead creased with his question.

"So far alright, but he won't say much about it while we're here."

Cade nodded.

"I'm super tired," he muttered. In seconds his words were followed by a soft snore.

CHAPTER 25

$\mathcal{N}$early a week later, we landed in Spokane. The late afternoon sun blazed in the bright blue sky as we loaded into Dad's limo at the airport.

Cade's wound was on the mend, but he still had to take it easy. Hendrix also had to allow his shoulder more time. Gemma's side had progressed nicely, and she was almost healed and back to normal activity. Pierce and I were the only ones not physically hurt. But mentally and emotionally? As long as I was alive, I'd never be able to forget that terrifying scene. The image of everyone lying on the stage not moving was burned into my brain for eternity.

Silence filled Franklin's limo while the driver headed toward Cade's house. My thumb traced the back of his hand, and he laced his fingers through mine. I'd been missing him next to me in bed. Franklin hadn't allowed me to stay with him overnight at the hospital. He said I needed my rest as much as Cade did. Even though I knew he was right, I didn't like it.

The limo came to a stop in front of Cade's house.

"I'm going to walk with him to the door," I said to Franklin.

Without a word, Pierce followed us out of the car and stayed within fifty feet.

"So much for privacy," I said to Cade while we strolled up the walkway to his tan house. The lawn was freshly mowed, and the bushes were newly trimmed. Bright orange and red roses added a splash of brilliant color next to the front porch.

"I miss you already," he said, stopping and tucking my hair behind my ear.

"Me too. I was planning on sneaking you in at night, but you can't crawl up the ladder and into my bedroom window while you're healing."

"Maybe we can try the front door?" he asked, a sad smile easing across his face.

"Yeah. Call me later?" I asked.

"Count on it." He leaned down and gave me a gentle kiss. "Your dad is watching, so I had to keep the kiss PG."

"As soon as you're better we'll make up for lost time," I said quietly.

"Promise?"

I nodded.

"I love you, Mac. I'll see you in a few days."

"I love you, too. Get some rest."

He squeezed my hand, then I reluctantly let it go, leaving my heart with him as I made my way back to the car.

Pierce opened the back door and settled in behind me.

"Are things serious?" Franklin asked without missing a beat.

I peeked at Hendrix, who sat next to Gemma, holding her hand.

"We aren't seeing other people, if that's what you're asking," I confessed.

Franklin rubbed his chin, pinning me with his steady gaze. My nerves hummed. Here it was. Cade hadn't been gone for even a minute, and Franklin was going to tell me I couldn't see him again or whatever else. I loved Franklin like my own Dad, but sometimes he tried to control people. He should have known by now it wouldn't work with me.

Franklin leaned over to Hendrix. "Son? Do you think Cade's settled down for your sister?"

Hendrix's gentle blue eyes landed on me.

"Yeah. I've never seen him like this before. He's committed to her, Dad. I think you should give him a chance. He's a good guy with a lot on his shoulders, but the moment he thought he had a chance with Mac, he dropped all the extracurricular activities and partying. The last month has been about what's best for the band and my sister."

Franklin relaxed in his seat again and stared out the window.

"Alright then, let's have him over for dinner."

I nodded and flashed a grin at my brother. Although I knew it wasn't over, the first step had been taken, and Franklin had accepted we were seeing each other. Now the rest was up to Cade.

Ten minutes later, the limo pulled up the winding drive in front of Franklin's mansion. Pierce exited first and approached two men at the front door. I leaned forward, attempting to get a better view of them.

"Who are they?" I asked Franklin.

"Zayne and Vaughn, our new security team."

"Who has who?" I asked, wondering if Pierce would have a small break from Gemma so his heart could heal.

"Pierce will stay with Hendrix and Gemma, Vaughn will be my bodyguard, and Zayne will be yours."

My eyes widened. "We could switch it up," I suggested.

Franklin's brows knitted together. "Is there a reason Pierce shouldn't continue guarding Hendrix and Gemma?"

There was no way I could explain to him I was trying to protect Pierce's heart.

"Nope, I thought he might be getting bored." It was a lame excuse, and Franklin saw right through it.

"Since you and Cade are together, I don't need to worry that you've developed feelings for Pierce, right?"

"Me? Oh lord no," I sputtered. I glanced at Gemma. She knew what I was up to. It wasn't only Pierce's heart I was trying to protect, it was also Hendrix's. My brother had to be tired of having Pierce around and knowing he was into his girlfriend.

I gave a half shrug. "Ya know, Dad, I'm exhausted and talking out of my ass."

He frowned. "I know the last days have been intense, but promise me if there's a problem you'll let me know."

My leg began to bounce. "It's all good. I promise. Pierce and I had some time to hang out, and I got used to him being my body-guard is all. We were backstage together when—"

The limo door opened, and Pierce bent down. "We're all clear, sir."

"Thank you. The driver will bring in the bags. Let's get everyone settled for the night."

I slowly inhaled a deep breath as I entered the foyer. Even though I'd lived with my mom most of my life, I'd stayed here for the last few months. It had been a good opportunity to spend time with Franklin one on one. When he and my mom were married, he worked nonstop, building his law practice. I don't know all the details, I was only seven at the time, but he just went off the rails and started drinking heavily. When it turned into the bender from hell, Mom packed up and we left. Shortly after that, Hendrix gave up on Franklin as well and moved in with us. I guess Franklin was trying to return the favor by paying for my college tuition and letting me live here.

I noted the sparkling white and black swirled marble that not only graced the entrance but expanded down the hallway for as far as I could see. The housekeeper must have recently cleaned it.

My stomach growled, and I made a beeline straight for the kitchen.

Hendrix's chuckle filled the hallway, and everyone followed me. I dropped my purse down on the tan marble countertop.

"Home," I said, flinging myself against the large stainless-steel doors of the refrigerator.

"Hungry, Mac?" Franklin asked, leaning against the counter and smiling.

"They starved me, Dad. We only got to stop for food once a day."

Gemma giggled. "I'm sure you really believe that. You of all people know how large your son's appetite is."

"Fine," I said, pretending a Southern swoon. "I missed Ruby's cooking."

"Aww, my Mac!" Ruby cried, slipping through the back door with a bag full of groceries. She placed it down near the stove and crossed the kitchen, her plump hips swishing with her steps. Ruby smoothed her white apron over her black uniform and gave us a warm smile.

"Ruby!" I said, jumping up and down. I flung my arms around her. "I'm so glad you're here."

"Where else would I be when all my favorite people arrive home safe and sound?"

But we hadn't all arrived home safe and sound. John's family was currently mourning that fact. Before I could stop it, I burst into tears.

"Now, now," Ruby said, soothing me. "Franklin told me. You're home now, it's going to be alright."

My emotions erupted while I allowed myself to be wrapped up in one of the safest places I knew. Ruby's arms. She was so much more than our chef, she was another mom to all of us.

I pulled away, blinking rapidly. "Sorry," I mumbled.

"Don't you apologize, Mac. Come. Sit down and I'll make dinner."

I slid my butt onto a bar stool and nodded to the one next to me. Gemma and Hendrix joined me.

"I'm making beef stroganoff with French bread. For dessert, I have Mr. Hendrix's favorite."

My eyes grew wide, and I grinned. Hendrix and I looked at each other and said in unison, "Chocolate peanut butter pie!"

"But I made a sugar free pie for you, Mac," Ruby said, grinning.

"You're my hero! Too bad Miss Ada Lynn didn't have your sugar free recipe the first time she fed me a piece of her pie." I glanced at Gemma and cringed.

"I can't say I'll ever forget that night, Mac." Gemma shook her head and sighed. "I've never seen anyone talk as much as you did."

"Sugar and ADHD don't mix well for me. Hyper doesn't even begin to describe what happens."

"I guess I missed this?" Hendrix asked, his attention bouncing between Gemma and me.

Gemma shook her head and laughed. "Yup. Mac had just arrived in Louisiana, and we were having dinner with Ada Lynn. Mac had mentioned in passing that sugar and she weren't a good combo, but I had no idea how serious she was. Anyway, three bites into Ada Lynn's pecan pie and Mac blurted out all the details of Brandon harassing me on campus. I hadn't told Ada Lynn anything about him because of her heart condition. However, it all ended up okay. Mac actually did me a favor by nudging me to open up and share with Ada Lynn."

"Glad I could help?" I asked, shrugging off the awkwardness I still felt.

Gemma laughed and turned her attention back to Ruby. "Dinner sounds wonderful. I'm with Mac, eating on the road for a month ... well, you really appreciate a nice home-cooked meal."

Ruby winked at us and busied herself in the kitchen, humming under her breath.

"Kids," Franklin said, motioning for us to follow him.

We filed out and followed him to the living room. My jaw

dropped when I saw the two guys standing next to the fireplace with Pierce.

"Mac," Gemma whispered. "Shut your mouth." She muffled her giggle.

I was full on drooling.

"I want to officially introduce you to Zayne and Vaughn."

"Hi," I squeaked, then quickly cleared my throat. If I weren't so in love with Cade, I'd definitely be throwing myself mercilessly at either Zayne or Vaughn. Or maybe both of them.

I shifted from one foot to the other, chewing my thumbnail while I took in Zayne's light brown hair, chiseled jaw, and emerald green eyes. His dark washed jeans hugged thick, muscular thighs, and a whisper of ink peeked out from the right sleeve of the maroon polo shirt stretched taut across his broad, muscular chest.

I think I might have whimpered before I tore my eyes away to look at Vaughn. "Shit."

"Mac," Franklin scolded.

"Sorry! I've never seen—Wow, dude. How did that happen?" I asked, moving closer to him.

"You'll get used to her," Hendrix said, watching me make a fool of myself and grinning.

"Gemma, do you see this?" I asked her, pointing at Vaughn.

"I do."

"You're beautiful," I said. "I mean—I."

Vaughn's expression never changed while I ogled him. His tanned bicep sported a serpent tattoo that slithered around his arm and disappeared across his chest. A few lines of the ink could be seen near the V of his shirt. His blonde hair was short and messy, but more than the muscles, tanned skin, and perfectly angled jaw. It was his eyes. One deep brown. One glacier blue.

"It's called heterochromia iridium," Vaughn said, his silky baritone voice rippling through the room.

I stepped back and chanced a look at Gemma. Even though it

wasn't obvious, I knew she was inwardly drooling. Her cheeks were flushed.

"Oh boy," I said, sighing. "Is this anything like the hot nanny fantasy, Dad?"

"Mac," Franklin said, holding up his finger to silence me. "I apologize for my daughter's behavior gentleman. As you're about to find out, Mac says what she's thinking most of the time. It's not always appropriate, but it can be rather humorous on occasion."

Hendrix chuckled. "She's hours of entertainment." Hendrix tossed his arm around me and pulled me against him, fondly kissing the top of my head.

"Nice to meet you all," Vaughn said.

"You're Dad's bodyguard, right?" I asked him.

"I am."

"It was by design I'm sure, and lucky for you. I wouldn't get a damned thing done all day because I'd be staring at you. You'd have to wear sunglasses even inside, or you'd be like a mega huge distraction. I'd feel like Mowgli in the Jungle Book when he saw the snake, Kaa. You could hypnotize me to do anything you wanted, like rob a bank or something totally illegal. I mean, never mind you're a walking cream cycle. All of you are for that matter, but good God. Pierce, where did you find these guys?"

I didn't miss Gemma's giggles beside me. Even Pierce was attempting to hide his grin.

"Don't worry, she won't attack. She might lurk in the corners and drool, but she's harmless. She has a boyfriend," Hendrix said, teasing me.

"Whatever," I said, holding up my hand. "Dammit, I do. I have a boyfriend I'm mad crazy about. I miss him already." And in five seconds flat, my mood took a major nosedive. "Nice to meet you. I'm here for your entertainment all week long." I waved at them, then made my way up the broad staircase, down the hallway past Gemma and Hendrix's room and to mine. I closed the door and flung myself across my California King. I'd trade this bed in a nanosecond to have Cade next to me.

My phone buzzed in my back pocket. I pulled it out and glanced at it. Suddenly my silly outburst and ogling seemed insignificant. There was only one guy who owned my heart, and he'd just messaged me.

It's only been a few hours, and I'm losing my mind without you.

I rolled over onto my back and held my phone in the air as my thumbs danced across the screen.

It seems like forever. Are you sure you can't sneak in through the front door tonight?

The three dots flickered across my screen while I waited for his response.

Yeah. Count me in. I thought I could make it a few days, but apparently my will power is nonexistent when it comes to you.

I couldn't stop the silly grin that eased across my face.

Do I need to pick you up since you can't drive yet?

Dammit. I forgot. No, I'll call an Uber. See you at 10:30? Mom and Missy will be asleep by then.

Guilt tugged at me. He was leaving his family to come over.

Now I feel guilty.

They'll be passed out. Seriously. I'll be staring at the wall or texting you anyway. I'm going a bit stir crazy not being able to do anything with this chest wound.

He wasn't the only one who wanted him to hurry up and get better. The doc had given strict orders *no sex* until he'd signed off on regular activity again.

Alright. If you're sure. I don't want to be a bad influence.

☺ *You can be a bad influence anytime you want.*

I paused a minute and replied.

I might have a nurse's costume in my closet from a few Halloween's ago. I giggled as I hit send.

Dammit. I dropped my phone. You're killing me, Mac.

Sorry? Not sorry? You're welcome?

Doc didn't say anything about a hand job.

I barked out a laugh.

And pop a stitch in your chest? No way. Sorry babe, I won't tease you and give you a boner.

Too late.

I'll see you tonight.

I can't wait.

Me too.

Mac?

Yeah?

I love you.

My heart fluttered with happiness.

I love you, too.

I tossed my phone on the bed and rubbed my forehead. In the space of thirty minutes, I'd run the full gamut of hormonal female emotions—giddy one second, foul mood the next, followed by tears and happiness. Sometimes I even annoyed the hell out of myself.

CHAPTER 26

"I almost feel like we need to arrive in an armored car," I said to Gemma. We were getting ready for John's funeral in her bathroom since it had a vanity mirror and enough room for both of us. Before she and Hendrix had started touring, we used to do each other's makeup and get silly in here while prepping for a night out. There was no silliness today.

"I know. It sounds as though Franklin doesn't even want us to go," she said, applying mascara to her lower lashes.

I spun around on the vanity bench and looked at her. "No way. I get he's scared, and so am I, but I'd risk it to say goodbye to John. We owe him that much," I said. It was more than fear I was attempting to control, though. The itch for some Xanax and alcohol had returned with a vengeance today. It had hit me hard. Although I knew I could pick up the phone and call my therapist for a refill, I didn't. I continued to surround myself with people who loved me. And bottom line? I couldn't risk losing Cade.

John's smiling face flickered through my mind and a quiet strength flowed through me. There was no doubt in my mind, he was supporting me from above.

"I do, at least." Gemma shoved the mascara brush back in the tube and tossed it on the counter.

"Gemma," I said, my voice thick with emotion. "I know if John had jumped in front of me, I'd feel guilty, too. But it wasn't your fault. There's nothing you could have done differently."

"I could have told Franklin I wouldn't testify against Brandon."

I gasped. "You don't mean it."

"I do. If it would have kept John alive, I would have gladly not provided a testimony."

"Gemma, you realize Brandon won't serve time if you don't. We both have to get on the stand."

She shook her head, her red wavy hair framing her face.

"You don't get it, Mac. Even if we do, we risk the chance of a corrupt judge or a jury member that's been paid to vote not guilty."

I ran the brush through my dark hair, then wrapped a section around my curling iron. Most days I either braided it or it hung straight past my shoulders. But today, today was for John.

"I get it. We're not dealing with a normal situation. Dillon has connections and is an incredibly powerful man, but Gem-ma," I said, slapping my leg, "so is Franklin. We have to do everything in our power to put not only Brandon behind bars for the rest of his life but to bring down Dillon and the entire, nasty, gnarly society."

She sank into the other chair. "Do you really think we have enough for the charges to stick?"

I nodded furiously. "I believe it with every fiber of my being. Plus, what would John want? Would he want you not to testify? No. And I've known him longer, so no way in hell would he have saved his own ass if it meant Brandon walked. It's who John was. It's why he became a bodyguard and whatever else he was up to we didn't know about. He's always been the guy who would sacrifice himself for the greater good. This time, you were the greater good. You have to know he's at peace with his decision and you need to be as well."

"I know you're right, but my heart isn't being logical. We shouldn't be attending a twenty-three-year old's funeral, Mac. It's wrong."

"I'm not going to argue with you, but what about any of this fucked up situation with Brandon isn't wrong?"

Gemma stood, smoothing her simple but elegant black dress. We had decided to buy the same one, John would have gotten a kick out of it. With a heavy sigh, we each stepped into our heels and stared at each other.

"Thank you, Mac," Gemma said, taking my hands in hers. "I'm so glad you weren't hurt during the shooting. I don't know what I'd do without you." She leaned in for a hug.

"I don't know how, but we're going to be alright. As long as we have each other we'll be okay," I whispered.

OTHER THAN ADA LYNN'S, I'd never attended a funeral before. Especially not for anyone my age or even worse, someone I'd grown up with. John's family sat in the first row of the church, and we settled behind them.

Pink and white lilies graced each end of the closed coffin along with a large bouquet of red roses in the center.

"I can't believe we're here," Cade said in a hushed tone.

"I know," I said, gripping his hand in mine. My focus traveled over his black jacket and silver tie. Cade didn't wear a suit often, but when he did, he was breathtakingly masculine and sexy as hell.

"I keep going over all the details in my mind to see if I could have done anything differently," he said, his voice cracking with emotion.

"Babe," I turned in my seat to face him, "you weren't anywhere near him on the stage. There was no way humanly possible you could have reached him or Gemma."

Cade looked at me, his expression filling with more pain than I could handle seeing in his beautiful eyes.

"How are you feeling?" I asked, redirecting the conversation. If he didn't want me to break down and sob in front of God and everyone, I needed to focus on something else for a second.

"Alright. I'm ready to return to playing, but I can't yet."

"Playing your guitar or me?" I whispered.

Cade flashed me a sad smile and kissed the back of my hand.

"Both, and I miss you more than I thought was possible. It's bad enough John's gone, but now that you're not next to me every night ... I feel like I'm losing my mind."

"Do you have someone to stay with your mom and Missy? I mean, you came over for a while the other night."

"Yeah, I can leave whenever I want to. It's ... I'm not supposed to be doing much anyway while I heal, and when I see you, it hurts just as much when I have to leave."

"Then don't," I said in his ear. "Stay with me and leave early in the morning."

He stared at me like I'd said he had three wishes.

"Through the front door," I added.

"I can't imagine Franklin would be alright with it," he commented wistfully.

"Pu-lease, Gemma and Hendrix have slept together at his house for like ever. I'll talk to him. If he's going to believe we're serious, I need to be honest with him and not sneak you in. Are you on board?"

"Yeah," he replied.

"Family and friends," the pastor said, stepping up to the microphone.

"We'll finish this later," I said, turning toward the front of the church.

233

The next forty-minutes were almost the longest in my life. The first had been when I was with Brandon in that warehouse.

~

FRANKLIN HAD OFFERED to host the post-funeral reception at our house. John's parents had accepted his help, and the downstairs floor was now brimming with over sixty people. I'm not sure whose bright idea it was to entertain people after someone had died, but it sucked. All I wanted was to hide and allow myself to grieve, but I had to continually plaster a fake smile on my face.

Even though Cade was with us at the house, he'd had to settle in on the couch and rest. Dark circles had formed beneath his eyes. I knew he was tired, losing John had kicked all of our asses leaving us exhausted. But Cade was still recovering from his gunshot wound too.

"Hey," I said gently, sitting next to him on the sofa.

"How are you holding up?" he asked, tucking my hair behind my ear.

I responded to his question with a shrug. "I'll be glad when it's over, and I can have some time to wrap my head around it all. I keep expecting John to walk through the door."

"Me too," Cade said.

"Do you want to stay tonight?"

Cade's expression softened. "I'm exhausted, babe. I think I'd fall asleep on you."

"I'll take it, but you need to be comfortable since you're healing, and if it's in your own bed for a while I understand, but I don't have to like it."

"I know," he said, kissing the back of my hand.

"Kids?" Franklin said, approaching us. He looked strikingly handsome in his soft blue button-down shirt and navy tie. The last year had added a smidge more silver to his dark hair, but he wore it well. "How's everyone doing under the circumstances?"

"Ugh," I replied.

"There's nothing easy about this situation," Franklin agreed. He pulled a chair up and sat down with us, his gaze falling on Cade. "I know my son has known you for a long time, Cade, but I haven't. I need to know what your intentions are with Mac."

"Aw hell," I muttered. "Right now, Dad?" My voice teetered on whiny, but I didn't care. We'd lost John, and Cade had the weight of the world on his shoulders. We all did.

"Yeah, I think it's a good a time. It's not like we'll all wake up tomorrow and feel better about losing John, and it seems you two are pretty close. Why don't you go find Gemma and Hendrix, and allow me to speak with Cade?" He posed it as a question, but I was well aware it wasn't up for debate.

I slouched forward in defeat. I knew when to push Dad and now wasn't the time. "Good luck," I said, kissing Cade's cheek before I got up and reluctantly made my way into the kitchen. If we hadn't had a house full of people, I would have grabbed Gemma, hidden around the corner, and eavesdropped on Franklin and Cade.

Anxiety hummed beneath my skin, and I rubbed my arms. What if Cade said the wrong thing, and Franklin pitched a bitch over us seeing each other?

"There you are," Gemma said, strolling into the kitchen and joining me at the counter. "I've been wondering what happened to you."

"I was hanging out with Cade for a bit when Franklin decided right now would be the perfect time to have the father to boyfriend conversation."

"Now?" Gemma asked unable to hide her surprise.

"I know," I said, plopping onto the bar stool. "Doesn't he know today is about John?"

"He does, Mac. But there's not a single person here that hasn't seen how Cade looks at you. It's clear he's in love with you, and as a father, I'd assume Franklin wants to learn more about him.

Regardless of where John is, Cade's feelings aren't going to change for you, and I think Franklin realized it today."

"You think so?" I asked, my concern calming down a little bit.

"I do. You're lucky," Gemma said, releasing a soft sigh. "Franklin loves you, and he wants to be involved in your life. A lot of fathers are too busy or don't make their kids a priority. He's candid with you and Hendrix, too. You always know where you stand with him. Give him a chance to accept your relationship."

"I'm scared. What I have with Cade is so different and special. I'm afraid I'm going to wake up and it's going to disappear."

"I get it, but trust me. He's not going anywhere, from what Hendrix has shared with me. You can't tell him I told you, though," Gemma said, rubbing my arm. "Let's see what happens with Franklin, and we'll figure it out together. We should probably check on John's parents now."

I nodded. I knew she was right, but at this point my heart was on overload. It would simply break into a million pieces if I lost anyone else.

It was after nine in the evening when the house finally emptied of all the guests. Franklin had hired some staff to clean up, but I found myself wandering around aimlessly, picking up paper plates and glasses. None of this made sense. John should be with us, alive, laughing, and licking my cheek.

The minutes had ticked by slowly as I waited for Cade to call me and tell me how things had gone with Franklin. Honestly, I wasn't sure if Franklin would talk to me first, but either way, I needed to know something soon.

The doorbell rang, pulling me out of my melancholy thoughts. I strolled through the living room, into the foyer, and opened the door.

"What are you doing here?" I asked Cade. "Are you alright?" I quickly assessed him for any signs of bad news.

"I'm fine. I wanted to see you. It was so crazy today." A small smile eased across his face as he leaned against the doorway.

I motioned for him to come in and closed the door behind him.

"You look exhausted," I said, standing on my tiptoes and giving him a quick peck on his lips.

"I am, but I needed to be next to you tonight," he said, twirling a strand of my hair around his finger.

"What? You're staying with me?" I asked, my voice filling with surprise and a little bit of hope.

"I am. Franklin and I had a good talk. He knows I'm here."

"Wait? You let *him* know before you showed up?" My eyes narrowed at him. "What happened to girlfriend privileges?" I asked, teasing him.

Cade chuckled softly. "This time, yeah. I did."

"Tell me everything, but first let's get you into my bed. This is our first night here together. I mean, you've spent a lot of nights at my house, but not like this."

"I'm ready," he said, taking my hand and following me upstairs.

Fifteen minutes later, I turned off the lamp on my nightstand, and we snuggled together underneath my teal and white comforter. Even though we were no longer on the bus, I curled up against his right side. It seemed natural to sleep on this side of him now, and I had to be super careful since his chest was still healing.

"You're going to have a scar." I traced the edge of the bandage gently with my finger.

"Yeah, I know. Maybe I'll do something cool and get some ink in memory of John."

I sat up and stared at him. "That would be amazing," I whispered.

"I think so, too."

I laid back down, my mind drifting to all the times John had talked about getting a tattoo. I wondered if he had. My chest tightened with the deep ache I had for the loss of my friend.

"Wait!" I popped back up like a jack in the box.

"Shit," Cade said, grabbing his chest.

"Omigosh, I'm so sorry, are you alright?"

He grimaced and nodded. "Yeah, maybe we can work on not jostling the bed too much?"

"Yup," I said, nodding emphatically and gently placing my hands on the bed. "But you're here, and I got so wrapped up in John and your scar I forgot you're *here*. I mean, in my house ... well Franklin's house, and in my bed. But Franklin knows, so does it mean the talk went okay? Did he embarrass you and ask if we're using protection? And omigosh, we didn't the last time, but you didn't tell him, right? Talk about TMI." I groaned and rubbed my face. "I know, I know, you can't tell me if I don't hush."

Cade grinned and took my hand. "I love you, Mac. You're adorable when you chatter."

"Really?" I asked, suddenly shy.

"Most of the time, yeah."

"Let's hope you don't change your mind," I replied. "What if you get tired of my adorable chatter? Think about how many couples grow to hate their significant other's quirks or qualities they initially thought were endearing and cute."

"You forget I've known you for a long time. I don't know what you've been through in the past with Asher and Jeremiah, Mac, but I'm not going to break up with you over your ADHD. You're so much more than a label."

My body visibly relaxed with his words.

"Thank you."

"Are you ready to hear what Franklin and I talked about?"

"Is it bad?"

"I'm here next to you, babe."

"True. Alright, spill."

"He's a little scary honestly."

"Dude, he's an attorney, of course he is!"

"I forget sometimes, though. To me he's always been Hendrix's dad, and now he's my girlfriend's dad. It's different."

I couldn't stop myself from grinning. "I love the sound of being your girlfriend."

"Me too. I think Franklin is adjusting as well."

I wiggled down in the bed and propped my head on my hand, staring at Cade while he talked.

"He asked if I was in love with you, and I told him yeah."

"What did he say?" I asked, my eyes widening. I knew first-hand how intimidating Franklin could be.

"He asked if I'd considered a real future with you, and what it looked like with me in the band. I told him I had, and I was in this for the long term."

"Ohhh," I said softly.

"I told him after I was healed, I wanted to get our own place."

"What?" I squeaked. "Are you serious?"

"Well, I was."

My heart sank. "What do you mean?" How did I go from the idea of living with my boyfriend to not in one breath?

"Franklin asked me not to at this time. He said you'd be alone when I was on the road and with Dillon loose, he would worry about your safety."

"I fucking hate Dillon. He and his son ruin everything." My chin quivered as I fought back the unwanted tears.

"He's right, Mac. Until this is settled, we need to keep you safe. I'd never forgive myself if anything else happened to you. So after talking with Franklin some more, I agreed to wait. But if you want to tour with us and take online classes for a while, he's totally cool with it."

"Really? I guess I should choose a major so he knows I'm

serious about getting a degree. And you're alright with it, too?" I asked, hope filling my voice.

"Yeah. I think about not being with you for weeks at a time, and it rips right through me."

"Me too," I admitted.

"So if this works for you, I'll stay here at night, and go home during the day to see Mom and Missy until she goes to bed. When we set the tour schedule again, well, you'll be with us. Eventually, we'll get our own place to live, but for now, I'm going to side with your dad and stay in his good graces."

"Yes." I grinned at him. "It sounds perfect." I leaned over and kissed him softly.

His hand slipped around the back of my neck, pulling me closer. Our lips parted, and his tongue swept across mine.

"I miss being with you," he whispered.

"I miss you inside me," I replied between kisses.

Cade moaned his response, our kiss deepening as my hand trailed over his ripped abs and disappeared beneath the cover.

"Be really still," I said, wrapping my hand around his erection. "Let me do the work and try to keep your heart rate down."

"Babe, I'm not sure this ..."

"If you get too worked up, I'll stop."

"Hell no," he responded.

I wiggled beneath the covers and ran my tongue along his long shaft.

"Jesus," he muttered, bunching up the blankets in his hand.

Slowly, I eased him into my mouth, inch by inch. I savored every moment as I stroked him, tasting every part of him. Need pulsed through me, and I carefully released him and moved out from under the covers.

His amber eyes darkened with desire, and I pulled my tank top over my head.

"Hi girls," he said, grinning and cupping my left breast. "How I've missed you."

I sighed, his touch igniting a fierce desire inside me. Nothing I'd had in the past compared with him on any level. Emotionally or physically. Cade touched my heart and soul like I'd never been touched before.

His thumb brushed across my nipple, then trailed down my stomach and dipped between my legs.

"Cade," I whimpered while he teased me through the thin material of my G-string. He moved the satin material to the side and slipped a finger inside me.

"You're so beautiful," he whispered. "I miss tasting you."

My breath hitched in my chest as he stroked me.

"That's it, Mac."

I moved him away, and confusion clouded his face.

"Hang on. I'm going to be so, so careful, but you tell me if it's too much."

His gaze never left mine while I slid my G-string over my hips and tossed it on the floor. I gently straddled him, and eased myself down, guiding him inside me.

"I love you, Mac," he said.

"I love you too, but you've got to stay still and let me guide you." I held onto his wrists for balance as I timidly rocked my hips against him. "Am I hurting you? How's your chest?"

"Stop talking, babe. I promise I'll tell you if it's too much, but for now, I want to be inside you. It's been too long."

I guided his hands to my breasts and shifted my weight backward, allowing him deeper inside me. A soft moan escaped me while I took control of our pace, and he caressed every part of my body as we made love.

"Mac," he panted.

Leaning forward, I placed my palms on the mattress above his shoulders and carefully balanced my upper body above him. I dug my heels into the bed for leverage, my pace quickening. The familiar swirl of heat spread through my body.

"Cade," I said. "I'm going to come."

.A. OWENBY

His fingers dug into my ass cheeks as my body tensed, and I lost myself to him.

"Babe," he grunted, his muscles flexing beneath me. Seconds later he relaxed, and I sat up slowly.

"Are you alright? Did I hurt you? Omigosh, we shouldn't have done that." I eased off him carefully.

"I'm good," he said, a lazy smile spreading across his beautiful features.

"Let me look at your bandage and make sure you're not bleeding. What was I thinking? How selfish of a girlfriend am I? I just missed you so bad. If anything happens to you, Cade; I'll never forgive myself. I'm so sorry." My voice rose in pitch as I continued.

Cade gently grabbed my wrists with one hand and tilted my chin toward him with the other.

"Mac, I'm grown and capable of making my own choices. I'm fine, you were great. Please don't panic. I've missed you, too. I'm okay."

My jaw tensed, and I quickly glanced away.

"Hey, what's the matter?" he asked, sitting up.

"I was afraid I hurt you," I muttered. "But, as much as I wanted to … the last penis in my mouth was Brandon's," I hiccuped. "At the moment I was fine, but it just hit me."

"The video," he whispered, brushing a stray hair from my face.

I nodded, unable to articulate my crazy emotions.

"As much as I love it, seeing you like this isn't worth a blow job."

"But I enjoy it, Cade. I want you to feel good, but the last thing I need is to remember what he did to me. It just all came rushing back after we were finished."

"Come here," he said, wrapping his arm around me and pulling me to him. "I love you, and we never have to do anything that brings up bad memories." His lips gently brushed mine. "It's been a really emotional and intense day, are you able to get some sleep?"

"Yeah," I said and settled in next to him. "I'm glad you're here, Cade."

He kissed the top of my head. "There's no other place in the entire world I'd rather be than next to you."

CHAPTER 27

$\mathcal{T}$he next several weeks flew by and Labor Day was around the corner. Cade's wound had continued to heal nicely, and he was returning to more and more normal activities.

"I'll see you in a few hours," I said, standing on my tiptoes and kissing him goodbye.

"I love you," he replied.

Although Franklin hadn't objected to Cade spending most nights, he slipped out around six-thirty every morning before anyone saw him. This gave him time to get home before his sister woke up and the nurse left. But today, the nurse would stay, and Cade would meet me here before we left for the courthouse.

My stomach flip-flopped after I closed the door behind him and leaned up against it. This would be the first time I saw Brandon face to face since he had kidnapped me. Thank God I wasn't in this alone.

"Morning, hon. How are you doing?" Franklin asked, appearing just outside the kitchen with a cup of steaming coffee in his hand.

"I feel sort of sick," I said, walking to him.

He wrapped his arm around me and pulled me in for a hug. "We'll all be there with you."

"I know. Thank you."

Franklin's phone buzzed on the kitchen counter, and he stepped away to answer it. I rubbed my eyes and made my way to the coffee pot.

"Do we know what this is about?" Franklin asked.

Grabbing a coffee cup, I filled it and turned toward him. He had his attorney poker expression in place, and I couldn't get a read on the conversation.

He ended the call and looked at me. "I have a meeting before court, so I'll need to get there half an hour earlier than planned. Pierce, Vaughn, and Zayne will also be with us today."

"Really? You think we're going to need them all? That's not a good sign, Dad."

"I don't want you to worry, but I'm taking extra precautions." He rubbed his chin and frowned. "Is there any way you can talk Cade into not going?"

"What? Why?" I asked, my volume louder than I'd intended.

"I'm concerned about everyone's safety today, Mac."

My mouth dropped. "You mean like if another shooter showed up to finish what they started?" I asked, my voice hovering above a whisper. Terror snaked down my spine as I recalled the band's last performance and the sound of gunshots.

Dad didn't answer me right away. "We have to be prepared for every possible scenario."

I leaned against the counter and blinked my tears away. "I need him there, but if he's in danger, I'll tell him not to come. I couldn't stand it if he got hurt again. Or worse." I swallowed hard, forcing the ball of emotions down. I had to keep my shit together today.

"I'm sorry, Mac. I think you're making the right decision, though. Sometimes the best decisions are the hardest, and when you're in a relationship, they should be based on what's best for your partner. There's no doubt in my mind if Cade could switch places with you today, he would."

"I agree, he'd do it in a heartbeat," I said, nodding. Even though I didn't want to hear what Franklin was saying, I realized he was right. "I'll call him in a little bit."

"Thank you. It will be one less person I'm worried about today."

The back door opened, and Pierce strolled into the kitchen.

"Mac, sir," he said and nodded slightly at us.

"Morning," I mumbled and took a sip of my coffee.

"Vaughn and Zayne are keeping an eye on the perimeter this morning."

"Thank you," Franklin said, placing his cup in the sink. "Mac, we have a phone call to make, but when you see Gemma and Hendrix, please let everyone know we need to leave here by nine."

"I will."

The men walked out of the kitchen silently. Maybe Franklin, had his poker face in place, but there was no way anyone could miss the tension in the air.

CADE and I had our first argument an hour later.

"I don't like it either, but if Dad says it's dangerous, then I have to listen to him. He's right, you're first in my life now. I have to make decisions based on what's best for both of us, not simply me anymore."

"Dammit, Mac. I'm not okay with this."

"Listen to me," I said, sinking down on the edge of my unmade bed. "The minute it's over and I'm safely back in the limo and on my way home, you can come over. I'll need you more then." I had just lied to my boyfriend, and I inwardly cringed.

A heavy silence filled the line.

"I wanted to be there for you when you testify," Cade said softly. "I feel like I'm failing you."

"No. You can't think of it like that. I need you to be safe so I can get on the stand and not worry about you. This is the best way you can support me."

"I don't have a choice, do I?"

"Not really, but I didn't want to come right out and say it."

"And I suspect Pierce, Zayne, and Vaughn will be with you all, too?"

"Yeah. We have the full crew today."

"Mac!" Franklin called up the stairs. I stood, not wanting to say goodbye to Cade.

"I have to go. I'll call you the minute I'm done."

"I'm going to be a fucking mess until I hear from you."

"Try not to worry. We're in good hands," I assured him.

"Mac?"

"Yeah?"

"I love you."

My heart ached for him. I'd lied. I needed him next to me. I wasn't sure if I was strong enough to look at Brandon and testify against him. On the other hand, maybe not subjecting Cade to every gory detail of what the monster had done to me was for the best.

"I love you, too," I said, my voice cracking with emotion.

I ended the call, gathered my purse, and hurried down the stairs.

"I'm here," I said, smoothing my navy-blue silk blouse and slacks.

"Are you ready?" Gemma asked me while she nervously tugged on her beige skirt. The soft blue blouse she'd paired with it accentuated her eyes. Hendrix waited next to her, fiddling with his tie that nearly matched Gemma's top. His hair was a bit of a mess, which told me he'd run his hands through it multiple times, a nervous habit when he was stressed out.

"No. Are you?" I asked.

She shook her head. My attention drifted to her and Hendrix's hands. My best bestie was terrified. Hendrix's thumb stroked the back of her hand, causing her to ease up on the death grip she had on his fingers, allowing the blood flow to return.

"Let's go, kids," Franklin said, picking up his briefcase and holding the front door open for us. He grabbed his black suit jacket and slipped it on over his white dress shirt.

We filed out the door and into the limo. I stared out the window as Pierce, Vaughn, and Zayne settled in next to us.

"Nice and cozy," I mumbled, scooting over and smashing myself against the door. Not even steamy hot bodyguards could help my mood today.

The tension increased in the car as we grew closer to the courthouse. Franklin didn't have any words of advice or wisdom, either. He wasn't entirely clued in on what to expect since he wasn't an attorney on the case. The only reason he knew anything was because he and Pierce were looped in through courtesy and the FBI. Under normal circumstances, Franklin would have to call in a lot of favors to be as involved as he was now.

The car pulled into the parking lot, and my heart pounded against my chest.

"What if I can't do this?" I blurted. "Dad? What if I can't look at the son of a bitch and testify?" I clenched my teeth together in an attempt to hold back my tears.

"You don't have to do this, Mac. We still have Gemma's testimony."

I looked at Gemma, sharp guilt stabbing me in the pit of my stomach. How could I ask my best bestie to do this and not follow through myself?

"No. I can't do it. She gave herself to save me. I'm fine." I inhaled sharply and chided myself for allowing Brandon to fuck with my mind.

"If at any time—" Franklin started.

Flashes of Gemma, Hendrix, Cade, Pierce, and John collapsing on the stage in front of me stirred my anger.

"I'm fine. Let's take the bastard down and go after his sorry excuse of a father next. Today, this is for John." I squared my shoulders and glanced at my family.

Gemma winked and nodded at me.

"I'm proud to call you my sister," Hendrix said to me.

Only he would know what to say to give my heart the strength to walk through those doors.

"Thank you."

The bodyguards exited the limo first and opened the doors for us. The minute we were outside the vehicle, each of them took their place, creating a tight circle around us.

Franklin led the way up the stairs, and I slipped between Gemma and Hendrix, taking each of their hands in mine.

Cade's words whispered through my mind while we walked through the doors of the courthouse, renewing my strength. *I see an amazing, smart, funny, loyal, beautiful woman. You're full of fire, and you're all heart at the same time.*

Mine and Gemma's heels clicked against the tile floor of the hallway, bringing my thoughts back to what I was about to do. Franklin's phone buzzed, and we turned the corner as he answered it.

"We're here."

We came to a stop in front of the courtroom's large wooden door, and my heart jumped into my throat.

"Mac," Gemma said gently.

I dropped Hendrix's hand and turned toward her.

"I'll love you even if you don't testify. We're family, and I know how gut-wrenching this is. I'd protect you from all of it if I could."

Speechless, I threw my arms around her.

"I love you, best bestie."

J.A. OWENBY

"You too, Mac," she said, returning my embrace.

"I'll be right in," Franklin said, ending his call. He cleared his throat before he faced us. "Pierce, the judge wants to see you and me in his chambers. Vaughn and Zayne, take everyone to the conference room. Don't let anyone in or out."

"Wait? What's going on?" I asked, puzzled. "Aren't we supposed to go into the courtroom?"

"Now." Franklin's tone was stern.

Hendrix led the way down the hall as my mind scrambled for an answer to the schedule change.

"When I'm done, I'll meet you all in here," Franklin said as we settled into the plastic chairs. Zayne stood next to Hendrix, and Vaughn remained in the hallway, the door clicking closed with a finality that made me jump.

"What do you think is going on?" Gemma asked, standing and wringing her hands together.

"We won't know until Dad's back," Hendrix said. "Try not to stress. It could be anything from a postponement to ... hell, who knows. This entire thing has been fucked from the beginning."

"I couldn't have said it any better, bro." I leaned back in my chair, my fingers drumming on top of the wooden table.

"So Zayne?" I asked, attempting to redirect my attention.

"Yes?" He didn't move anything except his emerald green eyes when he spoke.

"Where did you get your ink?" I asked, pointing to his right arm. I wasn't sure if he had more tats or not underneath his suit.

"Portland," he said, his voice clipped.

"Since you're my bodyguard, for now, I'll eventually see it, right?"

"I'm not hiding it from anyone."

My lips pursed. "I can see why you and Pierce get along so well, you're both exceptional conversationalists," I said dryly.

Gemma released a nervous giggle, and Hendrix arched his

eyebrow at me. I raised mine right back at him. If Zayne was going to be my shadow, I wanted to know something about him.

"What's in Portland other than a tattoo parlor?"

"I'm from there. So are Pierce and Vaughn."

"Oh, really?" I asked, standing with this new information. "How long have you known him?"

By this time, Gemma's and Hendrix's attention had also piqued.

"Since we were twelve."

"Holy Hannah! You knew little Pierce?"

"Yes," Zayne replied.

"Fine, since you're rushing to fill us in on the details, I'll ask Pierce about it."

"Good luck with that. He doesn't like to discuss his childhood," Zayne said.

A flicker of something I couldn't identify crossed his expression.

"Did you know Pierce was from Portland?" I asked Gemma.

"No. He's never told us anything about his life before he started working for Franklin."

"He's so full of secrets," I said, sitting back down and staring at my brother. "You're awfully quiet, Hendrix."

"Mac, I know you're stressed right now, but I don't think we need to pry into Pierce and Zayne's background," Hendrix's tone held a hint of disapproval.

"Fine. I'll do it later when you're not around."

My leg bounced underneath the table and my anxiety returned. Thirty painful minutes later, the door opened, and Franklin walked into the room.

CHAPTER 28

*W*hatever had happened in the judge's chambers wasn't good.

"Kids," Franklin said softly, shoving his hands in his pockets. "I need you to trust me and just do what I tell you. We're leaving."

"What?" I gasped, jumping out of my chair.

"Mac, you need to stay calm. The second we're in the limo, I'll explain what happened, but for now we're to leave the court-house the same way we came in."

I glanced at Gemma and Hendrix. They appeared as confused as I was. Without another word, we left the room and walked into the hallway.

My head snapped up at the sound of his voice, and I clutched Gemma's arm. In seconds, my knees turned to Jell-O and Brandon Montgomery sneered at me from across the hall. His eyes flashed with hatred before Zayne stepped in between our line of sight.

"Keep walking," Franklin ordered.

"I can't wait to bury my cock in your girlfriend, Harrington!" Brandon called after us. In one quick movement, the guard whirled Brandon around and shoved him in the opposite direction.

"No!" I screamed when Hendrix stopped in his tracks, spun around, and took three steps in Brandon's direction. Brandon peered over his shoulder and flinched as my brother gunned toward him.

"You keep your filthy fucking hands off my girlfriend and sister," Hendrix growled.

Pierce moved in between them, and an additional deputy entered the hallway, blocking my brother from nailing Brandon in the jaw. Vaughn grabbed Hendrix's arms and hauled him backward.

"Hendrix," Franklin said, their noses only an inch apart. "If you don't want to spend the night with Brandon in jail, I strongly advise you turn around right now."

"Do me a favor and lock me up with the sick bastard. I guarantee you only one of us will walk out alive," Hendrix said, his voice low and thick with hatred.

"Babe, I need you here with me," Gemma said calmly from behind him.

I gawked at the entire shit show in front of me. If anyone could calm down Hendrix, it would be Gemma. But not even the threat of jail would get him to back off right now.

"Hendrix!" Gemma pleaded. The anguish in her voice halted him in his tracks and he turned around. "I think I'm pregnant, Hendrix."

Time stood still as everyone's eyes landed on her—including Brandon's.

"What?" Hendrix said, walking away from Brandon and the guards.

My mouth hung open and my attention traveled from Gemma to Pierce. I didn't miss the brief shock on Pierce's face, but Hendrix had the full-on deer in the headlights look.

"Are you sure?" he asked, taking his hands in hers.

"The home pregnancy test was positive, but I have an appointment tomorrow with the doctor for a blood test. I'll find out for sure then. I need you with me, not here in jail."

He nodded. "Yeah. Let's get you out of here." He slid his arm protectively around her waist while the guys surrounded us again.

"Fuck," I muttered under my breath to Pierce. Glancing over my shoulder at Franklin, a pang of sadness ripped through me. This was not the news he'd hoped for yet. Maybe someday, but we all wanted a calmer life before bringing an innocent baby into the picture.

My mind whirled a million miles an hour as we entered the limo.

The moment the door closed, my mouth opened without my full consent.

"What. The. Fuck?" I asked, gawking at Gemma. "You're pregnant and didn't tell me?"

"I'm so sorry, Mac. I was trying to get through today and the appointment tomorrow." Tears streamed down her face. I knew for a fact Gemma didn't want kids, but Hendrix did. Crap just got even more intense.

"We'll figure it out," Hendrix said, wrapping his arm around her shoulders.

"I'm sorry, Franklin. This wasn't the way the conversation had played out in my mind. But Hendrix was about to get himself tossed in jail, and it flew out of my mouth."

"I understand why you did it, but I think I need some time to wrap my head around this. Not to mention I need to talk to you all about what happened in the judge's chambers."

"Omigod." I rubbed my forehead with the palms of my hands and groaned. "What the hell happened? Why are we not in court testifying right now?"

"Since the immediate danger is over, I'd like to take a few minutes to collect my thoughts and talk to you all at home."

"That bad, huh?" Hendrix asked.

A heavy silence filled the car on the way to the house. I pulled my phone out of my purse and messaged Cade.

Shit hit the fan. I'm on my way home, but I can't see you yet. There's more to come apparently.

Black dots flickered across my screen.

Are you alright? Did you see him?

I snorted. Yeah, I saw him alright, but I'd have to wait to tell Cade the full story.

Yes, but we didn't have to testify. I don't know why yet. I'll let you know when the coast is clear, and you can join me.

Thanks for letting me know you're safely on your way home. I love you.

Love you, too.

I shoved my phone back in my bag and thought about the only thing in the world that made me happy: Cade.

It was only one in the afternoon, but I made a beeline for the bar the second we got home. After a few healthy slurps of my vodka and cranberry, I joined everyone at the table. No one said a word to me about my beverage while we settled in at the table. Pierce, Zayne, and Vaughn disappeared the second we were safely in the house.

"What happened?" Hendrix asked, still holding Gemma's hand as though she were made of porcelain. I wondered if Cade would be attentive if I were pregnant. God knew I didn't want any munchkins, not even with him. One pregnancy, although brief, was enough to last me a lifetime.

"You didn't have to testify because Brandon pled guilty to a lesser charge."

"What?" Hendrix snarled. "How did you let this happen?" He stood up suddenly, knocking his chair backward.

"Hendrix, we need the entire story. Please," Gemma said, holding her hand out to him.

He ran his hand through his hair and remained standing.

"How did this happen?" he asked Franklin quietly.

"Since he pled guilty, the judge gave him a reduced sentence. He received three months in the county jail since he had no priors. Brandon has never been in trouble before. Well, none that could be proved. We know he's done plenty but walking into a courtroom with charges that will stick is another matter."

"How could he have pleaded down? He had a gun on Gemma and me. That doesn't count for some prison time?" I asked, my voice trembling.

"Although he sexually assaulted you and attempted to rape Gemma, he didn't. There was no ransom, and he didn't transport you across state lines, so the charges were reduced."

"Then what the hell good is the system if it doesn't protect us from monsters like him?" I cried.

"I know, Mac. But there's more ..."

My body shook with sobs as I brought my knees under my chin and curled up in the chair.

"Mac," Gemma said, hurrying toward me and wrapping her arms around me. "We'll figure this out."

I leaned my head on her shoulder as my tears flowed. What the hell would we do in three months when Brandon was released? We lived in the same city, attended the same school. Would I have to change my entire life in order to not run into him? What if he waited for me again?

If anyone else in this world understood my inner turmoil, it was my best friend. But she might have two people to take care of now. I'd not missed Brandon's twisted, hate-filled expression when he'd heard her news. But I wasn't sure if it was for Gemma or Hendrix. I suspected in his mind it should be his baby, not my brother's.

Gemma released me and grabbed the box of tissues from the china hutch.

"Thanks," I said, taking one and blowing my nose.

Instead of returning to Hendrix, Gemma sat down next to me and took my hand.

"What else?" Gemma asked, her voice betraying her brave facade.

"The FBI was behind the plea deal. They want Brandon out in hopes he'll lead them to Dillon. They're looking at the bigger picture."

"Well will they have a tail on him or what? I mean, if they know who he is and what he's capable of, will it at least keep other girls safe?"

Franklin nodded. "I fought for them to step in if Brandon was harming another girl, Mac. You and Gemma are my daughters, and I'd hate for anyone else to go through what you two have."

"What do you mean?" Hendrix asked.

"Brandon will have a tail, and if he's seen harming someone, the FBI will call it in. They can't step in and stop anything, but the cops will be on the way."

"Won't it tip Brandon off?" I asked. "I mean, he's typically at a party or on campus."

"Right, as long as it's not too risky to the overall operation ..." Franklin said, his voice trailing off.

I pursed my lips to keep from screaming at the top of my lungs. There was no way this deal was fair.

"They will do everything to keep other women safe. You have my word."

"It's a gamble, Dad. I mean, if I'm understanding correctly they'll call it in only if it doesn't blow their cover," I said.

"Yes."

"Is that all?" I asked.

"There's one more thing," Franklin said to us, the color visibly draining from his face.

CHAPTER 29

"You have a few days to consider the offer," Franklin said.

I sat rooted in my seat, unmoving. There was no way I'd heard him correctly. The Witness Protection Program? Fuck. This was serious. How in the world had we ended up here?

"I can answer any questions for you," Pierce said, entering the dining room.

"I—I," I stammered. "What the hell do I even do with that?"

"I know, Mac and I'm sorry it's come to this. You all have a choice, though. But you have to make it together."

Gemma's cheeks flushed bright red with the information, and Hendrix sat wide-eyed at the table, staring at us.

"Would we stay together?" I asked.

"Yes. The program protects families all the time."

"But we'd leave our entire life behind? Our friends? Cade?" My voice hitched as I considered the consequences if we went or if we stayed.

"Cade would have a choice to go with us. If he wanted to, but it would mean leaving his sister and Mom, Mac." Franklin's expression softened.

"I can't ask him to choose, Dad. Hell, I can't even choose. If we stay, we risk running into Brandon everywhere we turn, maybe even another shooting. If we leave, you give up your job, your friends, our house."

"Those are all *things*, though. We can have all of those again, Mac. This is about keeping us safe while the FBI goes after Brandon and his family."

"Can we come home after it's over?" Gemma asked Pierce.

"I'm sorry, Gemma. No. We don't know how deep this goes, and unfortunately, Dillon is well connected. You'd be looking over your shoulder for the rest of your life."

Hendrix ran his hand through his hair and glanced at Dad.

"Where are you at with all of this?"

"I realize you all are grown, but my choice will be whatever you three decide."

"Dad, it's not fair to you," I added. "What do you want? What's important to you? You've made a good life here."

"I have, but my life is with my family wherever it may be. Not to mention I might be a grandfather, so there's that to think about as well."

Gemma bit her lip. "I'm so sorry. I'll know one way or another tomorrow. It might help everyone with their decision."

"Let's not jump to conclusions yet. Take tonight to talk to each other, see how the appointment goes tomorrow, then we can talk again. Whatever you decide, I'll be there."

"I'm done for now," I said, standing and taking a gulp of my vodka. "And Hendrix?"

"Yeah?" he asked, looking perplexed.

"Wrap. That. Shit. Up. This is the second time she's thought she was pregnant. You saw what I went through. Like, why would you not be more careful? And here we are about to make life-altering decisions based on a baby's safety."

"Mac, the first time wasn't his fault. I was new on the pill and simply got scared remember?"

I sighed, and guilt washed over me for being a bitch to my brother.

"I'm sorry. I'm sorry. I don't want either of you to have to go through the heartbreak and hell I did. Regardless if you keep it or not, it fucks with you."

I walked away before they could say another word to me. On the way to my room, I grabbed the bottle of vodka. I didn't miss Pierce's disapproving looks, but he didn't say a word. I wondered if Zayne would give me the same disapproval. For now, I didn't have to deal with him much since he kept an eye on the outside of the property along with Vaughn.

I hurried up the stairs, down the hall, and into my bedroom. Kicking the door shut with my foot, I strolled across the room, placed my glass down on my nightstand, and unscrewed the lid of the vodka. I tilted the bottle back and grimaced as the alcohol burned my throat. Replacing the cap, I set it down, then picked up my phone.

Need you ASAP. Please.

Cade's message was on my screen before I could blink. The poor guy had probably been a wreck all day while he waited for me.

On my way. See you in ten.

I splashed some more vodka in the remainder of my cranberry juice and downed it. There was no way I could have this conversation with Cade without some liquid courage.

A KNOCK SOUNDED at my door, and it creaked open slowly.

"Mac?" Cade asked, poking his head around the door.

"Hi, sexy," I slurred and grinned, noting how his shirt hugged his muscular chest. I rolled over on my side and propped up on my arm.

"Dammit," Cade said, closing the door behind him. "You're

drunk." A deep frown creased his forehead as he spotted the half-empty bottle of vodka.

"Tipsy," I said, patting the bed.

"Was it that bad?" he asked while he joined me.

"You can make it better," I said, wiggling my eyebrows at him.

He took my hand and kissed the back of it. "Talk to me. What happened."

I groaned and flopped back on my pillow.

"The motherfucker got a plea deal. He's a free man to rape and pillage the town square in three months. The only hope we have is if the townsmen take him in the middle of the night, slip a noose around his neck, and hang him from the tree on the edge of our cherished city." I placed the back of my hand on my forehead for extra dramatic emphasis. Even though this situation was deadly serious, I couldn't resist being a smart ass. It's what I did when I was stressed. That and eat.

"What?" Cade asked, his brows knitting together in confusion.

"Oh, it gets so much better. Would you like a drink now?"

He shook his head, and I continued.

"We didn't have to testify at all which was good, but lemme tell ya. Fucking fireworks exploded in the hallway when we were leaving. Some goon decided to walk Brandon back to wherever he needed to go at the exact minute Hendrix, Gemma, and I walked out of the meeting room they'd stuck us in."

"Oh shit."

"Right?" I rubbed my temples, attempting to regain a little bit of focus. "The second Brandon saw us, he tells Hendrix … Brandon said he's going to bury his cock in Gemma."

"The son of a bitch," Cade said, hopping off the bed. "Where were the guards?"

"They were there, and Pierce stepped in front of my brother right as he was about to land a punch in Brandon's face."

Cade's hands clenched and unclenched while I talked.

"But it's not what stopped Hendrix."

"What did?"

I barked out a drunken laugh. "Gemma," I whispered loudly. "She tells him he needs to calm down so he's not arrested."

Cade motioned for me to hurry up and spill the details.

"Then she announces in front of *everyone* she thinks she might be pregnant."

Cade's mouth hung open with the news. "Holy hell. Like, in front of Franklin and Brandon, too?"

"Hell yeah. In her defense, she was scared shitless Brandon was that close to us again, and Hendrix was going to get his ass tossed in jail. She just blurted it out. Gemma is actually a really private person, I know she didn't do it on purpose. But dude! You should have seen the look on everyone's face, including Pierce's!" I whisper yelled.

"What do you mean Pierce's? Why would he care?"

I raised my eyebrow at him and picked up the vodka bottle, topping off my drink. "Want one now?" I asked again. "It gets even better."

"Are you serious?" he asked wide-eyed.

"Mmmmhmm," I said, taking another sip.

"Yeah. I think a drink would be good."

"There's a glass in the bathroom, help yourself."

I chewed my lip as he walked out of the room and returned with a glass. How God could have made him any hotter, I had no idea. Between my really good buzz and being terrified I was about to lose him forever, all I could think of was how badly I wanted to jump him.

"Mac?"

"Huh?" I asked, my gaze raking up his muscular body and peering up at him. "Sorry, I was thinking about you naked."

Cade chuckled and sat down next to me, taking a hefty drink.

"What happened next?"

"No clue. Where was I?" I asked, peering at him out of one eye.

"Pierce's reaction and Gemma's possible pregnancy."

"Ohhh, yes. So, gotta ask you something and don't take it personally, but do guys not have a clue about these situations?"

"Not sure what you're referring to." He took another drink and waited for me to reply.

"Crayons. Box," I muttered under my breath, recalling what I'd said to the girl that wanted to suck my boyfriend's dick at the concert.

"Huh?" Cade asked, his expression clouding with confusion.

"It's alright, I'll draw you a picture," I said, grinning at my own joke. "There's a certain bodyguard who's very much in love with your best friend's girlfriend."

Cade gagged on his drink.

"Dammit, sorry babe. I didn't mean for you to choke on that one."

"Are you serious? How did I not see it?" he asked, wiping his mouth off with the back of his hand.

"Right? That's what I meant. Do you guys not see what's happening right in front of you?"

"In my defense, I wasn't paying a bit of attention to anyone or anything besides you," he said, trailing his fingers down my cheek.

I leaned into his touch and kissed the palm of his hand. "I love you so much it hurts," I confessed.

"Babe," he said, brushing his lips against mine. "I'm right here. I'm not going anywhere. You have my heart."

Raw emotions balled up in the pit of my stomach. I inhaled sharply, the seriousness of the situation weighing on me.

"Anyway, Gemma's confession had a huge impact on all of us. We'll know more tomorrow after she goes to the doctor."

I scooted back and rested my back against the headboard. My fingers tightened around my glass.

"Cade," I said, softly. "When I was with Asher, it was … we were young, and he was my first. I didn't really understand what a relationship should really be about. Then, when I went to Louisiana, I met Jeremiah. I thought I was in love with him, but he was my rebound guy. It wasn't until you walked into my life that I really began to feel whole. You're the first guy I've dated that really saw me for me and loved me regardless. I didn't have to pretend or try to hide my ADHD or mood swings. When you showed up it was like a part of myself had been missing all this time, and it had finally made its way back to me." I paused, glancing up at the ceiling in order not to turn into a puddle of tears.

"Mac? What is it?" he asked, taking my free hand.

"Please know that whatever happens ... it was you ... you were the light during my darkest days I've ever lived through."

"Babe? You're scaring me. Are you breaking up with me?"

I shook my head, the tears finally streaming down my face. "No, but you might break up with me."

CHAPTER 30

"Mac, I've told you before I'm not going anywhere."

I held my hand up, not wanting him to say any more until I could explain.

"Hear me out," I pleaded. "When we learned Brandon would be free in three months, Franklin and Pierce approached us about—. The Witness Protection Program."

Cade's eyes widened. "What?" he asked, his voice cracking. "You're leaving?"

"I don't know. And if I do, we all do. It's a decision we have to make together."

"Fuck." He rose slowly. "Do you want to go?" he asked, pain etching across his face.

"I don't want to leave you, Cade. You're the only person I care about other than my family, and they'd all be with me."

"Fuck," he said, rubbing his hands over his hair and pacing across my room. "When will you know?"

"Tomorrow. If Gemma's pregnant I think we'll all want to keep her and the baby safe. I think at that point we're all in." I choked on my words. "I don't want to lose you," I cried.

In a few short steps, Cade was next to me on the bed, pulling me into his lap.

"I love you," he said, his words thick with emotion. "I love you so much."

I clutched at his shirt and held onto him with everything inside me.

"Is there any other way?" Cade asked.

I nodded. "Yeah, but I don't expect you to do it."

"What? What is it?" Desperation hung from his words as we continued to cling to each other.

I sat up, my attention on him. "You can enter the Witness Protection Program with us."

Cade's expression changed in slow motion while he realized what I'd offered him.

"I told you I loved you, and I meant it. I would be willing to take you with us. At the same time, because I love you, I can't ask you to make that kind of sacrifice for me."

Cade's eyes glistened as he stroked my hair. "It's all or nothing then?"

I nodded. "I'm so sorry. For both of us. My heart was literally ripped out of my chest when Franklin talked to us this afternoon. All I could think about was seeing you, and how I couldn't ask you to do this for me. At the same time, I don't know how I'm going to make it without you." I hiccupped.

Cade wrapped me in his arms and rocked me as our tears flowed together. "I don't know how to get through this … I've lost John, and now there's a good chance I'm losing the love of my life, my best friend, and my career all at once."

"I'm so sorry," I whispered, kissing him. "Make love to me, Cade. If this is our last night together, I want to remember it in your arms."

He leaned me back onto the bed and kissed me deeply as he took me to heaven and back.

~

THE RAIN PATTERED against my window, waking me the next morning. For a brief moment, my mind recalled the amazing sex I'd had with my boyfriend the night before, then reality came tumbling down around me.

"Cade?" I called out to him.

His place in bed was cold. Had the idea of me leaving been too much for him and he'd left without telling me goodbye? I slipped out from under the covers and grabbed my shorts and shirt off the floor. I dressed and hurried out of my bedroom.

Ruby's voice carried through the living room, and my bare feet padded against the soft carpet while I ran toward the kitchen.

I rounded the corner, nearly smacking into Franklin as he was strolling out.

"Whoa," he said, raising his cup of coffee up to keep it from spilling.

"Hey," I said, peeking around Dad. My heart stuttered when I saw him. His smile lit up his entire face, the flecks in his amber eyes flashing while he talked with Hendrix. Their laughter filled the kitchen. What was going on? Had yesterday been a nightmare, and I'd not had to tell my boyfriend we were over?

"Are you alright?" Franklin asked, worry lines creasing his forehead.

"Yeah," I nodded, my eyes landing on Cade again. "Are you? I mean, yesterday was pretty crappy."

"It was, but we'll have more information this afternoon. Hang in there and know we're family. We'll stay together."

"Fuck." I grimaced. "Sorry. What about Mom?" Panic shot through me. How in the hell had I forgotten about her? "Dad? She can come with us if we go right?"

"It will be up to her, Mac."

"This whole thing sucks. How am I supposed to leave half the people I love behind?"

"Try not to worry about it right now. Spend the day with Cade, and we'll meet after Gemma's appointment. I'll have time to talk to your mom by then, too."

I swallowed the ball of emotions that threatened to erupt inside me. All I needed to focus on right now was being with Cade.

"I'll try."

"I'll be in my office if you need me."

"Thanks, Dad," I said, pushing up on my tiptoes and kissing his cheek. "I love you."

"Love you, too."

And I knew beyond a shadow of a doubt Franklin really did love me. There was no difference between Hendrix and me in his eyes. He may not have been my biological father, but he considered me his daughter.

Cade glanced up and gave me a tight little wave.

"Morning," he said, standing and giving me a gentle kiss. "Did you sleep well?"

"Yeah," I said, smiling up at him. "Hey," I said to Hendrix, joining them at the bar.

"Are you hungry, Mac?" Ruby asked, bringing over fresh biscuits, gravy, sausages, and scrambled eggs.

"Oh, you know what I'm like when I'm stressed!" I cried, grabbing a biscuit and taking a bite. "Mm, melt in my mouth yummy. What would I ever do without you?" My words stopped short as my focus bounced between my brother and Cade. My mood immediately plummeted. "Ruby, I love you. Thank you for taking care of me."

She halted in her steps toward the stove. "Thank you. It means the world to me. I've worked for families that didn't care, but you all … you're my family." She said, fisting her hand against her heart.

I blew her a kiss and returned to eating my biscuit. If I didn't, I'd lose my shit in front of her. I didn't dare look at Hendrix or Cade. I'd fall apart. How were we supposed to leave everything behind? We had a fantastic life except ...

"Where's Gemma?" I asked, finally realizing she wasn't with us.

"She's training," Hendrix said, his mood growing serious.

"I suspect nothing too high impact?"

"Yeah, at least for now anyway."

I nodded. "Is she scared?"

Hendrix leaned his elbows on the table and steepled his hands together. "She's terrified. And, she won't say it, but she's hoping she's not pregnant."

"Hendrix, I love you, but I can't blame her. You guys have plenty of time. The band is finally taking off, and I think she'd really resent being at home taking care of a baby."

"She'd come with and so would the baby. Bands with families do it all the time."

"Yeah, but considering what she went through ... I think she's afraid she wouldn't be able to protect her bambino."

"Me too."

I grabbed his hand. "I know I can be a brat sometimes, but I love you and Gemma so much. Please don't take it the wrong way if I don't want her to have a baby right now."

"I don't think she would choose not to carry it, but you're right. I guess we'll have to see."

My heart broke for him. "I've been there. I know how hard this is. Let me know if I can help with anything."

"Thanks." He patted my hand and stood. "Her appointment is in a few hours, and I've got some stuff to do before we go."

"Let me know the second you hear."

"I will." Hendrix leaned down and kissed the top of my head.

"I thought you left me this morning," I said around bites of my breakfast.

"Nope. I came down to spend some time with my best friend while you slept."

I paused mid-chew. "This morning allowed me a glimpse into what my life will be like without you," I whispered.

"Not now," he said. "We have today. I don't want to lose that. Please." His voice was soft and pleading.

I nodded, unable to articulate how much my heart was breaking.

"I have a day planned for us," Cade said, sipping his coffee. A smile eased across his handsome face, and his gaze flickered with desire.

"Yeah?" I asked, grinning at him. "In bed? In the shower? On the floor? On my desk?"

Cade chuckled. "All of the above. You and me, naked. But more than that, I want to hold you. I need you in my arms, Mac. I need to hear your heartbeat, I need to hear my name on your lips, and I need to be able to keep today with me for the rest of my life."

Now I understood what people meant when they said they'd found their soulmate. Cade was mine, I knew it for certain. How could I watch him walk away forever and not fall apart?

"I'm done," I said, tossing my fork down. "Let's go. I don't want to waste another minute."

Cade stood and reached for my hand.

IT SEEMED the days I wanted to last forever flew by, and the days I wanted to fly by dragged on for years.

By four in the afternoon, we were all on pins and needles, waiting for Gemma and Hendrix to return from their appointment. I almost felt bad for her. She had a full-on audience lying in wait and ready to jump her.

At four thirty, the front door opened, and Hendrix and Gemma walked into the house hand in hand.

I released Cade's fingers and jumped off the couch.

"Am I going to be an aunt?" I asked.

CHAPTER 31

*I*t was bad enough waiting for your own pregnancy results, but when an entire family's future hung on the balance, it was crazy.

"No," Gemma flashed a sheepish smile. "It was a false alarm and a faulty home pregnancy test. The doctor said the stress and travel most likely threw my cycle off even though I'm on the pill. I'm so sorry I scared everyone."

Hendrix pulled her into him, kissing the top of her head. I collapsed on the couch, crying. The relief I saw in Gemma's face, or because the whole ordeal had stirred up memories of my own pregnancy and how devastating the experience had been. Cade pulled me against him and gently rubbed my back. He knew what this meant. We could make a decision concerning the Witness Protection Program based on what was right for us, not what was best for an innocent child.

"I'm not going to lie," Franklin started. "I'm relieved. Under the circumstances ..."

"We agree, Dad," Hendrix said. "It's a bad time."

"I don't even know if I want kids," Gemma whispered. "Franklin, I might never give you grandkids. At this point I don't know."

I wiped my tears away while Franklin walked toward her. "Gemma, you've overcome so much, I don't think there's anything wrong with not wanting children. This decision is between you and my son, and I'm supporting you both. It's a huge life changer."

"Thank you," she said, glancing nervously at my brother.

"So where does this leave us?" I asked.

"Let's all sit down," Franklin said, settling into the brown, leather, wing-backed chair across from the couch. Gemma and Hendrix picked up and moved a few chairs closer so we could all face each other. It was crazy to think this moment, this conversation, had the possibility to change my life forever.

"I spoke with your mom, Mac. She's on board with whatever we decide."

"Whoa, you two would be in each other's life again," I said, unable to stop my grin.

Franklin raised his hand, stopping any additional thoughts I had on the subject.

"She made it clear it would be for you."

"Oh." I frowned, sinking back into my seat. Cade squeezed my hand.

"It would be sort of cool to have you two back together," I muttered.

Franklin cleared his throat and paused. "I'd like to know what you all are thinking. Hendrix?"

My brother gripped his girlfriend's hand and took a slow, deep breath. "We want to stay, Dad. We feel if we run, it will encourage Brandon's behavior. We'll be touring with extra security, and we understand the chances we're taking."

"Gemma? How do you feel? Are you in agreement?"

"Yeah, I'm with Hendrix," she said.

"Mac?"

"I want to stay and take this motherfucker down."

Franklin barked out a laugh.

"Are you sure you're up for the fight? He'll be released in three months. That may seem like a long time, but it'll fly by fast. You'll have constant protection, and no privacy."

"Yeah, I get it, but I'm not willing to give up my life because of him and Dillon. I want to fight. I want to win. And I want to stay in Spokane. This is home, Dad."

Franklin hesitated and took a deep breath. "Are you sure you're not basing your decision on Cade?"

"Sir, if I may?" Cade said, leaning forward.

"Of course, Cade."

"I had a conversation with Pierce earlier today, and he said I could also take Mom and Missy. I'm on board with the program."

"What?" I squealed.

He turned toward me. "I told you, I'm all in. Whatever it takes. You're stuck with me."

Before I could stop myself, I threw my arms around him and peppered his face with kisses.

"I love you," I said.

He rested his forehead against mine, "I love you, too, babe. I meant it when I said I'm not going anywhere."

"That tells me a lot about how you feel for my daughter," Franklin said, "Thank you."

"Thank you, sir," Cade said.

"I've watched Hendrix and Gemma's love deepen over time, and honestly, I don't think anything could tear them apart. You two may not be there quite yet, but I recognize the same signs. It's a rare gift to find your other half. Don't throw it away like I did."

"I won't," Cade replied, his expression stern.

"This is it then? We're not leaving?" I asked, my voice filled with hope.

"I need each of you to understand that in three months, you won't be able to use the bathroom without security tagging along. Brandon will be back in Spokane, and you will all be in danger. Can you live with that? Is it *really* what you want?"

Silence filled the room as my focus fell on Cade. He nodded. I looked over at Hendrix and Gemma. They nodded.

"Dad, it's up to you. What do you feel is right for our family?" I asked.

"I've never run from a fight, but I won't lie, this is one I'd run from," he admitted, frowning.

When your badass attorney dad admits he'd take off in the opposite direction and hide, it startles you to the core.

"What? You've taken every one of your cases head-on. You're not a coward," I leaned forward on the couch. "Are you telling me this is the one case that has you rattled?"

"Yeah," he said softly. "Dillon isn't someone I take lightly. He tried to murder my family. He shot my son, my future daughter in law, and he killed John. I'm afraid we've met our match. There's nothing worse than burying your child," he said, his voice cracking with the weight of the memory. Kendra, Franklin's youngest child had only been four when she died.

I hopped off the couch and wrapped my arms around him. "This is different. You're different. Forgive yourself," I encouraged. "We have." My attention drifted to Hendrix. From the obvious pain on his face, I knew his thoughts were with his little sister, Kendra. John wasn't the only one who should still be with us.

And for the first time in my life, I watched Franklin Harrington break down and cry.

"I'M SO glad your bandage is off," I said, trailing my fingers over Cade's chest.

"Are you okay with the decision not to go into the Witness Protection Program and stay in Spokane?"

"Mmm, so much better now that I know you're beside me for the long haul."

He rolled over in my bed, facing me. "I would have gone with you, Mac. I would have put my family in the Witness Protection Program for you. I love you that much. But I didn't want to influence your decision. You had to do what's best for you and your family."

"Thank you. *You're* part of my family now."

"I know my history with girls has been … active, but I don't want you to doubt how much I love you."

My hand slipped under the blankets, wrapping around his thick erection.

"Show me," I whispered.

"Come here," he said, tugging on my arm.

He slid down in the bed and guided my naked body over his face. His arms wrapped around my legs as his tongue worked magic on me as I sat on his face.

And for the first time, I was comfortable enough with him to try this position.

IT HAD BEEN a long time since I'd woken up happy and content.

"Morning," Cade said, kissing me.

"Morning," I replied sleepily. This was the life, waking up in the arms of someone you loved.

"I don't want to leave, but I need to get home."

"Mmm, I can't handle you leaving me every day."

Cade kissed the tip of my nose. "I know, but we'll be on the road again soon, and I'll be all yours."

I laughed. "Not really." I tilted my chin up and kissed him. "Will we ever have our own space? One we're not afraid we'll be murdered in?"

Cade cupped my chin. "Don't say that. Not a day goes by that I don't worry I'm going to lose you."

"I'm sorry. I ..."

Cade's mouth crashed down on mine. "I love you."

"Promise?" I asked, knowing it was a silly question.

"Always," he said. "I need to go."

Even though I wanted him to stay, I also needed to be supportive of his family, but my heart left the second Cade walked out my door.

"Sup, bestie?" I asked, strolling into the gaming room later that morning.

"Hey," Gemma said, patting the seat next to her on the leather couch.

I plunked down and smiled at her. "I still miss our college days."

"Me too," she said, grinning. "We had some long conversations, huh?"

"Yeah, but I think it's those talks that build lifetime friendships."

"Me too," she said, leaning her head on my shoulder.

"Are you happy you're not pregnant?"

She looked up at me, sadness evident in her expression. "You won't tell anyone?"

"Nope, never. It's between us girls," I swore.

"Mac, I don't know if I'll ever want kids."

"Gem-ma," I said, slapping my leg. "Do you understand not every female on this planet wants little rug rats running around and it's alright? There is nothing wrong with it."

"Maybe. But Hendrix ... I'd give him anything. I love him so much."

I sighed, trying to figure out the right thing to say to her.

"I don't want kids," I said. "I love Cade with all my heart, but kids ... not in my plan. I'm not sure where he is yet, and I know we're young, but ..."

"Me either, but I know Hendrix does," Gemma said.

"Honestly? I think all that matters to Hendrix is he wakes up in your arms every day. If you don't want kids, it's okay. You need to give yourself permission to not want them. I realize society thinks women need to procreate, but shit ... I don't want to, and we shouldn't be pressured into having kids."

"Really?" she asked.

"Yeah, really. And if we end up old spinsters because of it. Well, I guess we'll be roomies again."

Gemma giggled. "My life would not be okay without you."

"Right back atcha, bestie."

CHAPTER 32

The weekend after Labor Day, the temperature dropped twenty degrees. I slipped on my baby blue cashmere sweater and jeans and applied my make-up. Today, the band was making a TV appearance to announce their next tour.

"Are you ready?" I asked Gemma. Although I wasn't a part of the interview, my nerves were galloping full speed ahead. This was the first time since the shooting that everyone would be in front of the public. August Clover would also announce the new drummer, Asa Garner.

"No. All I can think about is the last time we were on stage," she said, applying the final touches to her eyeshadow in my bathroom.

"Me too," I said, turning toward her on the vanity chair. "But then I remember we're in this together. Gemma ... A part of me wants to fly a big fuck you to Brandon and his family ... like I refuse to let them to steal my life, but the other side of me ... I'm terrified when we leave on tour again, I won't make it back to hug Mom and Franklin. What if the shooter returns and doesn't miss this time? The only way I can console myself is that I figure we'd at least all die together. I can't take losing anyone else. John's gaping mouth and bullet hole in his head ... it haunts me every time I close my eyes."

"Mac, that's horrible," she gasped. "I'm so so sorry you had to see that. I can't even imagine. And you're definitely not alone with how you're feeling. It scares the shit out of me too. The only thing that helps me feel a bit safer is that we will have even more security around us. Plus, almost everyone I love will be with me, and I need to stay focused on that."

I nodded. She had a good point, and I needed to concentrate on the positive as well.

The doorbell rang, and I rushed down the stairs to answer it.

"Hi sexy," I said, opening the door to Cade.

He leaned over and gently kissed me. "How's my favorite person in the entire world?"

"Better now that you're here."

I took his black windbreaker and hung it up in the hallway closet.

"Are you excited?" I asked, beaming up at him.

"Yeah, I'm glad I'm healed and ready to play and sing again. But even more, I'm happy to have you next to me for another month."

I giggled and gave him a quick kiss. "The TV crew is setting up in the living room." I grabbed his hand and led him through the foyer.

I left the room while Gemma, Hendrix, and Cade mic'd up. This would be their first interview without John.

Stepping to the side of the foyer, I kept my focus trained on them. Although they smiled, it didn't quite reach their eyes. My chest tightened. No matter how hard I tried, I couldn't grasp the reality that John was gone. It just wasn't fair. He had a full life ahead of him, and he should be on the couch next to his best friends. I looked away from the band and tried to pull myself together before I burst into tears. Deep down, I knew John would want them to be happy and move forward.

"Are you ready?" I asked Franklin who had appeared next to me.

"No. I'm not," he admitted. "When your kids are putting themselves front and center, in harm's way and basically taunting an insane man ... No, you can't prepare for it."

There was nothing I could say to make him better. I leaned in and slipped my arm around his back.

"I guess we'll have to support each other on the sidelines then," I said.

～

THE MERE THOUGHT of Cade on stage and in front of a crowd again shook me more than I had expected it to.

"I'm not sure I like it," I said, pacing back and forth across my bedroom.

"We're all skittish, babe. We have extra security, and we're doing everything we can to be safe. But we all agreed we'd tour again."

"I take it back," I said, chewing on my fingernail. "Brandon is weeks away from being released from jail. I should have agreed to the Witness Protection Program."

"Is it what you really wanted?" Cade asked, rubbing my arms.

"No. I just want my life back."

The sound of the doorbell startled me out of our conversation.

"Hang on," I said, listening as Ruby answered the door.

My jaw dropped. "I'll be right back."

I hurried down the stairs. What in the hell?

"Mom? What are you doing back from Europe already?" My eyes popped open at the sight of her. She looked exhausted, but as beautiful as ever with her dark brown eyes and long sandy blonde hair piled on the top of her head in a messy bun. A bubble of excitement burst inside me.

"Hi honey, I'm home," Mom said, giving me a big hug.

"What are you doing here?" I asked, motioning her inside. "Are you alright? Why did you end your trip early? Omigosh, I'm so glad you're here. But you're okay? Nothing's wrong?" I asked, worry nudging at me.

"Franklin updated me on what was going on, so I took the first plane I could and came straight here before I went home. I couldn't stay in Europe any longer. I needed to be with my family. I needed to hug my kids."

Mom's expression softened as her eyes searched my face. It didn't seem to matter how old I was, I always needed my mom. Relief that she was home consumed me, and I pulled her in for a hug. We clung to each other for a long moment. When we stepped away from each other, Mom dabbed her eyes.

"How was your trip?" I asked, dragging her into the kitchen.

"Amazing. I'd love to take you some day."

"I'd love to go with you. Maybe a girl's trip," I said. "Do you want some coffee? Are you jet lagged?"

"Is that who I think it is?" Hendrix asked, entering the kitchen with a huge smile on his face.

"Hi! How are you?" Mom asked, wrapping him in a big hug.

"I'm good," he replied. "It's good to have you home."

"Same," she said, kissing his cheek. "Why don't you and Mac sit down and fill me in on the tour?" she asked.

"Janice, welcome home," Franklin said from the doorway.

Her head snapped up, and a shy smile eased across her face. I glanced at Hendrix and winked. There was a lot of history between Franklin and Mom, but I knew them well enough to realize they'd never stopped loving each other, life had just taken a crazy turn.

"So Mom, welcome back. I'm having sex with Cade Richardson, Gemma thought she was pregnant, and Brandon will get out of jail in a few weeks. Yup, that's about it." I hurried over toward Hendrix, pulled on his hand, and headed out of the kitchen.

"We'll see you in the morning!" I called.

"Mac," Hendrix chuckled. "Are you trying to give them some time together?"

"What was your first clue?" I asked, dragging him up the stairs.

I stopped when we reached the top step and sat down. He sank down beside me.

"Do you remember when we were little, and we couldn't sleep? We'd meet in the hallway with our pillows and blankets?" I peered at Hendrix.

"Yeah. It was when Janice and Dad argued all the time."

I nodded. "Even though they were in the process of splitting up, I never doubted my brother was there for me."

Hendrix reached for my hand.

"I felt the same way about you, little sis."

My attention traveled down the stairs and into the foyer. I loved this house. I loved being here with Franklin, Hendrix, and Gemma. And as crazy as the outside world had turned, I always felt safe here.

"We almost left everything behind, Hendrix," I said. "I realize we still would have had Gemma and Franklin, but what about Janice and Cade? I know I'm with Cade now, but he's your best friend. You've known him since grade school. I can't imagine walking away from everything we've known ..."

He turned toward me and held my gaze.

"I get it. We've been through hell and back together."

"Yeah," I said, propping my chin on my knees. "All of this ... the Witness Protection Program, losing John, Brandon being released soon ... It's really made me evaluate what is important in life."

Hendrix looked at me with a somber expression.

"I didn't understand for a long time that every choice we've made has affected our parents in either a positive or negative way, and every decision they've made has also affected us. We've all made mistakes, and even screwed up royally. But Hendrix, more than anything in the world I want us to be together as a family again," I said softly.

"Do you think Dad still loves Janice?" Hendrix whispered.

"Don't you? Whenever we mention Mom to Franklin, he gets this look on his face. Sort of sad and dreamy all at the same time."

Hendrix grinned. "Yeah, I've seen it too."

"What if they never stopped loving each other and they simply need some time to heal now that Franklin has been sober and back on track for a while?"

Silence filled the space between us.

"Guess there's only one way to find out," he said. "All I want for both of them is to be happy."

"Agreed."

After a few more minutes of silence, we made our way down the hall and to our bedrooms.

"Night," I said, giving Hendrix a little wave. My heart swelled with love and gratitude for my brother.

"Night," he said before disappearing into his and Gemma's room.

I pushed my door open, and my soul did a little happy dance. My boyfriend was waiting for me in my bed.

"Babe?" Cade asked sleepily.

"Yeah," I replied slipping out of my clothes and under the covers next to him.

"Mmm," he said, sighing. "This is the best part of the day. You next to me," he said softly.

"Mine too," I said.

Cade gave me a quick kiss on the forehead as I snuggled up to him and drifted off to sleep.

AT SIX THIRTY the next morning, I staggered down the stairs and to the front door with Cade.

"I'll be glad when you don't have to leave," I said quietly, my lower lip jutting out in a playful pout.

"Morning," Mom said from behind me.

"Mom?" I was stunned to see her still here.

She blushed at the knowing smirk on my face.

"I'll get some coffee started," she said, hurrying past us in her burgundy robe.

I waited until she'd slipped into the kitchen before I giggled.

"I think my parents spent the night together," I said, wrinkling my nose at the thought of them naked.

"I'd agree with the assessment," Cade said, grinning. "Maybe we're all back where we belong."

"Almost," I sighed, kissing him. "When you don't have to leave me in the morning ... then the world will be a perfect place."

"I couldn't agree more," he said, nuzzling my neck.

"Mm, you better stop or I'm going to take you back to my bed and have my way with you."

Cade's soft chuckle sent goosebumps down my back.

"I love you," he said. "I'll talk to you later."

"Have a good day. I better go and investigate my mom's activities." I couldn't hide my grin at the thought she and Franklin might be patching things up.

Cade kissed me goodbye and slipped out the front door. The house was quiet except for the drip of the coffee pot.

I made my way into the kitchen.

"I'm so happy to see you," I said, sitting down at the breakfast bar with Mom.

"You too, honey. I really missed you."

"Tell me about ... Europe?" I giggled. "No, wait, we're adults and you're at Franklin's house in your robe. Spill."

A shy smile eased across mom's face.

"I know he still loves you," I blurted.

"Mac," she chided. "We'll need to work some things out. I know the idea excites you, but one night together doesn't mean we're patching things up."

I planted my palm against my forehead. "Did you two have a one-night stand?" I groaned. "That's the last thing I want to hear my parents are doing."

Mom smiled. "I don't know what it means, yet. The one thing I know is I'm home to spend time with my daughter and her brother. When Franklin talked to me about the Witness Protection Program, it put everything into perspective again. In a way, I'm relieved we're not going to hide."

I threw my arms around her. "I missed you so much."

"You too, baby."

CHAPTER 33

EPILOGUE – ONE YEAR LATER

"*J*t's been a long-ass time coming," I said, smiling at my boyfriend as we unpacked our boxes of books and placed them on the large walnut bookshelves. I was absolutely giddy at the idea of finally sharing a closet with Cade, not to mention a bed we didn't have to leave at six-thirty in the morning.

Our new house wasn't far from Hendrix and Gemma's, and we shared the same view of the Spokane River as they did. We were also within minutes of his mom and Missy. The full-time caregiver was amazing, which helped us both feel more comfortable about finally taking the leap and moving in together.

I squished my bare toes into the new, plush, tan carpet while I lifted my dress shoes out of another box. The wall of windows was my favorite part of our new room. Well, other than Cade being a permanent fixture in it. He was by far the best part.

"It was well worth the wait, though. We finally have our own place, and I don't have to share you with a houseful of people anymore," he said, grinning and tossing the dark burgundy, king-sized sheets onto our bed.

"And the best part is you don't have to leave every morning!" I said, clapping my hands together. "At first I was worried about leaving Franklin alone in that big house, but when they announced Mom was moving in with him. Well! Problem solved. Plus, my family is back together, Cade," I whispered, my voice filled with emotion. "I'm so happy."

Cade sauntered over to me and wrapped his arms around my waist.

"Me too, babe," he said gently, placing a kiss on the tip of my nose. He held me for a moment, then pulled away, his expression growing serious. "We have a big day ahead of us. How do you feel about seeing Brandon?" He tucked a loose hair behind my ear.

Brandon's sentencing date and the anniversary of John's death had somehow fallen on the same day. Maybe John was up above, pulling some strings to finally end the madness. I placed my hands-on Cade's broad muscular chest and peered up at him.

"I don't think I'll ever be alright when I see that sorry son of a bitch. But over the last year I've learned that life is full of surprises and shit rarely turns out like you expect it too. But my life is filled with people I love and trust, which means I can make it through anything with them by my side."

Cade leaned down and kissed me gently. "I couldn't agree with you more. Losing John, getting shot … it really put things into perspective. I'm ready to see Brandon get what he deserves, and I'm definitely looking forward to the celebration ˙ later tonight."

"At least Brandon will get a minimum of twenty years in prison and maybe life. It'd be nice to know the world would have one less rapist and kidnapper walking around."

"I'm just stunned he didn't learn anything the first time. Granted, he only served three months for kidnapping you, so maybe he thought he could get away with grabbing an underaged girl and driving across state lines. The second he did that, it became a federal offense."

"Brandon's sneaky and manipulative, but his narcissism was the noose around his neck, and it brought him down." My inner voice cackled with glee.

"I'll take it," Cade said, kissing me.

I glanced at the clock. It was nearly noon, and we needed to meet Gemma, Hendrix, Franklin, and Mom at the courthouse in an hour.

~

I PULLED my burgundy windbreaker around me a little tighter as Cade and I walked up the courthouse steps accompanied by Zayne, my security guard. Cade looked sexy as hell in his navy-blue suit and white button-down shirt. My mind easily drifted to what was waiting for me beneath his clothes.

The afternoon sunshine warmed the bright blue sky, and the air carried the crisp, fresh smell of autumn. Thoughts of hay rides, scented pumpkin candles from Bath and Body Works, and Thanksgiving were enough to calm my nerves for a minute. It was also crazy to think that, in a few short months, Spokane would be covered in snow and Cade and I would spend our second Christmas together.

Cade opened the door for me, and I immediately spotted Gemma's red hair. She smiled and waved, her one and a half carat solitaire engagement ring flashing on her petite finger. We walked over to the group hand in hand.

"Are we on schedule for the sentencing, Dad?" I asked Franklin, giving Vaughn a quick wave who stood behind Mom. Dad looked as spectacular as he always did in a black suit, but now his eyes gleamed brighter. My mom just had that effect on people.

"Yes, everything is going according to plan," he said, smiling and leaning down for a hug.

"Hi, Mom," I said, kissing her on the cheek. She'd opted for a simple black dress that hugged all her curves, giving her a sexy but classy look.

I quickly hugged Hendrix, Gemma, and Pierce while we waited outside the courtroom to be called in. Although I knew Brandon would be locked up for a long time, my nerves were still on edge.

Ten minutes later, the door opened, and we filed into the stuffy room and sat down on the wooden pew. I was stunned to see the rows of seats fill so quickly with the victim's family, reporters, and what I assumed were other girls Brandon had harmed. I'd never know for sure how many he'd hurt, but at least there was a good chance he'd never harm another person again. Cade laced his fingers through mine, his thumb tracing soothing circles on the back of my hand. I leaned against him, thanking the universe he was next to me. Although I'd found my own inner strength, Cade was still my rock.

The room fell silent when the judge entered and sat down. No way in hell would I want to have faced Judge Warner myself. He was an imposing man, his once black hair now peppered with gray. His stern expression and his commanding aura filled the room. He glanced around and began the proceeding. Over the next hour, we listened to the defense and prosecuting attorney's argument, Lily, the fourteen-year-old hostage, her family, and Brandon speak. As we had expected, the prosecutor was asking for life on multiple charges and the defense wanted only twenty years.

For the first time since I'd known Brandon Montgomery, he didn't have a nasty sneer on his face. In fact, he looked terrified. Anger reared to life inside me. No matter how scared he was right now, it was nothing like what his victims had felt when he'd assaulted them. Maybe it was wrong, but I still hoped another prisoner would stalk and terrify him.

I peeked over at Gemma when Judge Warner began to speak. "Brandon Montgomery, please rise."

This was it. My pulse raced and Cade's fingers tightened around mine while we waited for the results.

My heart galloped full speed ahead when Brandon stood. What if he only served a few years? What if the judge was in Dillon Montgomery's pocket? My leg bounced up and down uncontrollably.

"You've been a bit difficult to catch, but thanks to the FBI, Lily Weston was safely returned to her family. However, this left you with multiple charges, including rape of a minor, kidnapping and transporting across state lines, and several counts of child pornography. I've listened to all sides of this case, and I'm hereby sentencing you to forty years in the Washington State Penitentiary without parole."

My hands covered my mouth, muffling my cry of happiness while cheers filled the room. A soft cry came from Lily's family while they embraced each other. I turned to hug Cade then Gemma and Hendrix. Pierce had done it. He'd literally hunted Brandon down and brought him to justice, just as he'd promised.

WITH ALL THE news of the shooting and John's death, the band's fame had skyrocketed. It was nearly impossible to go clubbing or out in public anymore without fans bombarding them. But tonight, we celebrated the win of Brandon's conviction as well as John's life. Even though we'd invited Layne to join us, he politely bowed out since he'd not known John.

Zayne and Pierce exited the car first then opened the back door of the limo.

"Dude, is the coast clear?" I asked Pierce, poking my head out of the car. Gemma giggled as we waited. Pierce hurried to the tattoo parlor's door and held it open for us while Zayne stayed near the car. Laughing, Gemma and I ran for it first, and Cade and Hendrix followed behind us. Once we were safe inside, Pierce locked the door behind him and grinned.

"Let's do this," he said.

Cade had rented the tattoo parlor out for the night. We each took a chair, and my heart fluttered. I was about to get my first tattoo.

"Hey, guys, welcome. I'm Mike the owner and one of your tattoo artists tonight," a burly dark-haired guy said. "I've got shots for everyone to toast the evening."

A petite blonde handed out the drinks, then left the room.

Cade raised his glass first, and we all followed suit.

"To John," he said softly. "To the life he led and the lives he saved."

"Cheers," we all said in unison and downed the tequila.

"Brrr," I said, shivering from the burn of the alcohol.

"If I understand correctly, you all want the same tat but in different areas?"

"Yup," I answered for everyone. "Cade can show you the sketch we all came up with."

Cade shifted in his seat and grabbed a piece of paper out of the back of his jeans pocket. He unfolded the drawing and smoothed it out on the chair. We all gathered around it and held each other's hand. My throat tightened with emotion. I couldn't think of a better way to honor John.

"It's beautiful. I can even add some shading that will deepen the image too," Mike said.

We all nodded as we stared at the drum with wings. Inside the snare drum, it held a red heart on fire. That was John, always loving life and living it to the fullest while he loved everyone around him with his whole being.

"MM, those shots were strong, but at least my tattoo hurts less," I said to Cade, staring at the plastic bandage over my ankle. "I can't believe Pierce had so many tats!" I giggled.

"I'm not surprised, but he's had a lot of loss in his life, and tonight he honored one more." I didn't miss the heaviness in Cade's voice. Even though it had been a year, emotionally it felt like John had left us only yesterday.

I sighed softly and lay back on our bed next to my boyfriend.

"It's going to feel really strange not having Pierce around as often. I mean, he's not just a bodyguard, he's our friend," I said.

"I know, but he'll have other cases to work on, and I think he needs some time to get over Gemma."

"Poor guy. But yeah, I agree."

I rolled over on my side and glanced at Cade's new tattoo. Cade's gunshot scar had been positioned in the center of the heart.

"Does it hurt?" I asked him.

"A little. It hurts more that John's gone. It just reminds me to not take life or the people I love for granted."

Silence filled the room, and I laid my head on Cade's chest. The soft rise and fall of his breathing calmed my racing thoughts. It had been a great day with Brandon's sentencing and our group celebration, but I was still processing the events. I stifled a yawn and glanced up at Cade.

"You're so beautiful," he whispered. "And tonight is the first night in our own place. It's the first night of our life together." He smiled and smoothed my hair while I snuggled up against him. "I love you, Mackenzie Worthington," he said softly.

"And I love you," I said, leaning up and kissing him gently.

Peace flowed through me. Everything I'd ever hoped for was falling into place. My eyes fluttered closed, and I drifted off to sleep with his arms wrapped protectively around me.

~

Don't miss the Love & Consequences bonus scene, and get an inside look into who he really is ... Click here!

Want more of the hot and mysterious bodyguard, Pierce? Don't miss Love & Corruption! It's full of suspense and a second chance romance. Just click here! OR Start the series from the beginning with Gemma & Hendrix's story in Love & Ruin.

A NOTE FROM THE AUTHOR

Dear Readers,
If you have experienced sexual assault or physical abuse, there is free
confidential help. Please visit:

Website: https://www.rainn.org/
Phone: 800-656-4673

Edited by: Deb Markanton

Cover Art by: iheartcoverdesigns

Photographer: CJC Photographer

First Edition

ISBN: 978-1-949414-90-5

Gain access to previews of J.A. Owenby's novels before they're released and to take part in exclusive giveaways. www.authorjaowenby.com

Made in the USA
Columbia, SC
08 May 2023

16218620R00181